Allison flushed.

113

"There's no use arguing about it, Thorne. I won't be your pensioner, you won't have me for your wife, and I won't take a lover. It would be best if you left now."

Thorne folded his arms and glared down at her. "Be sensible, Allison. A beautiful woman like you cannot live on her own without a man to protect her." He turned her around and held her pinioned by his strong hands on her shoulders. "I swear I would never dishonor you," he growled.

Allison struggled in his grasp. "I am sure you have no intention of doing so. But now that we have become aware of the potent attraction between us, can you honestly say no danger exists? That we won't ever be gripped by passion? For if you are that sure of your self-control, I am not!"

SIGNET REGENCY ROMANCE
Coming in January 1999

Diane Farr
The Nobody

Rita Boucher
The Poet and the Paragon

Allison Lane
A Clandestine Courtship

My Lady Ghost

by

June Calvin

A SIGNET BOOK

SIGNET
Published by the Penguin Group
Penguin Putnam Inc., 375 Hudson Street,
New York, New York 10014, U.S.A.
Penguin Books Ltd, 27 Wrights Lane,
London W8 5TZ, England
Penguin Books Australia Ltd, Ringwood, Victoria, Australia
Penguin Books Canada Ltd, 10 Alcorn Avenue,
Toronto, Ontario, Canada M4V 3B2
Penguin Books (N.Z.) Ltd, 182–190 Wairau Road,
Auckland 10, New Zealand

Penguin Books Ltd, Registered Offices:
Harmondsworth, Middlesex, England

First published by Signet, an imprint of Dutton NAL, a member of Penguin Putnam Inc.

First Printing, December, 1998
10 9 8 7 6 5 4 3 2 1

This book is dedicated to the on-line community that has been of so much help to me while writing this book, especially the loop-troops of the Beau Monde, the members of the Georgette Heyer list, and the English Civil War reenacters;

To my niece Wendy Toscani, for helping me with my rusty French;

And to my son, Craig, for smiling at just the right moment.

Prologue

Sputtering torchlight illuminated a scene of grisly chaos in the courtyard below. The gates had opened: Silverthorne Castle's garrison was surrendering. Tears ran down Lady Marpold's face as she turned from the window slit at the urgent request of her maid.

"My lady! Come quickly. Your father is injured."

Her face as pale as her silver blond hair, the dowager Baroness Marpold left her observation post high in the castle's keep. She hastened down the wooden stairs to the great hall, where two soldiers struggled to carry an older man to a bench before the fireplace.

"Father!" She knelt by him, her hands already seeking to lift away his blood-soaked shirt.

"No, leave me be, Elena. The wound is mortal." Baron D'Aumont raised a trembling hand to prevent his daughter's ministrations. "No time for tears, either. Sir Broderick has surrendered, at my command. One more cannonade and the north wall would have been breached. This way my people will not be put to the sword. Armstead, Geoffrey, go back to your posts, and send Sir Broderick to me."

He closed his eyes for a moment. "Blasted Roundheads. Damned Royalists. To think of Englishmen killing Englishmen, and I with a son on either side. Which side was I to serve, pray tell? Regicides or Papists? Bah! Neither of them worth shedding blood for. All I care for is to keep what is mine!"

"Shhh." Elena took a flagon of water from her handmaiden and began bathing his bloodstained forehead. "Do not excite yourself; you'll only bleed the more."

"Nay!" He brushed aside her hand. "Dismiss the servants."

With a glance and motion of her head, Elena sent the watching group in retreat.

"Your daughters are safely away?"

She nodded.

"I would have you go, too. This minute."

"I'll not leave you thus!"

"You must!" He grasped her sleeve, pulling her close to him. "You alone know where the treasure is hidden—the treasure that will restore the house of D'Aumont once this cursed war is over. It is to preserve my father's hard-won legacy that I have fought off all attempts upon this castle. You'll keep my secret?"

"You know I will—to the death."

"And what good would that do, pray?" The baron's voice cracked with an ironic chuckle. "You must live, to pass the treasure on to my grandchildren when England shall be at peace again. Now, swear to me you'll go this instant." He fixed her with piercing grey eyes.

Tears streaming down her face, Elena nodded. "It shall be as you say."

"God go with you, daughter."

"And you, father."

"Nay, daughter, this day I go to God. Broderick!"

Elena turned her head. Her father's second-in-command, Sir Broderick Ramsey, had joined the servants standing at a respectful distance.

The tall, ferocious-looking soldier strode forward. "My lord?"

"Take Elena to safety. You know how. She may have need of your sword. I will live long enough to surrender, but not long enough for them to torture into giving up my wealth. When once you are safely in France, you have my permission to marry her." He handed a long, round ivory tube to the attentive knight. "My testament. See that my property passes to my children and their children, never to that traitorous brother of mine!"

"It shall be as you command." The two men's hands joined briefly, before Baron D'Aumont's fell weakly to his side. Sir Broderick raised Elena to her feet, saluted the baron with his bloodstained sword, and half dragged the weeping woman away from her father's side. The sounds of horns and marching feet lent urgency to their steps as the two fled into the dim interior of the castle's keep.

Elena turned for one last look. "I'll guard your treasure with my life," she whispered, her tear-blurred eyes focused on the supine form in front of the fire. "Your children will restore the castle, and the D'Aumont name and heritage will blaze forth in glory once again."

Chapter One

The tinkle of glasses mingled with the buzz of dozens of voices as Allison Weatherby stood talking with, or rather listening to, her dance partner. Victor Mangus, Lord Bertland, was holding forth on his favorite subject, the need for sterner vagrancy laws. The other members of the small conversational circle echoed agreement. Allison turned her attention elsewhere, for if she continued to listen, she would surely say something pointed about the way such laws would affect disabled soldiers, veterans of the late war, many of whom now begged for coins to keep themselves alive.

Thus it was that she chanced to listen in upon a conversation between two elegant and very young ladies standing next to her.

"Silverthorne has twenty thousand a year, Mama says. And though he is old, he is well enough looking, you must agree."

Thorne old? Allison smiled. *Well enough looking?* She glanced across the room to where he stood in conversation with two of his political allies, Lord Langley and Lord Pelham. Both handsome men, they were put quite in the shade, in her opinion, by the tall, broad-shouldered marquess. Hair the color of rich, dark chocolate threatened to escape its careful arrangement in the Brutus style and break into ringlets. In profile his nose hinted at the Roman. Thorne stood in his habitual commanding posture, one long leg forward, arms folded, looking down gravely at his companions.

"He has an air about him, that I will allow," responded the second girl, causing Allison to think sardonically, *Once those piercing grey eyes looked down into hers, and that sensual mouth gently touched her hand, the foolish chit surely would realize how ridiculous was her faint praise.*

"But I do not think you should set your cap for him," the high, breathless voice continued, "for Mama says he has never shown the least inclination to marry, and besides, he will soon be involved in a scandal."

"Oh! Do tell me, Mary. You know my mother will not allow me to gossip."

"He is living with his mistress, you see. A Mrs. Weatherby, a widow. Very pretty, they say. Doubtless she hopes to marry him, but Mama says such a high stickler as Lord Silverthorne will never marry his mistress."

Allison stiffened and felt heat coloring her cheeks. *Is that what the tabbies are saying?* She looked more closely at the speakers. Judging by their white muslin dresses, the two young women were in their first season. *The real scandal is that someone has discussed such matters with you*, Allison thought. She turned her back on them.

"Living with her? How shocking! But I am persuaded you are wrong, for are not Lady Catherton and her daughter, Mrs. Weatherby, his house guests? They are related to him, I believe."

"Distantly related, yes, but . . . Oh, good evening, Lady Langley." Allison could hear the slight crinkle of muslin as the two gossiping minxes curtsied to their hostess.

"Good evening, Mary," a pleasant female voice responded. "And Catherine. You are both in looks tonight. But where are your partners? Shall I look about me for someone to stand up with you for the next set?"

"Thank you, Lady Langley, but they have merely gone to bring us some lemonade. Such a delightful party, ma'am! We have just been talking about your charming decor."

Little cats! Allison turned to catch Lady Langley's eye. Immediately Gwynneth excused herself from the young ladies and hastened to join her friend.

"Allison, there you are! Your mother is looking for you."

"Thank you, Gwynneth. Before I go, will you present me to your two friends?"

Lady Langley looked a little puzzled, but agreed. Allison had the satisfaction of seeing the girls blush as her name was spoken. "Is this your first season?" she asked, looking from one to the other.

"Yes, Mrs. Weatherby," they both chimed.

"Ah. Delightful. I remember my first season so well. I always went in terror that I might commit some terrible *faux pas*, but found it was as my mother said: 'If you never speak ill of others, you need never fear the malice of the tabbies yourself.' "

The shame-faced looks of the two young women before her told her that the medicine had been unpleasant. *I only hope they swallow it right down and that it may do them some good!* Allison bade them good evening. They made haste to retreat to their mothers' sides.

Laughter danced in Mrs. Langley's eyes. "What was that all about, Allison?"

"You know what they say about never eavesdropping, lest you hear something bad about yourself . . ."

"I do beg your pardon for neglecting you, Mrs. Weatherby." Lord Bertland interrupted them. "I know that such political discussion is incomprehensible to the female brain, and therefore quite boring. Shall we take the floor again?"

"Thank you, Bertie, but I must decline," Allison replied through clenched teeth. "Lady Langley tells me my mother wishes to see me." She escaped gratefully, linking her arm in Gwynneth's as they went in search of Delphinia, Lady Catherton.

Allison was silent as the carriage rattled through London's streets, carrying them home to the Marquess of Silverthorne's town house on Curzon Street. Her mother required few responses as she recounted the highlights of her evening of whist. *I can never understand how she remembers every card played in every hand, and yet cannot recall how many debts she may have incurred.* Glad enough to be left to her own thoughts, Allison nodded and murmured occasionally in response to Delphinia's chatter.

Across from them Thorne looked at her through hooded eyes, that look he often gave her that spread a slumbrous warmth through her entire body.

A man ought not to look at any respectable female in such a way unless she be his wife or fiancée. It was precisely that look which made her mother so sure Thorne would offer for her before the season ended. But Allison's view was less sanguine. There was no doubt that Thorne desired her, just as she was powerfully attracted to him. But he had never even hinted at any interest more particular than helping the two widows return to society after their period of mourning.

So the tabbies think I am his mistress. Allison turned her head away and frowned at the rainy streets passing by her carriage window. *I wonder if he thinks along those lines?*

Allison lifted her chin proudly. Many men thought she would, as a recent widow, be desperate for a man in her bed, but she had quickly set them to rights. If Thorne thought to make her his mistress, he would find himself very sadly mistaken. She might feel desire, but she would never be a slave to it.

And if it is marriage, as mother thinks? Allison would have been satisfied to remain single, for unlike her mother, she liked her independence, though to be sure it would be much more agreeable had she a better income. Yet her feelings for Thorne went deeper than mere desire, much deeper than a wish for the security and status that marriage to a marquess would bring.

She had been acquainted with him forever. In addition to their family ties, their fathers had been friends from school days, so she, Thorne, and his double first cousin James had been playmates during their early childhood. Thorne, older than she by four years, had made a warm place for himself in her heart by allowing a very young girl to play with him and James, always seeing that she took no hurt from their sometimes rough-and-tumble games. James, two years her senior, had followed the example of his adored older cousin. As a result, she and Jamie had been as brother and sister long after their fathers' estrangement had separated Thorne from his playmates.

In the few weeks she had been living in his household, her feelings had ripened from friendship to admiration to deep affection. She had never known a kinder man, nor one more devoted to his duties to family, land, tenants, and country. Nothing would make her happier than marriage to him.

If they had become objects of gossip, though, she must consider her future. Thorne had always maintained he did not intend to marry; that he had reached the age of twenty-eight without being leg-shackled indicated he meant to keep this resolution. *It is time to bring the Marquess of Silverthorne to the point*, she decided, *or leave his household, before my reputation is ruined.*

*   *   *

Adrian Thorne D'Aumont, 9th Baron D'Aumont, 5th Earl of Riggswheel, 3rd Marquess of Silverthorne, let Delphinia's flood of words wash over him as he studied Allison in the flickering light of the carriage lamp. He enjoyed looking at his distant cousin, who was an attractive woman, though her beauty by no means fit the classic mold. She was tall and slender, with the small high bosom of a miss just out of the schoolroom, in spite of her twenty-four years. Her straight, narrow nose was more pert than classical in profile. She hadn't the perfect oval face, either—heart-shaped, rather, with her wide forehead and small, rounded chin.

A phrenologist would say that forehead hinted at intellect far in excess of the ideal for a woman, and he would be right. She had an almost masculine understanding and loved to dispute with him on almost any subject from politics to music to literature.

Still, she enchanted him. He liked that nose, and the brilliant sapphire eyes. He liked the way her full mouth slanted higher on one side than on the other when she was amused. She enjoyed laughing and frequently teased him into laughing with her. There had not been enough laughter in his life. As for her intellect and tendency toward argument, to his surprise he had begun to look forward to their lively discussions. No stranger to argumentative females, he had been amazed to find one who could use reason to carry her point, rather than tears or tantrums. Better still, and even more surprising, she could admit to being wrong and seemed eager to repair the defects in her education.

He longed to kiss that pert nose and run his hands through her silky silver blond hair, which always seemed to glow. As if sensing his wayward thoughts, Allison suddenly turned her head away, staring moodily out the window. He had seldom seen her in the megrims, at least not since he had rescued her and Delphinia from the decaying dower house they had been forced to live in since Lord Catherton died.

Has anyone insulted her? he wondered, clenching his hands at the thought. *Or is she upset that neither Jason Westingham-Jones nor Ronald St. John asked her to dance tonight?* His conscience twinged at that thought. He had sent away two of her most ardent admirers with a flea in their ears, because he suspected they wanted more from her than friendship, though less than marriage.

He had encouraged Lord Bertland, however, for he could find no fault with the man except that he was a Tory, and boring. *Allison would say that was a redundancy*, he thought, smiling. Perhaps after Delphinia went upstairs, he would tell her of the plans he, Langley, and Pelham had made to prevent the passage of more legislation limiting the freedom of England's people to peacefully assemble and seek redress of their grievances. She always took a lively interest in politics.

Thorne allowed the ladies to exit first, into the capable hands of his first footman, who had carried a huge black umbrella out of the house to shield them from the light rain. Indoors, he stopped them at the foot of the stairs to ask if they wished to join him for tea or sherry before they went up. As expected, Delphinia declined. She always pretended to be exhausted, yet he suspected she wished to give him and Allison time to be alone together. That thought made him uneasy, though his mind shied away from examining it.

Unexpectedly, Allison also declined. She often lingered with him when they returned from the evening's entertainment, discussing the day's events. He had come to look forward to that time.

"Not tonight, Thorne. I . . . have some letters to write." Allison had often made mistakes when she acted impulsively. She wanted to think matters over for a day or two before taking any steps either to head off scandal or bring Thorne up to snuff.

Thirty minutes later, Delphinia entered her daughter's room to find her brushing out her long hair absentmindedly. Her maid had already brushed it once.

"What is it, dear? You were so quiet in the carriage, and didn't join Thorne for a sherry. Have you the headache?"

Allison jumped a little, for she had not even noticed her mother's entrance. "Not at all, Mama. I just needed some time to think."

"I wish you had stayed below with Thorne. He looked quite disappointed. Perhaps this was the evening he was going to offer for you."

"Hmmm. If so, he will find another time. The way he looked at me in the carriage, I declare I wonder if he had some less honorable proposal to offer me."

Delphinia drew herself up proudly. "Impossible. Even if Thorne were so lost to decency as to offer such an insult to his own kin . . ."

"It is a very distant connection, Mother."

Delphinia continued as if she hadn't spoken. "Which he is not, for a more upright and moral man I have yet to meet! He would not dare to do such a thing with me under his roof. No, my dear. He has been most particular toward you. And do you really think if I had been a widow alone, he would have taken quite as much interest in my plight when that wretched William neglected me so?"

Allison did not want to get her mother started on the sins of her father's cousin William, now the third Baron Catherton. Not that his sins against her were undeserving of censure. He had refused either to remit to her mother the money due her as part of her marriage settlement, or to give her all of her dower rights, maintaining that as her husband, the second Lord Catherton, had deliberately bankrupted the estate, William had no obligation to her.

"Many men think widows may take lovers with no disgrace to themselves," Allison said, moving the conversation in a direction she knew her mother could not resist following.

"Now *that* I have never understood, for may not a widow sin? And it is a sin, my dear. Forgive me for showing my religious upbringing, but . . ."

"*Pax*, Mama. You long ago convinced me on this subject."

"And if that were not reason enough, there is always the danger of a child, for at twenty-four you cannot be said to be past the age of childbearing, which is all to the good since Thorne will want an heir."

Allison nodded, a familiar, unwelcome pang gripping her heartstrings. *If only Charles had wanted an heir.* She turned away from the mirror and rose to kiss her mother on the cheek. "I expect I do have a bit of a headache. Or perhaps I am missing Charles again, for after dancing with Lord Bertland, how can I help but remember how light on his feet my husband was, how very unlikely to tread on my toes."

Delphinia frowned. "He is a worthy man. If Thorne does not come up to scratch, he would do very nicely for you."

Allison grimaced. Lord Bertland was indeed a worthy man, and a kind one. But he was patronizing and self-important and stout and fifty and . . . *Must* she marry? If it were only herself, she would supplement her small income with a position as a governess or companion rather than marry for money. But clearly her mother expected her to find a husband who could provide for them both.

Allison turned away as a familiar anger swept her. *How can I ever forgive Father for not paying Charles all of my dowry? For gambling it away as he did all of Mother's portion?* She had found it difficult to mourn her father properly after learning the straits in which he had left her mother and herself. She tried to tell herself that he would have mended his ways and made up her dowry if his death had not followed so quickly on the heels of Charles's. It was what her mother always said, but Allison thought she did not believe it, that acknowledging the truth of her husband's lack of concern for them was just intolerable for her.

Delphinia put her arm around Allison's shoulders. "Do not fret, love. You do not have to accept Lord Bertland, or anyone else for that matter. I am sure that when Thorne completes his research into my legal position, I shall have a comfortable income."

Allison smiled and allowed her mother to think she was reassured, but she strongly suspected such optimism would not be justified. She had thought from the first that Thorne sponsored them this season in the expectation that she would make an advantageous marriage.

Lord Silverthorne looked at his reflection in the mirror and frowned. *Why are you so blue-deviled?* It was Thorne's wont to conduct dialogues with himself when he needed to sort through problems. *Since when do you worry so about a woman's moods? And when did your minutes alone with her become so important to you?*

His reflection regarded him somberly. *Face the facts, man. The widow of your good friend has become your treasured friend.*

There is naught in that to be so down-pin about, though.

Lust? His reflection showed a sardonically lifted eyebrow.

That, too.

But there's more? You aren't falling in love with her, are you? For you know where that leads, at least with a woman of your own class.

Not for me it doesn't. No marriage for me, and most particularly not a love-match. I learned my lesson well, at my father's knee.

Then you must bed her. Lust flames out quickly enough once satisfied, and the wench is not unwilling, I think.

Thorne frowned even more fiercely. Had he really allowed himself such a thought? *Not a very honorable thing to do. She is a lady, my kinswoman, and a houseguest.*

Not to mention tiresomely well-chaperoned, for Delphinia is still too much the parson's daughter to turn a blind eye on even a well-managed affair.

Thorne nodded agreement to his reflection and turned away. *So we stay friends, and that is that!*

Hmmph! Thorne's internal opponent couldn't resist a parting shot. *Something tells me a chaste friendship will be exceeding difficult for you to maintain with her living under the same roof. Best get her married off as soon as possible.*

Thorne had no answer for that. It was clearly the correct solution. *And until she is married, I'll be taking a great many ice-cold baths*, he thought grimly as he rang for his valet.

Chapter Two

"Jamie!" Allison jumped up from her chair by the window and flew into the arms of James Betterton. "How wonderful to see you!"

"Heard you were staying with Thorne, thought I'd pop in to see you and Aunt Delphinia." James returned her hug, then stood her away to study her face. "It's good to see the bloom on your cheeks again, Cuz."

Thorne watched the two greet one another with no great enthusiasm. He felt left out by this evidence of their closeness. James and he had once been as close as brothers. *Drat Uncle Leo for making me James's guardian*, Thorne thought, not for the first time. Thorne had been twenty-one, James nineteen, when Leonard Betterton died, leaving Thorne in charge of James's finances until the age of thirty.

After James hugged Delphinia, he offered his hand to his older cousin. *Well might you look wary*, Thorne thought grimly. He had ordered James to stay in the country until all his debts were retired.

Once they were seated, Allison quizzed James on his late arrival in town for the season. "I made sure there was a pretty young lady in it," she teased, "for what else can have kept you in the country so long?"

James's eyes darted to meet Thorne's briefly, and he smiled ruefully. "Had to take a repairing lease, you see. A stroke of bad luck put me all to pieces until quarter day." He had come to London to renew his request that Thorne purchase colors for him. In the army he might find some purpose for his life, as well as an escape from Thorne's control.

They chatted happily in the brief periods between visitors, for this was Allison and Delphinia's afternoon to be at home to callers.

Thorne surprised Allison by staying all afternoon. Usually he did not put in an appearance at all, being much too busy with his estates, charities, and political activities.

One of their visitors was Claude Springfield, of whom he heartily disapproved. He had not bothered to warn Claude off as he had Jason Westingham-Jones and Ronald St. John, because until this day Allison had never shown any signs of encouraging him. But today she flirted most charmingly with the man, who was an accredited rake. He noticed that Delphinia, too, was frowning a little as she watched the two.

Just as Springfield took his leave, Mrs. Pendleton and Mrs. Larchmont and their daughters Catherine and Mary were announced. Both Allison and Delphinia were surprised by their arrival, though for different reasons.

I had not thought the minxes would have the nerve! Allison greeted these visitors coolly, reluctantly acknowledging their introduction the night before. Her mother was even more frosty. The reason soon became apparent.

"Lady Catherton, you may perhaps remember my sister, Antonia, now Lady Dyshart," Mrs. Pendleton said.

"I daresay I remember her at least as well as she remembers me," Delphinia responded.

Here was unexpectedly plain speaking. Mrs. Pendleton decided to meet it head-on. "She does remember you, and longs to renew the acquaintance. It quite broke her heart when Dyshart made her cease writing you. But Lord Catherton's unseemly behavior . . ."

"My husband's heavy gambling and the resulting bankruptcy were indeed unseemly. Some people were unable to make allowances for the fact that he had recently lost his only son and heir."

Allison turned her head to one side and bit her lip. The death of her younger brother, Phillip, in a carriage accident had hurt her no less because she was with Charles on their honeymoon when it happened.

"It was a terrible loss for you both," Mrs. Larchmont inserted, hoping to smooth the troubled waters. "We all felt for you. What mother could not?"

Delphinia's rigid posture relaxed slightly. "There is nothing so devastating as losing a child. But it is different for fathers than for mothers. We feel the loss of the dear flesh that we carried beneath our bosom and brought into the world, the merry, delightful child, the promising young adult. But for a father, the loss of a son is all that and more. It is a loss of his posterity, his chance of immortality in this life. My husband never quite recovered from it. While I could weep, gaming and roistering were his only way of dealing with grief."

Tears stood in Allison's eyes. Her heart contracted with pity and love. *I never looked at it quite that way. My poor father.* Suddenly, the anger that had gripped her whenever she thought of him fell away.

Gratitude and a desire to give her mother time to recover her composure made Allison join the conversation, encouraging the young girls to talk of their experiences in their first season. Mary Larchmont boldly launched into a humorous account of her presentation at court, addressing herself particularly to Thorne, who listened with an indulgent smile.

Catherine was more reticent, but Allison noticed that her eyes frequently strayed to James's profile. *And why not? He is almost as handsome as Thorne*, Allison thought. For his part, James had been caught up in some private reflections and was clearly woolgathering.

Mrs. Larchmont brought him back abruptly by her sudden exclamation. "I just realized that all three of the Silverthorne heirs sit here in front of us. Mary, Catherine, have you heard the tale of the Silverthorne treasure?"

Both Mary's and Catherine's eyes grew wide with fascination. "I didn't realize Mr. Betterton was one of the three," Catherine said. "Tell us, Mr. Betterton, have you ever seen the ghost—what is she called? The Silver Lady?"

Delphinia shook her head sternly. "That is merely a folk tale, Miss Pendleton. Everyone knows there is no such thing as a ghost."

"And very likely no Silverthorne treasure either," Thorne added, frowning at James as if daring him to disagree.

"Will you be attending the balloon ascension tomorrow, Jamie?" Allison interrupted before Thorne and James could fly at one another as they always did when the subject came up of the

lost wealth of their common ancestor. Not only was this a contro-
versial subject, but also a painful one for Thorne.

The distraction did not work. "Is it a very romantic tale? I
should love above all things to hear it." Catherine sat forward on
her seat, eyes fastened hopefully on James.

"James, I don't think—"

Thorne interrupted Allison. "It is quite all right. By all means
satisfy the young ladies' curiosity, James. I must see to some business anyway." He stood and formally took his leave of them.

Mary pouted. "Did we say something wrong? Lord Silverthorne
is not angry, is he?"

"His father and brother were killed trying to find the Silverthorne treasure," Delphinia said. "It is not a romantic tale to him,
but a tragic one."

"Oh!" Mary put her gloved hand to her mouth. "It seems I have
put my foot wrong again."

Allison primmed her lips and said nothing. She longed to go to
Thorne, to comfort him. But under the gimlet eye of the two ma-
trons and their gossiping daughters, she didn't think it wise.

James made a soothing response, obviously thriving in the sun-
shine of Catherine Pendleton's smile. "Not at all. It was years ago.
He's long since recovered. And it *is* a romantic tale. Shall I tell it?"
Ignoring the silence from both Allison and Delphinia, he launched
into his recitation.

"The founder of our line, Thorne D'Aumont, was one of those
bold gentlemen sailors known as privateers who helped England
drain Spain's treasury during the reign of Queen Elizabeth. He was
named "Silver" Thorne not just because he captured two rich
Spanish prize ships, nor because he owned a king's ransom in silver, but because from childhood he had a thick mane of silver
hair."

"Like yours, Mrs. Weatherby," Mrs. Pendleton observed. "I've
heard it said that prematurely grey hair crops up from time to time
in the bloodline."

"Allison's hair is not grey," Delphinia inserted. "It is pale blond,
and—"

Having little interest in the color of any woman's hair, much
less one as old as Mrs. Weatherby, Mary interrupted to demand of

James, "Catherine spoke of a ghost, a lady ghost. Pray tell me about her."

"The story is that after the reinstatement of the monarchy following the civil wars, Thorne D'Aumont's granddaughter and two grandsons disappeared while searching for the treasure that their father, the first Baron D'Aumont, had hidden from marauders. Various explanations have been offered, from their having found the treasure and fled the country to keep the king from confiscating it, to their being killed when the north tower of Silverthorne, D'Aumont's castle, collapsed. As Baron D'Aumont's sons were unwed and his grandchildren by his daughter were all females, his title passed to his brother, who spent the rest of his life trying to find the treasure—in vain.

"Through the years, numerous people have claimed to see the daughter wandering the ruins. And yes, Miss Larchmont, she is called the Silver Lady. She is thought to be the ghost of Elena, the first baron's daughter. Some say she guards the treasure from intruders, others that she tries to show where it is hidden, and still others that she deliberately lures to their deaths those who seek it."

"Which may be a romantic story, but quite a ridiculous one. Thorne is convinced that the treasure, if treasure there was, has long since—"

Interrupting Delphinia, Catherine asked, "Have you ever seen the ghost, Mr. Betterton?" She looked hopefully at James.

Allison bit her lip to keep from reprimanding the chit. *Both of them as rude as they can stare*, she thought, glowering darkly at them, for all the good it did her, for they both were looking at James, eager for his answer.

James sighed. "Unfortunately, no, but not for want of trying. As a boy I believed she would appear and lead me directly to the treasure." Then he grinned mischievously and, slanting his eyes briefly toward Delphinia, said, "Allison has seen her, though. Haven't you, Allie?"

"James!" Delphinia huffed, reacting just as he thought she would.

Allison shook her finger at him. "Shame on you! You know I was a very imaginative child, and Silverthorne is a very romantic place. It is easy enough for a child to see any number of ghosts and mythical beasts there." She smiled and spread her hands. "As an adult I have seen nothing but picturesque ruins."

For good measure, Delphinia added, "Dangerous ruins, too. No one is allowed there since Thorne's father and brother were killed."

"Which means the treasure will never be found." James's mood underwent a sudden transformation. "Pity. My purse could use an infusion of silver, gold, and precious stones. I must go. I have an appointment." He stood abruptly, his expression closed. He bowed politely and said all that was proper before taking his leave. The other four guests suddenly realized they had stayed far past the acceptable half hour allotted for a social call, and hastily made their retreat.

Allison was glad to see the back of them. They had managed to irritate or upset everyone, and doubtless were preening themselves on a successful visit. Still, the afternoon had not been a total disaster. Her plan to make Thorne jealous as a way of precipitating a proposal had been well launched. She had flirted shamelessly with Claude Springfield, surreptitiously studying Thorne's reaction.

Your face is too expressive for your own good, Thorne, she thought, smiling to herself. *I saw that look in your eyes.*

She would prefer to flirt with Ronald St. John, though, for there was little chance he would take any hurt by it, as he had no interest in matrimony. Claude had made hints that his rakehell days were over, so he might be looking for a wife.

"I wonder why St. John did not call," Delphinia said, voicing Allison's next thought. "He did not dance with you last night, either. And what has happened to Mr. Westingham-Jones? He had been most attentive."

Thorne spoke from the doorway. "If you hope to see your daughter married again, you should be grateful to m . . . ah, pleased that they have both concluded Allison is not suitable game. I am afraid neither of them would wish to be leg-shackled."

"Oh! I didn't know. They both seem such nice gentlemen." Delphinia rarely saw flaws in handsome men, particularly if they had generous incomes.

"And whom do we have to thank for their reaching that conclusion, my lord?" Allison asked in a sweetly lethal voice.

"Why, ah, I may have had a word with them. My duty as your kinsman, you know, to see that their intentions are honorable."

"That was very good of you, Thorne. I'm sure we are both very grateful to you, aren't we, Allison?"

"I shall try to think of words to suitably express my gratitude at another time." Allison tilted her nose up and turned away from him.

"I shall look forward to it," Thorne replied gravely. Allison looked up from her book to see that laughter lurked in his eyes—laughter and admiration.

It was such a beautiful dream, Allison tried to keep from waking up, but inexorably the sounds of early morning intruded. Her maid bustled about the room, and the scent of hot coffee lured her into opening her eyes.

She burrowed deep into her covers and tried to remember the dream. *Extraordinary*, she thought. *I saw colors, heard sounds—it seemed so real.* In her dream she had been at Silverthorne Castle, a place she had often visited as a child before her father and Lord Silverthorne had fallen out.

This dream was a recollection of a particular visit, the year she was nine. Prior to that, although she had often seen the Silver Lady, the spirit had never taken note of her, but only hovered about anxiously, watching the people who walked about the castle speculating about where the treasure might be. The second Marquess of Silverthorne had enjoyed taking visitors to tour the castle while he regaled them with tales of his ancestors' valor.

On the particular visit that her dream had re-created, Allison had tired of the conversation of adults; tired, too, of Jamie's boyish teasing. He kept trying to frighten her by jumping out from behind rocks and outbuildings, pretending to be a ghost. So she had slipped away and was exploring on her own when suddenly she saw the Silver Lady, closer and more clearly than ever before. Her hair tumbled about her shoulders, glowing in the sunlight. She looked right at Allison, a radiant smile on her face, and beckoned for her to follow. At the entrance to the keep, the Lady motioned for her to enter. Hesitating a little at the thought of braving the darkness beyond the entryway, Allison heard her mother's frantic calls. In an instant the Silver Lady disappeared.

That was the last time Allison saw the specter, for her mother had been frightened and angry at the same time. Warning her that the old castle was too dangerous for her to explore alone, she had sternly forbidden her daughter ever to wander off unaccompanied again. Since that day, Delphinia had always campaigned to convince her that there was no such thing as a ghost, and Allison had eventually come to believe the whole incident was a figment of her imagination.

Her dream had taken up where reality left off. In it, she had followed the ghost into the keep. It led her through dark tunnels in a phantasmagorical sequence that bore no resemblance to the real appearance of the old castle's stronghold, at least not any part of it that Allison had seen. Eventually, she was brought into a room filled with treasure. The Silver Lady stood in the center, shining radiantly as she spread her hands to welcome Allison. Golden goblets, swords, rubies, emeralds, and diamonds sparkled as they spilled out of chests. And everywhere there was silver, silver, silver—goblets, swords, coins, cutlery—a king's ransom of silver.

As Allison drew near the Silver Lady, she began to change. The beckoning arms became muscular, the figure grew and took on a man's shape, the clothing went from voluminous skirts to form-fitting trousers, and the ghost's glowing tresses became a top hat and intricately tied cravat. Allison did not dare to look at this new figure's face, but she knew somehow that it was Thorne. She moved into the welcoming arms that enfolded her and lifted her face for a kiss. It was at this point that reality began to intrude. She had tried to hang on to the dream, but sleep retreated, leaving her bereft of the strong arms and passionate kiss she so much desired.

She realized the dream had been triggered by the conversation the day before. *Is this how James pictures the treasure? If so, it is a compelling vision, indeed.* Allison shook her head. *Impossible!* Every square inch of the castle, above and below ground, except for that buried under rubble or threatening to collapse, had been searched over and over. Secret rooms had indeed been found— empty rooms. Whatever the childhood dreams she and James had spun around that treasure, as an adult she was as convinced as Thorne that it had long since been removed from the castle.

*   *   *

That evening, Allison found her opportunity to twit Thorne for his presumption in discouraging her suitors. They returned from another ball in the early morning hours. For once Delphinia was not feigning tiredness. She yawned even as she followed the footman's high-held candle branch up the stairs. Allison accepted Thorne's suggestion of a glass of sherry, so that she could beard him on his interference in her affairs. He had given her fresh cause: This time Claude Springfield had also eschewed dancing with her.

Thorne handed her a small crystal glass and, to her surprise, immediately turned away from her. He made his way to the French doors that opened out onto the small garden at the rear of the town house. "A beautiful evening, isn't it?" he asked, holding out his hand in invitation. "Shall we walk in the moonlight?"

At the expression on his face, all thought of quarreling with him disappeared. Heart pounding with excitement, Allison crossed the room and took his hand, allowing him to lead her through the windows and into the silvery light. They walked silently side by side down the narrow, winding brick path.

"Your hair glows like moonbeams," Thorne finally said, turning to face her. "In fact, in that silver-beaded gown you look like a moon maiden. Are you, in fact, a daughter of the moon?"

She lifted her eyes to meet his. Naked desire stared out at her and called an answering passion from her. Suddenly, she was in his arms, without knowing who had made the first move.

Thorne's first kiss was hard, urgent—the expression of long pent-up feelings—and she returned it in kind. Then his lips gentled on hers and began a slow, maddeningly slow sampling of her lips, proceeding by delicate nips, stopping to suck gently on the fullness at the center.

This was seduction, and Allison loved every minute of it. As her knees buckled, she slumped against him, and he gathered her close with his strong left arm while his right hand plundered her hair, plucking out pins and jewels to free it. Then he broke off his kisses to spread it about her shoulders, fingering it wonderingly and murmuring, "So soft, so silky."

Allison put her hand behind his head and pulled him down for another long, drugging kiss. Before it had ended, she felt herself being lifted off her feet. She kissed his jawline, reveling in the sensation of tiny pricks from his beard, as he carried her back into the house and lowered her onto the soft leather of the largest sofa in his drawing room.

Immediately, Thorne followed her down, pressing her into the yielding leather, kissing her face, her neck, her bosom. She pressed her breast willingly, eagerly, into his hand as he pulled the beaded lace away. Lost to reason, frenzied with desire, she lifted her hips as he began to work the material of her skirt higher, all the while raining kisses on her.

But just as he successfully worked the fabric free, Allison became aware of the meaning of the words that punctuated his kisses. She stilled beneath him. "What? What did you say?" Her voice was breathless.

"I said you would be the most cherished, indulged . . ." Thorne, too, stilled as he realized what she was reacting to.

" 'Mistress in all of England.' Isn't that what you said?" She pulled her hands out of his hair and pushed against his chest.

"Don't. Oh, God, don't deny me this. You want me, I know you do. I've been going mad with desire for you. I know it will be awkward. Your mother is an observant woman, but—"

"My mother is a principled woman, and so am I." This time Allison pushed with all her might, heaving with her body, too. Thorne began to slide off the sofa. He had to sit up to regain his balance. Instantly, Allison wriggled from beneath him. Springing from the sofa, she hastily reclaimed her bodice and smoothed her skirt.

"No wonder the gossips say I am your mistress! They know you better than I do. How dare you warn Jason and Ronald away because they might have dishonorable intentions, when you planned to offer me your own dishonorable intentions!" The sense of betrayal and loss Allison felt overwhelmed her. She turned and dropped her face into her hands, sobbing.

"No, no, my love, don't cry."

"Don't call me your love." Swallowing her tears, Allison turned on him furiously. "You could not possibly love me and make such an offer. You cannot even know me at all, to think that I would agree to be kept by you." She broke away from him. "What a fool I have been. And poor mother. She thinks you hung the moon. 'Dear Thorne, such a kind and decent man, to take us under his wing when William treated us so shamefully.' Little did she know you had nefarious reasons for your kindness."

"No, you and she were too busy spinning your silken webs, to entrap me in marriage." Thorne drew himself up angrily. "Well, it hasn't worked. Any number of women have tried, but I am not inclined to marry. I thought you understood that."

"We did not scheme!" Allison stamped her foot in fury. "In fact, in spite of mother's constant harping, I had absolutely no intentions of remarrying. I like my independence, and—"

"I rather thought you did, so I naturally assumed that if you accepted my attentions that meant you . . ."

But Thorne couldn't quite bring himself to complete that sentence. In truth, before this night he had had no thought of making Allison his mistress. For weeks he had been struggling with his growing feelings for her, knowing an affair would wrong her, but fearing that marriage to her would doom him to his father's fate. What had just happened was entirely spontaneous.

"Oh, yes. I know. Like so many men, you thought as a widow I was ripe for any number of affairs. While I believed myself to be falling in love with you, you were planning—what? To purchase a nice little house for me in Hampton? But no—you just said you meant to be generous. Doubtless you planned on leasing a house right here in Mayfair."

She sliced the air downward with her hand. "What a fool I am. I don't even know you. Well, our idyll is at an end. Mother and I will remove ourselves from your household tomorrow."

"You most certainly will not! Where would you go? What would you do? Your combined income would not support you in a genteel manner."

"Then I shall just have to find a position somewhere. I will not be a whore. Yours or anyone else's." Allison's voice broke. She turned and ran out of the room.

Thorne caught her at the bottom of the steps.

"You and your mother will remain here," he stormed in his most intimidating voice.

"Don't you presume to tell me what to do. I won't spend another night under the same roof with you."

"I shall be the one to move, then. I'll go to my club—something I should have done long ago, before temptation overwhelmed me."

"Ah, yes. And I am the scheming temptress. Let me tell you this, Thorne D'Aumont: I would have preferred the attentions of St. John to yours, for he at least made no pretensions of concern for my honor."

Stung, and not knowing how to undo the false impression he had given her without explaining a great deal more than he cared to, Thorne let her go when she pulled her elbow from his grasp. He watched her climb the stairs and felt a little like a man who had been milled down by an unexpectedly strong opponent—hurting all over, not quite sure what he had done wrong, and too dazed to know what he should do next.

Chapter Three

"I do wish Aunt Henrietta would not be so careful of our purse. I would gladly have paid more postage to be able to read this," Allison complained, holding the piece of crossed and recrossed parchment closer to the window.

"Let me try if I can read it," Delphinia started to rise from the sofa where she lay with a cold cloth across her forehead. "I can usually make out her hand."

"No, Mother. Puzzling it out can only make your headache worse." Allison cast a worried look toward her mother, whose headaches had intensified and become more frequent since their removal to Bristol two weeks before. *What does it signify?* she wondered. *Is her unhappiness the cause, or does she have a malady requiring a physician's attendance?* It little mattered, since her mother had resolutely refused to see a Bristol physician.

Delphinia swung her feet to the floor and held out her hand. "My headache has gone long since. I have just been too lazy to move." Allison reluctantly handed her the letter and watched as she frowned over the cramped writing.

"Hmmm. Something about a house party, and a . . . oh, a ghost," Delphinia said in a tone of utter disgust. "It's about the Ghost of Hammerswold supposedly selecting a bride for the Hammerswold heir. What a lot of nonsense. James would do well to cease keeping company with that disgraceful Jared Camden. I doubt marriage to Sylvia Patchfield can improve him."

Allison laughed. "True. If the ghost chose that little cat for Jared, his much vaunted wisdom must be called into question. But why is Aunt Henny raking those old coals?"

Delphinia squinted at the paper. "It seems to be something about a maid. How confusing. What has a maid to do with the ghost?"

She turned the paper sideways so that she could read the perpendicular lines. "This part I can't make out either—surely it doesn't say James and Jared have been riding donkeys?"

"A fatal jest for the donkey that had the misfortune to carry one of Jared's girth, I sadly fear." Allison grimaced in disgust.

"Another ridiculous wager, I have no doubt. Our poor Jamie will bankrupt himself yet." Delphinia's expression saddened as she lay back down and dragged the cloth onto her forehead once again.

"Perhaps James can explain it all to us when he arrives. I had expected him before now." Allison leaned forward to peer out the window of their parlor. "Not that I truly believed he would be on time. Let us call for our tea now, else it will be time for dinner, and Mrs. Peterson's tea cakes will be quite stale."

Delphinia rose once more and fluttered anxiously to the window. "I am sure he was unavoidably detained. Perhaps his carriage broke down, or robbers . . ."

Allison barely suppressed an amused smile at her mother, who could not bear to hear ill of any of her male relatives. Rather than believe James had been careless about his arrival time, she would accept that Napoleon yet lived and was on the march to London.

"Do not distress yourself, Mother. He'll be here soon, I'm sure. I'll call Peterson, shall I?" At Delphinia's nod, Allison moved to the parlor door. Their one male servant, an ancient man in an ill-fitting uniform, sat dozing on a bench in the hall.

"We'll have our tea now, Peterson." She had to repeat the sentence, bending to speak into his ear.

The butler awoke with a start. "Master Jamie here?"

"No, but we have decided to begin without him."

"Up to his old tricks," the elderly man growled as he limped away to do his mistress's bidding.

"Peterson's rheumatism is bothering him again, poor old dear." Allison returned to her chair by the window and picked up the book she had been reading.

"How I wish we could afford to pension him off." Her mother sighed.

"He likely wouldn't go, Mother. You'd never convince him you could do without him. But we do need a younger man for the heavy work. Oh, that foolish, foolish girl." Allison tossed her book down in disgust.

"Girl?"

"Yes, the heroine in this novel has refused a very worthy and very wealthy gentleman. And who is she? A nobody, with encroaching, ill-mannered relatives."

Delphinia clicked her tongue. "These romances—so unrealistic. I don't see why you read them. I suppose it has ghosts and haunted castles and other things to your taste!"

"Not this one. To tell the truth, I don't quite know what to make of it. It isn't precisely a romance. More of a satire. I suppose the silly creature will get her comeuppance in the end, but in her place I would certainly have swallowed my pride and accepted him!"

"Now dear, you wouldn't accept a man you didn't care for. Else why did you not accept Lord Bertland's proposal?" Her mother wagged a knowing finger at Allison.

"This Eliza Bennet does love her suitor, though she may not know it yet. You have the right of it, though. I won't remarry except for love, and now that I have no hope of Thorne, I do not look for that to happen." Allison suddenly stood and began pacing the parlor, straightening cushions and realigning the chairs. Her lower lip was trembling.

"You still have hope of Thorne," Delphinia asserted. "It was all a misunderstanding. That dear, kind, honorable man could not have meant to give you a slip on the shoulder. He is not in the least rakish, and even if he were, he wouldn't dishonor you, his kinswoman and widow of his best friend. When he returns from Paris, he'll set all aright."

Allison clenched her jaw. She had smiled over her mother's defense of James, but she found nothing humorous in this continued manifestation of her mother's worship of Thorne, her favorite representative of her favored sex. When Allison told her Thorne had asked her to be his mistress, Delphinia had flatly refused to believe it. She insisted Allison had misunderstood Thorne. And since he had decamped to Paris the next day, there had been no opportunity for Delphinia to hear from his own lips that he had intended an affair. She had only come to Bristol because Allison made it clear she would leave Thorne's home, with or without her mother's company.

Despairing of ever convincing her mother of Thorne's culpability, Allison sighed. "I do wish you would not pursue this subject, Mother."

Before Delphinia could, with the best intentions, rub more salt into Allison's wounds, a loud knock at the door announced the arrival of their visitor.

Allison jumped up. "I'll go. Peterson will take forever, even if he heard it." She hurried from the room, glad to put an end to their conversation.

"Jamie! Just what we needed to brighten up a rainy spring day!" She welcomed her cousin with a wide smile, which slipped somewhat as she beheld another man following him into the foyer.

"Look who I brought with me," James announced. "Captain Newcomb, late of his majesty's service. Do you know one another?"

As James introduced them, Allison grew uncomfortable under the intent regard of this man whom she knew by reputation as a gamester and rake.

"Ran into Newcomb in London. Wanted to come for the fight. It'll be a famous mill. Roads completely choked. Every sporting gentleman in the kingdom must be on his way here." Hanging up his own coat and hat, and peeling off his gloves as he talked, James Betterton motioned the tardy butler to assist his friend.

Allison retreated to the parlor, scowling. "What has he brought that rackety captain here for?"

"Hush, dear, your manners," Lady Catherton warned her, sotto voce. "He is very highly thought of, you know, and so very handsome. You might do a great deal worse."

She darted forward and embraced James, then welcomed Captain Newcomb warmly. "I told you what it was, Allison. 'The roads quite choked.' Dear boy, we had begun to fear your curricle had overturned—such a dangerous conveyance, those high-perch phaetons."

"Never fear, Aunt Delphinia. Came in the captain's coach, safe and snug." James patted her cheek soothingly.

After greetings had been exchanged all around, and the cool, wet weather remarked upon, and the captain had paid effusive compliments to both ladies, his bold eyes on Allison the whole time, they settled down to tea.

"We had a letter from your mother today," Allison said as she served James. "Full of gossip about your friend Viscount Faverill."

"Poor Jared. Quarreled with his wife already. He is inconsolable."

"He looked well consoled to me last night, with La Fontaine on his arm." Captain Newcomb winked broadly.

James frowned, and Allison felt the heat rising in her cheeks, but Delphinia chose to see no impropriety in this remark. Eager to turn the conversation in less disturbing channels, Allison addressed James again on the subject of Aunt Henrietta's letter.

"Your mother spoke of that unusual party you attended last Halloween at Hammerswold."

"Lud, what a show that was. You wouldn't believe the half of it! Ghosts all around, terrifying maids and guests alike. Poor Fotheringay—he decamped after the second sighting."

"Fotheringay saw the ghost?" Allison's brows lifted.

"But I heard he sees a great many things when he is in his cups," Delphinia countered, ever vigilant against ghostly manifestations.

"Not sure he actually saw it. The mere thought was enough to drive him from our midst."

"Of course he didn't see it. There is no such thing!" Delphinia cast her daughter a challenging look.

"Well, as to that, all of us saw something, and the young women in the party actually conversed with him."

"Ah, but those young women were doubtless vying for the opportunity to wed Jared. You'd be surprised what one can see, when it is to one's advantage to do so."

"Well, Aunt, how do you explain the Beasley chit's terrified maid? She had nothing to gain; indeed, she abandoned her post and fled the castle because she saw spirits everywhere. Lady Hammerswold said she was able to see ghosts that the family thought had faded forever."

"She abandoned . . . she left them without a maid?" Delphinia's eyes were wide.

James nodded. "Shocking, isn't it." He winked at Allison.

"Shocking!" Delphinia's agreement was heartfelt. Allison bit the corner of her mouth to control the smile that was trying to emerge. A pang of regret quickly supplanted her amusement. Her mother did love to have a personal maid, a luxury no longer possible for them.

"We misread her letter. I thought she said the maid saw a ghost at Fairmont." Allison picked up the letter and examined it once again.

"Really? I had no idea we had any of them about," James answered. "Told Mama not to hire her, but she would do it, as a favor to the Beasleys."

Captain Newcomb had left off ogling Allison to listen intently to James. Now he leaned forward, his florid face flushed with excitement. "You should take this maid to Silverthorne. That's where your ancestral treasure lies hidden, isn't it? Get her to follow the Silver Lady to it."

"I say! The very thing!" James turned admiring eyes on the captain. "Why didn't I think of that?"

Delphinia snapped, "Foolishness! Don't even think of going there, James, or you, Captain Newcomb, with or without that maid. The Silverthorne treasure, if it still exists, is buried beneath tons of rubble.

"And surrounded by unstable walls," Allison added. "Don't forget, Lord Silverthorne's father and half brother were killed seeking the treasure. He permits no one to go there now."

"But that is doubtless because they didn't know where to look. I say, James, think I'll call on your mother—see if the seer would take a look at some property I have in Ireland."

James looked doubtful. "That maid was terrified of spirits. Much chance she'd deliberately look for one."

"That explains it." Allison held his mother's letter out to James. "Does this say that the maid has left her service?"

James looked at his mother's crabbed handwriting and scratched his head. "Think so. Stands to reason, if the creature saw any ghosts at Fairmont."

Newcomb sat back in his chair with a disgusted sigh. "Pity, for I know of several sites where there are rumors of treasures guarded by spirits."

"Are you returning to your regiment, Captain?" Delphinia made a transparent bid to change the subject. Newcomb willingly launched into a recitation of his reasons for selling out, chief among which was the small chance of gaining advancement.

"Can't distinguish oneself for valor when the country is at peace," he asserted.

"Indeed, no, but your courage has more than earned your place in military history," Delphinia replied, eyes alight with admiration.

Allison listened without comment. Her dear deceased Charles had been highly skeptical of the account of Captain Newcomb's valor that had made him a nine-day wonder after Badajoz. "Never saw him do anything but hold back until someone else had done the dirty work," her husband had told her. "Then he and his troop arrived in time to join in the looting. It was a very near-run thing that Wellington did not have him hanged instead of decorated!"

Allison found herself growing less and less pleased with her cousin for introducing Newcomb to them. Though she knew James could be a sad romp, he never before had brought one of his rackety friends among his female relatives. Why had he done so now?

She didn't have to wonder much longer.

"By the way," James asked her under cover of Newcomb's loud retelling of his brave actions in war, "when is Thorne returning from Paris?"

Through clenched teeth she replied, "I haven't the least idea, Jamie. We are in no way connected now, as you well know."

James leaned forward to touch her hand comfortingly. "Sorry—didn't mean to open that wound. It's just that I'm somewhat beneath the hatches. Hoped he might be back soon. Hate to ask him for money, of course, for Thorne'll read me a jaw-me-dead and try to put me to work supervising some estate or other, but—"

"You've been gambling again, haven't you? Oh, Jamie. You promised me you wouldn't."

He could not meet her eyes. "Something came up—thought it was a sure thing. Truth is, the captain here loaned me a small sum—I'm sure to be able to pay it back on quarter day, but he doesn't want to wait that long."

"Perhaps I can help. How much is it?"

"No, no. I haven't come here to ask you for money. Know you are not plump in the pocket."

"Haven't you? For you read the court papers as well as I, and Thorne's sojourn in Paris was mentioned there."

James looked down at his highly polished Hessians. He had

asked her for a loan, of course, by his very mention of the problem. "Fifty guineas."

"Fif . . . Oh, James. I can't. Nothing even close to that. We spent almost all of our money on the move and leasing this cottage."

"You leased this wretched thing?" James looked around disdainfully. "It is so small, and I cannot like the situation, on this busy street."

"Which is one reason we could afford it."

"Afford what, dear?" Delphinia had apparently heard enough of Captain Newcomb's heroics.

"I was telling Jamie about the cottage. We made a very good bargain."

"Humph." Newcomb glanced disparagingly around the room. "I am surprised at Thorne for doing so poorly by you. You would have done better to remain in London. There you might have been much better entertained."

Allison suspected she knew how the captain thought she ought to entertain herself. *He thinks I was Thorne's mistress, and am now pensioned off. Another five minutes and he'll be offering me carte blanche.* She stood abruptly. "Why Mama, look at the time. We are going to miss vespers."

Delphinia quickly hid her surprise, for they never went to church during the week. "Oh, dear. That would be a pity. Would you care to join us, gentlemen? They have such a lovely service here."

Alarmed, James sounded the retreat. "By no means, Aunt Delphinia. We had best locate the field where the fight is taking place now, get our carriage in a good position. Going to be quite a crush."

As the men put on their coats, Allison went to her desk and took out a locked box. From the small pile inside she extracted ten guineas, which she slipped into James's pocket as she hugged him in farewell. He whispered a promise to return it by quarter day at the latest.

After they had left, Delphinia sat down by her daughter, who was staring moodily out the window. "What is it, dearest? You did not seem best pleased to have the handsome captain visit us. He was most taken with you."

"I cannot like him. You should know that Charles had no great opinion of him as a soldier."

"Well, but he isn't a soldier any longer, dear. Doubtless he is looking about him for a wife. And from the way he looked at you, I think with very little effort on your part he would search no farther. Small wonder, too." Lady Catherton's eyes swept her daughter's trim figure approvingly. "You are in looks today. I have ever thought that shade of blue quite lovely with your coloring."

"Captain Newcomb was looking at me as if I were Haymarket ware, Mother, not a candidate for a wife. Which is just as well, for I want nothing to do with him."

"I am very pleased to hear you say it."

Allison stared. "You perplex me, Mama."

"Yes, very pleased. You rightly think the heroine in this book of yours a foolish creature." Delphinia brandished the copy of *Pride and Prejudice* triumphantly. "Yet you won't even look at another man, which only proves to me that, whatever you say, you have not given up all hope of Thorne! No, indeed, so don't swell up. You hope to be reconciled when he returns. I doubt not he will offer for your hand as soon as the matter is cleared up."

On that, Delphinia swept grandly from the room, quite as if it had been the Prince Regent's most elegant salon, and not a mean little cottage parlor. Allison was left to argue, not with her mother, but with her own foolish heart.

Chapter Four

Thorne shuffled through the morning's post diffidently. In addition to several demands for payment of James's bills, there were no fewer than three billet-doux in his mail, but none of them were in the hand he yearned for. Not that he expected anything addressed to him in that hand, and particularly not a love letter. With a sigh he broke the seal on a thick packet from Edward Bartholomew, his secretary in London, and began reading.

Not three minutes later, a loud crash shattered the quiet of the stately Parisian residence. "My lord?" Thorne's butler inquired after cautiously opening the library door.

The marquess pointed to the clutter of books, letters, and what had once been a beautifully presented breakfast tray, now sprawled across the parquet floor. "Clean up this mess and inform my valet that I go to England immediately."

Martin stepped back out of the room and snapped his fingers at a footman, then followed in his employer's wake as he strode from the room and up the stairs. "Should the rest of the staff begin packing, my lord?"

"No. I will be returning within the week, once I have taught a certain headstrong young widow a lesson."

"Not those! Those are daisies. These are the weeds." Allison held out the offending plant for her young employee to study. "Keep this with you, and pull out only the plants that look like it."

The boy scratched his head in puzzlement. "They don' look that much diff'rent tuh me."

Patiently, Allison pointed out the differences in the daisy's leaf and that of plantain. Then she watched closely for a while as Danny plucked plants from the choked flower beds. Satisfied at last, she moved away to inspect the grapevine that dangled hither and thither, medusalike, from the arbor trellis it covered. Shears in hand, she set about the task of trimming it back, while still preserving sufficient limbs for some grape production.

As she worked, she mulled over her interview that morning with the headmistress of Purvey's Academy for Young Ladies. In spite of Lady Langley's letter, Mrs. Purvey had been openly suspicious of her, and had refused to hire her until she received written responses from Allison's list of references. Moreover, she found Allison's qualifications too limited for teaching anything but music and French, and Mrs. Purvey herself taught the French classes. This meant she could offer Allison only a half-day of work at best. *I should have harassed my governesses less, and learned more*, she thought ruefully. She had more than once wished for a better education while debating with Thorne, but had never expected to need it to earn her livelihood.

Her mother's voice interrupted her uneasy thoughts. "Allison, where are you? Come see who is here!" Lady Catherton stood in the French doors that looked out onto the garden, shielding her eyes from the morning sun. "Allison?"

"She be over there, ma'am," Danny volunteered.

Allison straightened, bracing her back with the palm of her hand as she did so. "Here, Mother. I'll be with you in a moment."

"Take this, boy. There's a gingerbread vendor down the street. And do not hurry back."

The deep masculine voice made Allison's heart jump. She whirled around and saw Thorne bestowing a coin on the beaming boy.

She set down her shears carefully, as if they might break. *Ah, why does he have to be so handsome?* Allison's pulse jumped at the sight of him. His dark wavy hair tumbled about his forehead in disarray, suggesting that he had traveled on horseback. His face was in shadow, so his expression was inscrutable. She hoped his clear grey eyes would be shining with love, and he would go down on his knees to propose to her, having learned that he could not live without her. She had fantasized this moment many times over the last two weeks.

"Thorne is here to take us back to London. It was a misunderstanding, just as I've said all along. Come, we will talk over lemonade, and he'll make all right."

Rooted to the spot, Allison could not respond to her mother's happy summons. Unless he lied to her mother, there could be no satisfactory explanation. Unless he came to propose, there was no way to make all right. Her fingers twisted nervously in the fabric of her gown.

Thorne turned and murmured something to Lady Catherton, who waved to her daughter and went back into the cottage.

All the way from Paris to London, he had worried about where she had gone. After learning of her whereabouts from his secretary, all the way from London to Bristol he had worried about what her situation might be. He had been right to worry, Thorne knew as he looked about the dusty, weed-choked garden. A tiny cottage on a main thoroughfare. No servants to speak of. Two impoverished women, living alone, one of them young and beautiful, though looking hollow-eyed and sadly downpin. Fury—at her, and at himself—had driven him to find her, and now it saved him from the urge to fold her in his arms.

He is angry! When he moved close enough for her to see his face, Allison's numbness began to dissipate. Her response was not fear, however, but an equal surge of anger.

How dare he look at me that way. What right has he *to be angry!* She fisted her hands and straightened her spine, holding her ground as he stalked close enough that she had to tilt her head back to meet eyes that were hard now, like grey marble.

"What the devil do you think you are about, Allison Weatherby? When Bartholomew wrote me that you had disappeared, I feared you might do something rash, but this . . . this is beyond anything!"

Instead of responding to this attack, Allison launched her own. "So, you've explained it all to her, have you, Thorne? And it was a misunderstanding? I am vastly relieved to hear it. That humiliating scene on the sofa was a figment of my imagination? A dream? No, wait. I have it. When I thought you said 'come to bed with me,' you really said 'come wed with me!' No wonder you were so surprised at my indignant refusal."

"That is quite enough! I cannot credit that you told your mother—"

"She thinks you embody all the knightly virtues, Thorne. How else was I to convince her that we had to leave your home?"

"You didn't have to leave my home. I left precisely so that you wouldn't—"

She stomped her foot and whirled around, giving him her back as she grabbed up her shears and began whacking randomly at the grapevine. "As if I would stay after that night."

Thorne took her elbow none too gently, turning her back around. "You cannot have believed I would importune you after your forceful rejection?"

"I don't know what to believe." Allison closed her eyes. She could see herself, standing in the moon-drenched garden, wrapped in his arms, her face lifted to receive his kisses. The thought of his caresses on the sofa as he punctuated each kiss with a word still had the power to flood her body with heat. But inseparable from that memory were his words. She shuddered at the memory.

"Until that moment I wouldn't have believed you intended to offer me carte blanche!" She spat out the words, all the pain of that humiliating end to the tender scene of lovemaking once again overwhelming her.

Thorne dropped her elbow. "I never intended it. I spoke in the heat of passion. That evening was all a mistake. Your mother understands—"

"She wants so much to believe in you, she has blinded herself to the true meaning of your behavior. From the first she believed that your insistence that we live with you grew out of your interest in me. She took the notion that you were courting me. she fully expected you to offer for me at any time. At first I disagreed with her, but you were so very attentive—"

"I am sorry if you mistook my intentions." Thorne turned away, wiping at his face as if to free it of cobwebs. "You were not only my kinswoman, but also my best friend's widow. I could not leave you in that rotting dower house. I enjoyed our friendship, but that was all I ever intended, until that night. Somehow, in the light of the full moon, with your hair glowing like silver and that green dress shimmering with silver beads, you drew me to you. I touched you as a man might touch a fairy maiden, to see if she was real."

"Ah, yes. Once again we come to it. It was all my fault. I seduced you."

"You weren't unwilling." He turned back to her, brows arrowed downward, eyes scanning her face for the answer to a question he had no right to ask.

"No," she whispered. "I wasn't. I wanted your touch, your kiss, your . . . everything—until I realized it wasn't marriage you had in mind."

"I am truly sorry for that, Allison. It was wrong—I admit that. But please believe it wasn't premeditated. Indeed, I fought a hard battle with myself all spring to keep our association platonic, because I knew I couldn't offer you marriage." He held out his hands in supplication. "I thought you understood—"

"I didn't understand then, and I don't now. Say you do not love me; that I can understand. But to say you cannot marry me? My birth is not inferior. I haven't a large dowry, true, but I thought you had riches enough."

"Shut up!" He seized both of her shoulders and gave her a little shake. "It's nothing to do with money!"

"I thought not. Your feelings are not engaged. It was simply lust between us. I do understand that now, but at the time I believed otherwise."

My feelings not engaged! Thorne's hands tightened almost painfully on her shoulders. Thank goodness she could not know how he had wrestled with his feelings these last two weeks in Paris, when he finally realized that he had fallen in love. It was an emotion he regarded as an illness, to be avoided like the plague.

Her eyes searched his, and the pain and yearning she saw there mirrored her own soul. They swayed closer to one another, until without being sure how it happened, she was almost in his embrace. She pushed her hands up his chest until they cradled his head. "Can it be true? You feel nothing for me, other than lust?"

For a long, dangerous moment he looked as if he would kiss her. She leaned against him, almost on tiptoe, making her desire for that kiss perfectly clear. But he was visibly struggling with himself, and when he gained control, he gently but firmly put her away from him.

"I cannot marry you."

Allison felt wrenching pain through the whole fiber of her being. She turned away. "You do not love me. Forgive me for embarrassing you further. It won't happen again." She sank onto the bench that her busy shears had revealed beneath the grape arbor.

Thorne knew he had hurt her. He tried to think of something to say to comfort her, to reassure her, to exonerate himself. But no words would come.

After a long while, Allison raised her head and looked directly at him. No tears blurred her sapphire eyes—she had herself well in hand. "Again you said cannot. Please explain the use of that word."

Thorne struggled for an answer. "I . . . we would not suit, Allison."

"I expect it was all the brangling. We were forever coming to cuffs over something, weren't we? You seemed to enjoy our verbal sparring as much as I did, but . . ."

"It was at once the most exasperating and the most exhilarating experience of my life." His face relaxed; he almost smiled as he reminisced. "Never had I guessed I would have to defend my politics, my religion, even my taste in literature, to a woman. And one who could make me think twice about my answer, too."

She cocked her head, puzzled by the affection in his voice. "But you want a biddable creature for a wife?"

Thorne hesitated. How could he explain to her that the overwhelming feelings she aroused in him made him less likely than ever to marry her? She wouldn't understand. She would try to overcome his objections, and God help him, she might succeed. Besides, if he married—and it began to look as if he must, given James's increasingly irresponsible behavior—she would be ineligible for a reason not subject either to emotion or argument.

Thorne sighed and turned away, remembering the day two years before when he had called on her at Lord Catherton's town home. She was staying with her parents while Charles joined the dual United States–British force in the Oregon territory. The war office had asked him to break to her the news that Charles had died of an inflammation of the lungs. She had sobbed against his chest over and over again, "If only I could have had a child." His heart had swelled with pity.

Yet sad though Allison's barrenness was, it affected her and Charles alone. If Thorne died without an heir, it would affect literally thousands of people dependent upon him for their employment. Increasingly, he had become convinced that he could not trust their fate to the tender mercies of his ne'er-do-well cousin. That consideration, and that alone, could make him marry. *It must be a marriage of convenience only. Not a love match! Never!*

Thorne knew if he pointed to her barrenness as the reason he could not marry her, she would understand. But that would only serve to pour salt into that old wound.

Thorne studied the dear, unhappy countenance turned up to him. *It surprises me that she doesn't guess.* Allison and Charles had been married for six years, and for much of that time she had followed the drum. There would have been plenty of opportunity for a child to be conceived. *Perhaps she can't bear to face it.* Well, he couldn't bear to grieve her again. Let her think it was her tendency to speak her mind and stand her ground in the face of opposition that made him shy away from marrying her. *It isn't exactly a lie,* Thorne thought, shuddering at the memory of his stepmother's scolding voice.

"You have the right of it, Allison. I did enjoy some of our discussions, but I am much too busy to be forever argufying with my wife. It would be fatiguing to have to justify my every decision. I want a peaceful home and obedient children. Think of the example you would set."

Allison raised her chin proudly. "Thank you for explaining matters to me, Thorne. Now I understand. I misinterpreted your kindness, your friendship. Will you forgive me for the unpleasantness I put you through?"

"Shall we forgive one another and resume our friendship?" He held out his hand, which she, somewhat hesitantly, shook. "Good. Now you and Delphinia can come home. How on earth did you select Bristol as a refuge, Allison?" He hoped his teasing tone would lighten the mood.

Allison stood up. "No, we won't come home, if by home you mean Thorne Hall or your London house. However unintentional those moments of passion in the garden were, they have changed everything. I could never be comfortable under your roof."

"I have told you I would not deliberately seduce you. Now we both know the danger, we will be on guard against it. Come, Allison. Say you will go to London with me."

She shook her head vehemently.

"Then go to Thorne Hall."

"No. Residence in your home would only provide fuel for the gossips. I don't care to be served up as scandal broth. Besides, now that I know there is no hope of mother recovering her dowry, I cannot like living on your charity."

"Damn that Bartholomew! I shall fire him!"

"I insisted on seeing the accounts. Don't blame him. Blame yourself for hiding from my mother and me the true state of our finances."

"If you know the true state of your finances, you know you cannot live on your own. I daresay your entire annual income would barely pay the hire of this cottage. Stay on Curzon Street or at Thorne Hall while I look about me for a suitable residence for you on one of my smaller estates."

Allison lifted her chin. "I do not intend to be one of your many pensioners."

"Then how do you propose to live?"

"I am going to teach at a very good academy for females nearby and give piano lessons. That is why I chose Bristol. Lady Langley recommended it because of her acquaintance with the owner of the academy. It seems there are many wealthy tradesmen with daughters who aspire to gentility."

He stared at her as if she had grown a second head. "You propose to earn your own bread?"

"I can and will support myself and my mother."

"My kinswoman hiring herself out to Cits? Never! I won't allow it."

"You have no authority to stop me."

"I am head of the family, and—"

"We are but distant cousins. I have male relatives on my father's side who are more nearly related."

"And who turned their backs on you when your father died in debt."

Allison flushed. "Yes. Which is why none of them will seek to prevent me from supporting myself."

"You forget, your husband appointed me your guardian."

"He appointed you my financial guardian, Thorne. But it seems I have almost no finances to guard."

"Such as you have, I control. You rented this place illegally, in fact. Bartholomew had no authorization to pay your quarter's allowance ahead of schedule."

"Nor did he."

The earl looked around him. The cottage, though mean by his standards, looked to be well built and boasted a large garden, a small stable, and outbuildings for livestock. "Then how did you manage to hire such a place?"

"I sold my pearls." Allison turned her head and stared unseeing into the distance.

There was a long silence. "The ones your father gave you before your first ball?"

She nodded, not trusting herself to speak above the lump that suddenly rose in her throat.

"My God. You must really have wanted this."

"I really didn't want to be kept by you."

He flinched. "It isn't the same thing."

"There is no use arguing about it, Thorne. I won't be your pensioner, you won't have me for your wife, and I won't take a lover. It would be best if you left now."

"That I will not do, not without you and Delphinia. The two of you will return to London with me. I will send my servants to move your things and close this house." His mouth set in a grim line, Thorne folded his arms and glared down at her.

"I will not return to London with you." She folded her arms in echo of his posture and set her lips into equally mulish lines.

"Be sensible, Allison. A beautiful woman like you cannot live on her own, without a man to protect her. You'll be beset at every turn, once it is known that we are estranged."

"My mother can be a formidable chaperone."

"And that is another thing. Your mother! Don't tell me she will be happy here. There is no society as she knows of it in Bristol, and even if there were—"

"With her daughter working, she would be considered declassé. I know, and it makes me feel very sad. But I must choose the honorable path, and that precludes a life under your roof." She turned her back on him.

Thorne once again turned her around and held her pinioned by his strong hands on her shoulders. "I swear I would never dishonor you," he growled.

Allison struggled in his grasp. "I am sure you have no intention of doing so. But now that we have become aware of the potent attraction between us, can we honestly say no danger exists? That we won't ever again be swept away by passion? For if you can vouch for your own self-control, I am not so sure of mine!"

Her words ignited something fierce in him. Her bosom rising and falling with strong emotion, her nostrils flaring, kindled desire such as he had never known.

At the sight of that hungry light in his eyes she laughed, a low triumphant laugh, and stepped forward to press herself against him. Instantly, she was engulfed in his arms, her lips claimed in a searing kiss that she returned with equal ardor. But when his hand moved between them to cup her bosom, she broke away.

"You see, Thorne? We can never again share house room. Our lives must be separated from now on, or—"

"Oh, that is of all things wonderful!" Her mother's cheery voice broke into their tête-à-tête. She was beaming at them from a few feet away. It was clear that she had witnessed their passionate embrace. "I knew you would explain it all to her and come to an agreement."

Chapter Five

Allison and Thorne turned equally dismayed faces toward Delphinia. Thorne cleared his throat uneasily. Allison felt responsible for his embarrassment, having deliberately provoked that kiss to prove her point.

"It isn't what you think, Mother. Thorne and I have mutually agreed that we will not suit."

"Mutually . . . will not suit? Had your father caught a man kissing you like that, and no engagement announced on the instant, he would have had his horsewhip out."

"Mother, we were only saying our good-byes. Thorne feels that I am too disputatious, and I cannot change my nature to suit his notions."

"Is this true, Thorne? She has not mistaken the matter? You do not wish to marry my daughter?"

A great shuddering sigh escaped Thorne. He swiped his large hand over his face. "I am very sorry to have allowed myself to be carried away yet again, for what Allison says is true. I—"

"Yet again! So! You *did* try to seduce her in London." The change that came over Delphinia was startling to both observers. Suddenly, she was Lady Catherton, standing ramrod straight, her chin lifted proudly. "I must tell you, sir, that you are no longer welcome here."

Allison bit her lip. She wanted Thorne to leave, it was true, but she had only to look at his face to know how hurt he was by her mother's sudden hostility. Thorne had always been fond of her mother. Allison sternly suppressed the instinct to defend him; it was best if her mother at last realized the truth about Thorne's intentions.

"Please believe me—I never had any intentions of seducing

your daughter. What happened between us just now, and what happened that night in London, occurred spontaneously. But if you feel she has been compromised . . ." He looked around for any evidence of spying servants, but saw none.

Delphinia shook her head. "Fortunately, scandal can be avoided. Allison deserves a husband who is eager to marry her."

Thorne realized with dismay that a part of him hoped Delphinia would make marrying Allison unavoidable. *I truly am my father's son*, he thought, scowling.

"I have refused Thorne's request that we return to London with him," Allison informed her mother.

"Indeed, no! I have been much mistaken in you, sir. I now see that for us to make our home with you will not do, not at all. My daughter and I are of one mind in this."

Thorne felt like a villain. With both women glaring at him sternly, he saw that he had lost the battle to carry them back to London. He would have to find some other way to help them and protect them, though how he was to do it with them in Bristol, he could not yet divine.

"As you wish, Lady Catherton." He bowed stiffly to each of them and stalked from the garden with all the dignity he could muster, though he felt like a naughty boy who had been caught out in some serious transgression.

Rain! Rain! Rain! Allison's mind screamed the words as she stared out the window. As the final notes died beneath the hands of her last piano student for the day, she turned back to the class. Some of the auditors were giggling and whispering behind their hands.

"Young ladies, I must remind you that learning to listen politely to the musical performances of others is as important a drawing room skill as acquiring the ability to perform yourself."

"But Mrs. Weatherby, Jane struck five wrong notes," the lively and mischievous Alicia crowed.

"And by publicly noticing, you have struck twenty wrong notes, for you have scandalized twenty well-bred young ladies." Allison's eyes scanned the room, her expression as severe as she could make it after so inaccurately describing the room full of giggly girls. "I wish to see a composition from you tomorrow on the subject of consideration for the feelings of others, Alicia."

"Yes, ma'am." Alicia lowered her eyes and bit her lip to stifle her merriment. Jane, red-faced, retreated from the piano.

After the last girl had ambled out of the room, Allison turned back to the window. *Will it never stop raining? And such a cold rain for June.* She sighed. Nothing for it but to summon a hackney cab. For the entire week she had been forced to hire a cab to and from Miss Purvey's academy. The expense would seriously affect their budget.

Briefly, she contemplated walking, but cast the idea aside. If she became ill, they really would be in the basket. It had been a difficult few months, with too little money to keep the cottage well heated during a spring that had seemed more like winter. Sufficient food for themselves and the servants had been difficult to come by, especially for Ian, the tall, strongly built young man Peterson had managed to hire for a pittance to assist him.

There was cause for hope, though. Allison scolded herself for despairing. After all, she had taken on two new private pupils in the last week. If she could but stay healthy, she would soon be earning an adequate living for herself and her mother. *Adequate!* She bit her lip. Could she ever earn enough to provide the kind of table that would tempt her mother's finicky appetite?

As she stared moodily out the window, she became aware that a fine coach-and-four had pulled into the carriageway below. This in itself was not unusual, for some of Miss Purvey's pupils came from wealthy families, and their parents enjoyed displaying this wealth at every turn. But this particular carriage! Even through the failing light, the crest was plain to see.

Thorne! Why has he come? Allison knew by the thrill of pleasure that flooded her that she must steel herself to resist temptation once again. The carriage door opened and a tall figure emerged, brushing away the footman's umbrella impatiently. But it wasn't Thorne. Allison didn't know whether to be relieved or disappointed to see that it was James Betterton who raced the raindrops into the entry.

She hastened down to the parlor. Miss Purvey had extremely strict rules about her teachers entertaining male visitors; it would never do for him to seek her out tête-à-tête in the music studio.

"Jamie!" She held out her hands to him. "How kind. You've come all the way from London to take me home."

To her surprise, instead of laughing at her jest, James studied her features gravely. "Of course I have," he responded. "Can't let my future wife get her feet wet."

"Future wife? What May Game is this?"

"May Game, is it? Why did you never hint to me of this grand passion? Why had I to learn of it from Thorne? At least now I know why he seems to despise me more each day."

Allison dropped his hands. "You speak in riddles and conundrums." She glanced at Mrs. Purvey, who was observing this reunion with disapproval from her seat by the fire.

"Let us leave. We can be private in the coach." She raced ahead of him, gratefully accepting the umbrella that James had disdained. Once settled in the coach, she turned to him anxiously. "Now tell me what this is all about."

James took her hand in a gesture at once pitying and loverlike. "Poor dear. We shall be married as soon as may be. You only had to give me a hint, you know. Devilish fond of you, always have been. Never thought of you in just that way, of course, but—"

She snatched her hand away. "Stop talking nonsense. To marry you would be to marry my brother, for as such I have always regarded you."

James straightened away from her, beginning to look relieved. "So I had always thought, but Thorne said . . ."

"Is Thorne trying to make a match between us. Oh! Of all the things! Will he never stop meddling in my life!"

"I wouldn't exactly say he was trying to make a match. Expressly forbade me to see you, in fact."

"Forbade you to see me! Worse and worse. But how on earth did you conclude that I am in love with you?"

"It came about because he called me in to ring a peal over me about my debts. I'm all rolled up, you know. Thorne auctioned all of my unentailed property and still could not cover them all."

"Oh, Jamie. No!"

"Yes. He bought Fairmont in the sale. Says he'll give it to me some day if I walk the straight and narrow. Give my own property to me! The devil fly away with him."

Allison had never seen James seething with fury before.

"Then had the gall to tell me if I would marry and assure the succession, he would pay my debts straightaway as a wedding present."

Allison thought this rather generous, but held her tongue on that point. "But I still don't see . . ."

"So I told him to get himself an heir, because I'd never marry so long as I was under his thumb. Asked him why he didn't marry you. No, don't look so angry. Needed to be asked. Smelling of April and May, the two of you, before you left London."

"I collect he told you he didn't love me, nor I him. But I think I shall go quite mad if you don't explain how this gave you the notion I had a secret *tendre* for you?"

"Not what he said at all. Let me see. Can't remember his exact words. Something like thanks to me, he couldn't marry you, no matter how much he might want to. I put it to him directly. 'I've come between you and Allison?' And he said yes. So I said I'd propose to you immediately, and he forbade it. Told me I must go to Fairmont as his paid overseer and learn to manage it. Orders me about like a child." James ground his teeth.

Allison felt miserable for the two of them. Thorne took his role as James's guardian as seriously as he took all of his other responsibilities. It was understandable, though, that James should resent being controlled by one so near his own age.

After taking several moments to compose himself, James asked her, "So you aren't dying of unrequited love for me?"

"No, silly. I love you like a brother."

"Dashed queer then! I don't understand. Why did he say I was preventing him from marrying you? Wish you would tell me what your quarrel was about. Perhaps that would shed some light on matters."

Allison had told no one but her mother that Thorne had offered to make her his mistress. What James might do with this information she could but guess, but she feared he might force a duel upon Thorne. The very thought of either of them injuring or killing the other was anathema to her. She blushed and turned her head. "I don't think it has any bearing on this subject, which is quite inscrutable to me. We parted with a very clear understanding that we would not suit. You never came into it."

"Smoky business," James said, shaking his head wonderingly. "He as good as admitted he loves you."

"I always thought Thorne a man of high character, but he has lied to you, or he has lied to me. A man who is in love doesn't turn his back on a woman because she quibbles with him occasionally."

"Quibbles? You mean all that argufying over things like phlogiston and electricity and mesmerism, and politics and the like?"

"Yes. He said he wanted peace and quiet in his home."

"But last season he told me he found you challenging. Said it admiringly." The wondering tone in James's voice made Allison smile. "Always thought he waited so long to marry because most women bored him. I'm going back to London and thrash it out with him." James took her hand in the brotherly fashion he had always employed with her. "You've been made most unhappy by all of this. Only think, Allison! What if there is some silly misunderstanding. You do love him, I think?"

Allison shook her head. "For a time I thought I did, but I have concluded that I don't really know him well enough to love him. Never would I have guessed that he would lie to one of us." *Never would I have guessed he would offer me carte blanche*, she added to herself, not daring to express this thought to her volatile relative.

"Well, I intend to find out the truth."

"I beg you will not confront him. It would humiliate me. Whether he is playing some sort of game with you, or you were mistaken in what he said, I wasn't the least mistaken. Your may ask Mother. She became so indignant she sent him away with a flea in his ear."

James reluctantly agreed. "Then I suppose I must push on to Fairmont. I am completely without funds. It seems that I, like you, must earn my bread."

"You don't mean to go tonight?" Allison gestured to the carriage window. Twilight gathered outside the coach.

James took out a pocket watch and consulted it. "Not tonight. Let Thorne pay for another night's lodging. He deserves it!"

"Won't you stay with us? It might cheer Mother up."

"I could see when I called at your cottage that she was not in plump currant."

"No, indeed!" Allison grimaced. "She seems to have a permanent case of the megrims. She spends all of her time in bed or lying on the sofa, and hardly eats anything."

"I doubted Bristol would agree with her. It doesn't appear to agree with you, either, now I think on it." He studied her in the dim light of the carriage. "Pale and thin. And that dress!"

"It is what the instructors at Miss Purvey's academy are required to wear."

"Black and long sleeves I can understand, but why the poorest dressmaking it has been my displeasure to behold?"

"If you must know, Mother and I made it."

"Oh, Lud." James clapped his hand to his forehead. "Have you sunk that far? The two of you together used to muddle the hemming of a handkerchief. Beastly of Thorne to play the skinflint with you, but what I'd expect from him."

"He offered to house us and continue the generous allowance that we thought was from the residue of Father's estate. Turns out his debts were much worse than Thorne told us. Mother is a complete pauper. That's why my cousin William was so unhandsome to us, refusing to repair the dower house or establish an annuity in lieu of housing Mother there. He was furious that there was nothing to inherit along with the title."

"So all you have is Charles's pension, which can't be much." James shook his head wonderingly. "And yet you turned down further assistance from Thorne."

Allison lifted her chin. "Of course. Once I knew the whole, I could not bear to be the object of his charity. Can you blame me?"

"You make me ashamed that I have done so."

"It isn't the same thing. You're his true cousin and heir. He and I are only distant relations."

"Still, I should have been a man, long before this, instead of drinking and gambling and hanging about London. I have certainly fulfilled my father's worst fears." James looked as if this notion had just occurred to him. "Thing is, bad habits are hard to break."

Allison patted his hand understandingly. "Carousing and gaming are so much more attractive than poring over tracts on drainage and crop rotation, I make no doubt."

He smiled. "Just so. I should follow your example and do something for myself. Suppose I'll have to go up to Fairmont and learn all about being a farmer, after all. Lud, that it should come to this!"

Allison could not help but smile at the chagrin in his voice. "Poor Jamie! Though I almost envy you the country. Right now I wish I could go with you to Fairmont. Bristol is the most wretched place in the world in the rain!" The carriage had reached their cottage. "Do stay, Jamie," she pleaded with him.

The carriage door swung open, and the footman set the steps before assisting her out of the carriage. Her pattens made a decided splash as she did so. From the door of the cottage she watched James argue with the coachman, who at last drove away.

"Not half pleased with me, is old Hepden. He'd be even less pleased if he knew Thorne had forbidden me to come here."

"However did you manage it?"

James grinned. "The noble marquess was rushing to Parliament to give a speech, so after ordering me to my kennel, he left without giving Hepden explicit directions on my destination, else I'd have been taken straight to Fairmont, you may be sure. I'd give a monkey to see Thorne's face when he gets the bills for this trip!"

Chapter Six

"Yes, m'lord, to Bristol to call on Mrs. Weatherby." Mr. Hepden, Thorne's venerable head coachman, turned his hat nervously in his hands. "Was that wrong? Hadn't no orders from you, m'lord, so what was I to do?"

"You did as you must, of course. Thank you for reporting to me."

After Hepden left, Thorne threw down his pen and jumped up to pace before the bow window. *What the devil did I say to him? Why did he run to her with it?*

Thorne had been enraged when James approached him with a hare-brained scheme to locate the treasure of Silverthorne using a maid who supposedly had the ability to see ghosts. He had advanced the idea as a way out of their difficulties for both himself and Allison. Thorne had shouted at his young relative, "Is it not enough that I lost my father and younger brother to that so-called treasure? Are there not enough ghosts haunting that ancient relic without you adding yours?"

All his patience had long since worn out. Not giving James a chance to reply, Thorne had ordered him to retire to Fairmont. "No further advances shall you have from me! You must learn to manage your estate profitably, else how can you ever hope to manage my vast holdings?"

James's response had completely demolished his self-control. "It isn't my estate anymore, is it? And I don't want to manage your holdings. Stupid notion, anyway. I'll likely stick my spoon in the wall long before you. Why in the name of heaven don't you marry and get yourself an heir, so we can be free of one another? I made sure you would marry Allison, before your quarrel. She'd make you an admirable marchioness. Then I could join the army, which is what I've always wanted."

Thorne shook his head. *What did I say to him then? I vaguely remember saying that because of him, I could not marry Allison. Before I could explain myself, what did he do but say he'd never guessed, and would propose to her on the instant.*

Learning that James had in fact gone to Bristol deeply disturbed Thorne. *After I expressly forbade him to do so. If he repeats my words to her, she can't fail to realize it is her barrenness I referred to. What purpose would be served by reporting my words to her?* In spite of his low opinion of James, Thorne knew his cousin would never knowingly hurt Allison, whom he loved like a sister. As for James marrying Allison, it was unthinkable. Thorne felt ill at the thought of her in any other man's arms.

You had best get used to it, he told himself. *She will remarry eventually.*

Not James, he debated with himself. *Not a gamester. Not . . .*

Someone you know, so that you have to be reminded of what your cowardice cost you?

Cowardice? Thorne shook his head at the unwelcome thought. *Wisdom! To marry for love is to become a woman's fool.*

That he could not resolve this internal argument did not matter, for James's reckless behavior seemed unlikely to improve. Which meant he had spoken the truth with no varnish on it, when he blamed James for the fact that he could not marry Allison, for it appeared he would have to marry to ensure the succession.

What did James say to her? Is she going to marry him? These questions tormented him so much that he found himself planning a trip to Bristol to see how matters stood.

It's time I called on them, anyway. That footman I sent to work for her does not write very informative reports. Thorne drew out the latest opus from Ian McDonald, which Hepden had delivered along with his account of James's truancy. "Mrs. Weatherby takes a hackney cab to school when it rains. Lady Catherton seldom goes out. Peterson thinks she has gone into a decline. The piano tuner said the sounding board was cracked, which distressed the ladies very much." This last item especially concerned Thorne. He knew Allison had taken on some private music pupils; a defective piano might make that impossible to continue, and she probably couldn't pay for expensive repairs.

Allison stood in the doorway to her cottage, watching her last private pupil leave without a lesson. She blinked away bitter tears. Just as the brougham that had brought the child pulled away, Allison saw a familiar coach bearing down upon her. *Why has James come back? How has he convinced Hepden to wander about England this way?*

A few days ago she had received a letter from him telling her not to worry, that he had a plan to solve both their problems once and for all. He had been deliberately mysterious, but she found herself growing more cheerful, until she realized her piano's poor performance was the result of something far more serious than merely being out of tune.

She stood in the doorway, watching, wondering what scheme James had hatched. *Fancy him keeping the carriage for so long. Thorne will be livid.* She almost smiled at the thought, but remembering James's penchant for wild starts sobered her. *Let it not be some mad gamble*, she prayed, watching the carriage door anxiously. She realized the minute the masculine leg emerged that it did not belong to James. His were not so long, nor so muscular.

Oh, heavens! Thorne! She ducked back into the house. "Deny me to all visitors, Peterson," she cried as she fled. But the sound of heavy booted feet behind her told her she was too late.

"Good afternoon, Peterson," a deep voice intoned. "No need to announce me."

How dare he sound amused, Allison thought, hastily scraping her cheeks dry with the palms of her hands before turning around. She stood and waited for Thorne to come to her. He stopped two feet away.

"You've been crying."

"What do you do here, Thorne? If you will recall your last visit, my mother said you were no longer welcome in her house, a sentiment with which I heartily agree."

"I will explain the purpose of my visit after I have paid my respects to Lady Catherton," Thorne replied with a manner of supreme self-confidence, which was somewhat undermined by the embarrassed flush that darkened his face.

"She is resting with the headache. I really do wish you would leave. This is rather a bad time for a visit."

"I think it is very good time. What is wrong?" He leaned forward and traced a tear track down her cheek.

"Nothing that I can't correct on my own." She tossed her head. "That is, if you will leave. I am very busy."

"Busy turning away your pupils? Or did you contrive to have your piano mended?"

"How did you . . . oh! You exasperating man. I've suspected all along that Ian was a spy. I should have known so strong and capable a young man would not have agreed to work for what I could pay him!"

"You did it out of consideration for Peterson." He smiled tenderly at her. One of the things that endeared her to him was her kindness and regard for her servants.

"Yes, but it is quite objectionable to have him reporting my business to you. And now I think on it, he acts like a guard rather than a footman!"

"I had to have some way to know how you are doing, and someone to protect you. You won't pretend that Peterson could deter any persistent suitor." He stalked past her and opened the door to their front parlor.

"Mother speaks most harshly of you. She won't be best pleased to see you."

"Oh, Thorne. I am so glad you have come." Allison heard her mother's quavering voice issue from the direction of the sofa, where she had been lying with a cold compress on her face, her hartshorn at the ready.

"Mother!"

"No, Allison, we must face reality. We cannot continue as things stand. Your salary as a teacher was never enough, and now with the piano pupils lost—"

"They will come back once I have it fixed."

"You know it will cost the earth." Suddenly Lady Catherton began to cry. "Who would ever have guessed that I would call a few guineas 'the earth?' "

Thorne knelt by Lady Catherton's side. "Delphinia! You look

quite ill!" He turned his head to glare at Allison. "I never thought you would carry this fancy of living independently far enough to injure your mother."

Allison sputtered angrily. Her mother gave her hand to Thorne. "It has been dreadful, dear boy. The cottage never warm enough, and the food such as I cannot eat, for you know how particular I have always been. But the worst . . ." She turned her head aside and gulped, struggling for control. "The worst has been having those dreadful Cits come here and stare at me, and cluck their tongues, pretending pity when they are delighted to see one of the first families thrown down. Or worse, try to befriend me! False friends—all they want to do is parade me about and brag about knowing Lady Catherton. But the very worst is that I do not dare to play whist, be it for ever so small a stake, for we cannot afford for me to lose even a ha'pence." Delphinia burrowed her face in her handkerchief and gave way to real sobs.

Allison felt the tears begin again. She had known her mother was unhappy, but had not guessed the depths of her feelings. "Mother, please, dearest . . ."

"I am sorry to distress you, Allison. But I can't continue. Thorne has long since repented of his untoward conduct, I am sure . . ."

"That I have, Lady Catherton."

"You were wont to call me Delphinia, dear. Won't you do so again?" She smiled sadly at him through the tears.

"I shall be delighted," Thorne quickly agreed.

"Allison, come here." Delphinia held out a long, thin hand to her daughter.

Allison took the outstretched hand, trying to ignore the fact that Thorne was so near she had to take care not to brush against him. "Yes, Mother?"

"You must put your pride aside, daughter, and let Thorne assist us. Not that you shall surrender your good name, for that I could never endure." Delphinia's expression firmed as she glared at Thorne, who shook his head vehemently.

"As the head of your family, it is my duty to see to your well-being, which includes preserving your reputation. There will be no problem on that score, I assure you."

Allison sighed and bowed her head. What was she to do? Her

mind had not changed about accepting Thorne's charity, but she did not want to contribute further to her mother's unhappiness. Delphinia's headaches and lack of appetite had begun seriously to alarm Allison.

Mrs. Peterson, try though she might, could not cook like the fine chefs of Delphinia's past, no, not even if she had at her disposal such delicacies as tender veal and out of season asparagus. The Petersons hardly let a day pass without representing to Allison their fear that Delphinia had gone into a decline and might not live out the year.

"I will give the matter some thought," she reluctantly agreed. "I cannot leave immediately; I would have to give notice to Mrs. Purvey."

Thorne ground his jaw, and Lady Catherton moaned softly. "That tiresome woman," she said. "She has threatened you with instant dismissal on several occasions, and would have, too, if you had not accepted her dicta without question."

"True." Allison smiled grimly. "But she was well within her rights to insist that I dress conservatively. Nor could a respectable academy for young ladies operate with a scandalous woman on the faculty."

"Dress like a dowdy governess, you mean!" Delphinia hated Allison's return to black so soon after finally coming out of mourning for first her husband, then her father.

"Scandalous lady?" Thorne's eyes narrowed.

"Some tiresome Cit or other is forever calling on Allison. Reports of carriages frequently pulling up to our door made their way to Mrs. Purvey's ears, and she leaped to conclusions."

To head off the storm of fury that seemed about to erupt, judging by Thorne's expression, Allison laughed. "Can you imagine? I had a good deal of trouble convincing her that I wouldn't accept carte blanche from anyone. Oh, do not look as if you are going to hit someone. Much room you have to censor the gentlemen, even if that had been their purpose, but I believe if I had given the least encouragement, I could be the wife of a wealthy shipbuilder or merchant by now."

Thorne flexed his hands, which had tightened into fists. "It is just the sort of thing I feared you might face, living where you had no male relative to protect you."

"And who will protect me from my protector?" she could not help but respond.

"Don't, Allison. It is cruel to keep throwing his lapse into dear Thorne's face when he has repented and is so concerned for us." Delphinia sat up. "We had best tell Mrs. Peterson there will be another for dinner, and—"

"I won't refuse to let Thorne help you, Mother. You may live with Aunt Agatha, or Miriam Sawyer, or any other of the numerous female relatives he is already providing for, or even make your home with him. Now I reflect upon it, that will make it possible for me to find a better position as a teacher. Or a governess. I think I should like that very much." Allison looked from her mother to Thorne, daring them to contradict her.

He did, of course, having the gall to laugh. "My sweet Allison, you have no chance of becoming a governess."

"I suppose you are going to tell me why?"

Thorne held up a large gloved hand and began ticking off the reasons. "Any wife would fear to introduce into her home a woman of your beauty. But suppose she did? You cannot sew a straight seam, much less do fancy work. You have some artistic talent, but not enough to teach the subject. By your own admission you paid little attention to your lessons in the globe, and learned as little mathematics as you possibly could. Your French is excellent, but as you learned it from that woman from Canada whom your father so unwisely hired as your governess, your accent is less than Parisian, to be kind. How shall you teach these necessary accomplishments to young ladies?"

"Exactly so," Delphinia chimed in. "And then you must remember that you hardly have the submissive nature necessary to a successful governess."

"Or wife, according to you, Thorne!" Allison tossed her head. "Well, I know I might not suit everyone, but I believe that somewhere there is someone who would appreciate my strengths enough to overlook my weaknesses. As a governess, *or* as a wife." She lifted her chin and gave Thorne a challenging look.

"Don't be pert, Allison," Delphinia said in her best "mother's voice." "Do as I asked, and inform Mrs. Peterson that Lord Silverthorne will dine with us. We can discuss this all calmly after dinner."

"No need to bother Mrs. Peterson. I shall take the two of you to an excellent inn for a dinner. And for goodness sake, wear something with some color, Allie." Not waiting for an answer, Thorne exited the room to give his coachman directions.

"Must I choose? Please, don't make me choose. Stay, Lady. Stay!" But she didn't stay. The white robes faded to grey, the sad, concerned face disintegrated, to be replaced by that of her mother, looking at her accusingly. "You might have chosen one or the other, at least, Allison. Now we shall be poor forever."

Tossing her head back and forth on the pillow, Allison moaned, "I am so sorry, Mother." She woke at the sound of her own voice and looked around her in a daze, hardly able to grasp that she had been dreaming.

Wondering if the near total darkness of the room betokened another dark, cheerless day, she tossed the bed covers aside and crossed the room. A peek out the curtains of her bedroom window reassured her that it was merely very early. The sky, while barely light, looked cloudless; there were even a few stars holding out against the dawn.

Another of those "treasure" dreams, Allison thought as she slipped back under the covers to await the wakening of the household. This one, however, had been decidedly unpleasant. In it she had struggled through a labyrinth of dark, narrow passages following the Silver Lady, who dimly glowed ahead of her. Sometimes Thorne was with her, sometimes she was alone and terrified, battling her way through unknown dangers.

I fought a brave battle with my bedclothes, Allison thought, noticing their disarray. *And no wonder. Of all things, to be alone, in the dark, in a narrow place!* Allison's experience of being shut in a closet as a child by a disagreeable governess had left her with a lively dislike of such places.

But at last the dream had brought her into the same room she had found during her dream in London, brimful of treasure, with the Silver Lady standing in the center. Instead of a welcoming smile, she wore an anxious look, and was pointing. Allison looked where she pointed and saw Thorne, arms folded, a furious expression on his face. The Lady said to Allison, "You must choose. You must choose."

Choose what? Why do dreams seem to mean so much and yet upon awakening make so little sense? Allison closed her eyes, hoping to resume the dream. She tried to picture the glorious treasure instead of the dark passages or Thorne's angry presence. Instead, she began to daydream about the changes in her life that finding the treasure would bring. She could take her mother to London, hire a skilled chef to prepare dishes that would tempt her finicky appetite, deck her in gowns that were the *dernier cri*. They would have a town house of their own, and a country manor, too! And a carriage, and a stable in which to house fine horses.

And James! He could be free of Thorne at last. Perhaps with independence would come maturity and more responsible behavior.

What the treasure couldn't bring her was Thorne's love. In that sense, the dream told the truth. Surrounded by all that silver and gold, she had still felt the sting of his rejection. However, if money could not buy her happiness, it could at least buy her independence, and just now that seemed a treasure in itself.

As Allison watched dawn turn into daylight, she pondered the dream and the reality of her experience with the Silver Lady. Had she, in fact, seen her at Silverthorne so long ago?

Between my mother insisting the ghost was a product of my imagination, and Thorne insisting that the treasure either never existed or had long ago been removed from the castle, I never really thought of the treasure as a real thing worthy of my concern.

Could it be that when the ghost led her into the keep, it had been trying to show her the treasure? Everyone always concentrated on the north face of the curtain wall, where some said the Lady had perished with her brothers and second husband while fighting off marauders. According to local tradition, it was in the area of the north wall that every other sighting of the ghost had occurred. It was there that Thorne's father and half brother had gone to search, presumably after a sighting of the Silver Lady. She alone had been led to the castle's oldest portion, the ancient keep. Could the treasure be hidden there?

That dream did mean something! Allison felt an unshakable conviction seize her that she must go to Silverthorne and seek the treasure herself.

She jumped up and began to pace the room, her index finger tapping her front teeth as she thought. As dawn gradually claimed the sky, she struggled with the difficulties involved. Finally, her plan complete, she hastily dressed and descended the stairs, eager to put the plan into effect.

Chapter Seven

A llison found her mother at the breakfast table, looking well
rested and cheerful.

"Where is Thorne?" Allison asked, surprised she had arisen before him, for he was usually up with the sun.

"Oh, he was off to talk with the landlord and some tradesmen."
Delphinia avoided Allison's eyes as she spread some butter on her
toast. Pleased to see her mother eating heartily, Allison raised no
objections to Thorne's interference in their affairs. Instead, she
waited until Delphinia had completed her meal and was pouring a
final cup of tea before launching her plan.

"Mother, I have been thinking."

Warily, Delphinia paused, the teapot held in midair. "Yes, Allison?"

"I was wrong to agree to return to London with Thorne."

"Oh, dear, I was afraid of that. Well, I am sorry, Allison, but my
mind is quite made up. I shan't live here any longer, subject to the
whims of headmistresses and Cits. She put the teapot down. "Really, Allison, how can you be so insensitive? Do you think that I
would accept his assistance if there were any other option? Yet I
shall never know a moment's peace if you stay here without me."

"I did not say that I would ask you to continue living here. But
surely you see that it is courting disaster for me to live under
Thorne's roof?"

"I won't leave you here alone! Rather, I would stay here and
starve."

"Nor do I intend—"

"I suppose you want us to live on one of his minor estates? We
shall die of loneliness! And how will you ever find another husband, hidden away in the north of England or some rustic Scottish

hamlet? For that is the only way around our difficulties, you know. You must remarry. Thorne was right—you don't qualify as a governess or teacher. Mrs. Purvey exposed the defects of your education in one fifteen-minute interview."

Allison put on her most demure, obedient look. "Yes, Mother, you have the right of it. I am definitely unqualified as a governess at this time. But relying on Thorne will only cause the kind of talk that will make another marriage for me very unlikely. No, I have decided that we must accept Aunt Agatha's invitation."

"Is this a jest? You cannot abide the woman." Lady Catherton stared, astonished, at her daughter. Agatha Keisley was the sister of Thorne's father's second wife. She lived in considerable comfort in the dower house near Thorne Hall. She had taken up residence there as a companion to her sister Lydia after Thorne's father died.

Quite possibly the most unpleasant woman I know, Allison thought gleefully. *No wonder Thorne despises her.* Thorne had not been on terms with either his stepmother or Agatha, but true to his strong sense of responsibility, had continued to support Agatha after Lydia died.

"She will welcome us, you know, and it is unlikely that Thorne will run tame in her home."

Delphinia giggled. "No, indeed. He flees from her like a scalded cat, not that I can blame him, for though Agatha has been my bosom beau since I left the nursery, she is most unkind to dear Thorne. Why she will blame him for the death of his father and half brother I cannot imagine, for he was away at Oxford at the time."

"So it would be acceptable to live with her, then?"

"Yes, though I am surprised you would wish it. I know how she frets you with her hovering ways. And then, she will forever be pressing you to play whist."

"After what we have been through these last few months, a little coddling and solicitousness for my well-being will not come amiss. As for whist, the two of you must look to the neighborhood for your partners, for I shall be too busy to oblige you. My plan is to make use of Thorne Hall's vast library to improve the defects of my education, to better fit myself to be a teacher. The picturesque countryside will serve to improve my skills at sketching and watercolors."

Delphinia's eyes shone with pleasure. "Why, then, I should like it above all things."

Each woman kept certain private expectations to herself. For Allison, it was the hope that she would see the Silver Lady once more, and that the spirit would obligingly lead her to the long-lost treasure. If not, she fully intended to pursue a career in teaching the second she felt improved enough to qualify.

For Delphinia, it was her newly acquired but deep conviction that Thorne shied away from marriage itself, rather than from Allison's disputatious tendencies. And why should he not, poor boy, after having seen the misery his stepmother brought upon his father. The proximity Allison feared was what Delphinia would rely upon to show Thorne the very different marriage he could have with Allison.

"That's preposterous, Allison. You know that Agatha Keisley will send you right round the bend."

"Now, Thorne, you yourself mentioned living with her as one of our options."

"But I never thought you'd do such a thing."

She cocked her head. "Then what, I wonder, was your purpose in suggesting it?"

Thorne flushed. He had hoped she would reject it out of hand, of course. He wanted Allison with him, though he knew he shouldn't. "Very well, check and mate. But I cannot escort you there now. You must come back to London with me until we get the bill we are working on passed."

"The bill ameliorating the poor laws?"

"Yes. I spoke on the subject yesterday. I will have to be there for at least the next two weeks to sway as many votes as I can."

"Of course you must." Allison felt the powerful lure of a political discussion. She longed to ask him details of the bill. She sighed. *I wonder if the wife he selects will be interested in his political causes?*

"Just as I must give Mrs. Purvey adequate notice. Mother and I shall do very well on our own. We made our way here, after all. I suppose we may make our way to Derbyshire."

"A damn fool thing to do. I suppose traveling here and there with Charles made you completely unafraid of the dangers of travel."

"Hardly. I never traveled with less than a regiment when following Charles! Still, England in peace time holds few terrors after Portugal."

His brows knit, Thorne pondered the issue for a few moments. "Give your notice. I will return in two weeks to escort you. Is that an acceptable compromise?"

"It is." *Oh, Thorne. Don't you see that we could learn to compromise. Don't you see that I am not unreasonably argumentative?* Her heart ached with the desire to plead with him for their future, but pride held her back.

Some three weeks later, Allison stepped down from Thorne's luxurious traveling carriage into the ample arms of Agatha Keisley. "Oh, my dear, you look so peaked. But of course riding for hours in a carriage will have made you ill. And you, Delphinia, quite done in, I can see. Come in, come in. You shall both have a nice lie-down with cold compresses for your eyes. Thorne, how can you have pushed them to travel so far, so fast? Just like a D'Aumont, no consideration for the delicacy of females."

Thorne dismounted and bowed to his in-law. He knew it was pointless to defend himself against her. He could do nothing right as far as Agatha was concerned. She shared that trait with his stepmother, Lydia. *Too bad she doesn't have Lydia's beauty. She'll be on my hands until she dies.*

"Now, Aunt Agatha, Thorne was all consideration," Allison objected. "We stopped over four times on the way, including last night at Buxton, when my father would have insisted on covering the short distance from there to Thorne Hall, isn't that so, Mother?"

"Hmpf," Agatha responded, not giving Delphinia a chance to reply. "Don't think you are going to enter my drawing room in your riding clothes, Thorne. You smell of the stable. Why could you not have ridden in the coach like a civilized man?"

Thorne leaned down and whispered in Allison's ear, "You have chosen your dragon well. Now I wish you joy of her!"

As Allison turned quickly away to hide her smile, Thorne said aloud, "No, Aunt Agatha, I wasn't planning on coming in. I'll just ride over to Thorne Hall to visit with my steward, and then I must get back to London."

"Well! Not even going to call this evening to pay your respects! Just what I would have expected from you. Come on, Allison. You are looking positively green, my girl. A hot posset is what you need."

A hot posset on a warm August day! Allison returned Thorne's rueful smile as she turned away to suffer herself to be cosseted. *My plan had better work! I can't stand much of this.*

Thorne had not warned Allison away from Silverthorne Castle, nor extracted from her a solemn oath to forgo searching for the treasure as he had James. This surprised her, but she supposed it was because it had never occurred to him that she might do so. But he *had* insisted that she be accompanied by Ian McDonald whenever she went riding.

"But Thorne! I was never wont to worry about riding out alone in this neighborhood before," she had objected, in spite of her mother's warning kick upon her shins under the inn's dining table, as if to say *Do not dispute him, daughter. What can you be about?*

"There have been incidents here. You cannot be unaware of the agitation in the countryside since the Coercion Acts were passed?"

"I see." *This could put a rub in my way,* she thought in dismay. But contending with him might only arouse his suspicions, so she agreed to this stipulation. Well pleased, he had recommended several horses in his stable.

The day after their arrival she began to put her plan into action. Ian brought Firefly, a dainty sorrel mare, over from Thorne Hall very early, so that Allison could make her escape before Agatha could voice a thousand objections and issue a dozen orders intended to see to her comfort and to guard her health.

She knew something about Ian that Thorne did not, else he might not have valued the man so highly as her groom. Ian was punctilious and hardworking, loyal to Thorne, and not afraid to speak up to Allison should she do anything of which Thorne would not approve, but he was an ardent trencherman, and he very much liked his pint or two or three of ale. After thus imbibing, he had a strong tendency to fall asleep, which she had heard Peterson complain of constantly while they lived in Bristol.

Thus it was that when he and Allison left the dower house, she made sure that the picnic hamper he carried for her was fully stocked with the county's best dark ale.

She did not approach Silverthorne Castle immediately. It would not do to arouse Ian's suspicions and have him writing to Thorne. Rather, in the first days of their tenure at the dower house, she explored in every direction. It was familiar territory, for she, Thorne, and James had often ridden in the vicinity as children, she on her stout, stubborn little Shetland pony striving mightily to keep up with the boys' longer-legged Welsh ponies.

She took along her drawing pad and pencils, glad that Ian could not know what an indifferent artist she was. Each fair morning she spent hours sketching, inviting him to batten himself on the provisions while she did so. Once he settled down on a cloth, a well-thumbed copy of *The Pilgrim's Progress* in one hand and a bottle of ale in the other, she strolled out of his sight to do her sketching.

A full two weeks passed before she first set their horses' heads in the direction of Silverthorne, which perched along a cliff above Thorne Hall.

"Be ye going to the auld castle?" Ian inquired.

"Yes, I wish to do some sketching there." She kept her voice even, though her heart raced with fear that Thorne had told the groom to prevent her from approaching Silverthorne.

"Ye'll no be finding it a restful place to do tha' drawing, I'm thinking," Ian said, his eyes crinkling as he looked into the sun toward the castle, which lay east of the dower house and about half a mile away. Silverthorne had been built on the farthest reaches of a cliff that loomed over a beautiful little valley. Thorne Hall, a fine Palladian mansion built in the last century, stood not far from the base of the cliff, looking down over the meandering stream called Riggswater and the tiny town of Riggswheel.

"Are they working on the north wall, then? I did hear that it was being dismantled."

"Nay, 'tis only when the harvest is in and naught to do on the estate that they work there. 'Tis the guards that'll be disturbing you, I'm thinking."

"Guards?" Allison swallowed hard. "He has placed guards around the castle?"

"Aye." Ian grinned. "Dozens of 'em, a noisy lot!"

The mischievous grin surprised Allison, for Ian had until now been a sober companion. Firefly slowed her pace as Allison guided her onto the rutted, little-used road that led up the hill to the castle. If there were dozens of guards, they weren't using this road to go to and from their work. And what a fortune Thorne was spending, what with paying some workers to dismantle it, and others to guard it. He truly meant to see that no more lives be lost by treasure seekers, whether of his family or not.

She made a silent vow to take no risks. Her plan called for the Silver Lady to show her the secret passage that led to the treasure without the least danger or inconvenience to herself. She would then inform Thorne, who would safely recover the family fortune.

An eerie silence descended upon them as they climbed the winding road to the summit of the hill. Only their horses' hooves clopping in the soft earth and the calls of birds disturbed the peace. As they reached the area of the outer works, long since destroyed, the ground leveled off, and through the trees she could see the gatehouse, looking just as it always had, and quiet as a graveyard. She cast a puzzled glance at Ian.

Allison never failed to feel a strong thrill of admiration for the castle. Not the largest or the grandest in England, it nevertheless had a Gothic charm all its own. Only the north side of the castle, where its walls curved from the cliff face onto the top of the outcropping, showed serious damage from the enemies that had once besieged it. The castle's fourteenth-century architects had not envisioned the heavy guns available during the civil wars.

Allison and Ian passed through the archway of the gatehouse unchallenged. Ian's grin grew even broader.

"Those guards are not earning their keep today," she began, when suddenly her ears were assaulted by shrieks and hisses, and it seemed that the ground around her had erupted in white furies. Firefly pranced and snorted nervously; Ian's horse reared up, nearly unseating him and sending the blurs of white flying in a whir of feathers.

Geese! Dozens of large, aggressive geese surrounded them, necks outstretched, wings raised in challenge. These were the guards Ian had spoken of, and they were very nearly his undoing. She watched him struggle to gain control of his mount amidst the indignant hissing of goose and gander.

I'm glad I did not obey my first impulse to dismount at the gate and walk into the inner bailey, she thought, not relishing the idea of being on the receiving end of those nips that were aimed at the hapless horses.

A man with a peg leg hastened toward them from the castle grounds. He was alternately using his cane to speed his progress and to shoo away the geese. When they had retreated, he came to her side.

"I'm that sorry for the bother, Mrs. Weatherby. They don't know friend from foe—all they know is that you are a stranger."

Allison studied the man's face. "Sergeant Bean, isn't it?" He nodded and made her a profound bow, showing impressive mastery of his wooden appendage.

"Just Richard Bean now, invalided out of her majesty's service, ma'am, and a privilege it was to serve under your late husband. It was a sorrowful day, the day he left us."

Allison's eyes misted over. "You paid quite a price, too."

"Yes'm, but I'm much more fortunate than most who are invalided out, for Lord Silverthorne has looked out for me finely. Though I never did quite imagine myself as a sergeant to a troop of geese." Bean smiled up at her.

"Did ye want to dismount, ma'am?" Ian called to her, red-faced with embarrassment for his recent lack of control.

"Yes, seeing that the guards have retreated." While waiting for Ian to assist her, she watched the geese gradually settle back to grazing. *They will complicate matters considerably*, she thought. *How am I to sketch, much less explore, with them on patrol?*

"Mrs. Weatherby is wishful of making some drawings of the castle," Ian explained to Richard Bean.

"Will that be possible, without being attacked?" Allison inquired anxiously.

Bean stroked his chin. "I can pen them up, of course. Would ye be here just this once, or . . . ?"

"I was thinking of a series of sketches, actually." Allison turned around, pointing out features she would like to draw.

"Then it would perhaps be best if you let them get to know you.

Bring them corn a few days in a row, and they'll soon be your friend, ma'am. And once't they've accepted you, you can walk all over the castle quite secure, for they'll warn you of any danger. But m'lord said—"

Bean scratched the end of his nose worriedly.

He's been told not to let me near the place. Allison held her breath, fearful of what would come next.

"Said I was to make sure no visitors go near the north wall. Got it fenced off, and said no one was to cross that line. Don't want no more tragedies, you see."

"Very understandable. Nor would I wish to go there." Allison could say that quite truthfully. She had often wondered why Thorne's father had gone into the most dangerous part of the ruins, full knowing the risk it posed for him and his younger son.

Ian looked around uneasily. "Seen any signs of that ghostie, lad?"

"Never a one," Bean answered emphatically. "I agree with the master. Ain't no ghost, just a lot of ignorant talk. Still 'n all, ma'am, if you was fearful, I could stay nearby while you sketched."

"*I'll* do that," Ian asserted stoutly, though his face looked a bit green beneath his freckles.

"Not the least need, for either of you. Ian knows I can't abide being watched while I sketch. And I haven't any concern about the ghost, I assure you."

"Well, then, that's all right." Bean looked relieved. "I've a carpentry shop in the gatehouse, and a mite of work to do there, too. I'll get some corn, shall I? You can give the troops a morning treat."

The geese were hardly less intimidating in a frenzy to get their share of the corn she scattered for them, but Allison made herself stand in their midst, letting them flap and honk around her. She soon learned that Bean had named them all, goose and gander alike, after well-known military men. The largest gander, the most aggressive and ill-tempered of the flock, he had named Blücher after the crusty German general who had given such a good account of himself during the late Napoleonic wars.

*   *   *

Allison sat in the center of the bailey, facing the eastern corner of the castle, sketching the watch tower. After a week of feeding the geese, she knew they had accepted her, so she did not fear interference. Once she had fed them a ration of corn, they either grazed and waddled companionably around her, or totally absented themselves. They were in a fair way to furthering her scheme, moreover, for they had never fully accepted Ian, who gladly took her hint to visit with Bean while she sketched.

Today was the first day she had placed herself entirely out of view of the two men. The geese had taken themselves off somewhere. She was alone. She dutifully pursued her sketching, but glanced around several times, hoping against hope to see the specter she had glimpsed in her childhood. So far she had not once caught sight of anything remotely ghostly. Perhaps what she had seen as a child was indeed the product of a fertile imagination.

The dancing shade of the trees allowed more of the sun to shine upon her face than was strictly good for her. She decided to turn around and sketch the keep instead.

She repositioned the easel, turned the page of her sketchbook, and began lightly stroking in the lines of the solid central portion of the castle. The door, she recalled, was of recent construction, for the original keep could be entered only by well-defended stairs that led to the upper stories. As she held up her pencil to get the proportions correct, her hand froze in place. She blinked once, twice, to see if the shimmer in the doorway was an effect of the sunlight. Her mouth went dry as she watched the shimmer begin to assume human form.

Chapter Eight

A thrill of fear ran through Allison despite her determination in seeking this moment. The whiteness gradually coalesced into the shape of a female, dressed as a wealthy lady of the seventeenth century might have been except that she wore no cap. The long silver blond hair, so like Allison's, flowed freely about the lady's shoulders.

Swallowing her fear, Allison lowered her hand and looked directly at the ghost. Instead of looking sad and anxious, as she often had when Allison was a child, the Silver Lady smiled joyfully. As she became more and more solid in appearance, she beckoned to Allison.

Slowly she stood, placing her pencil against her sketch pad. Absentmindedly wiping her hands against her skirt, she cautiously drew near. As she approached, the specter retreated. The Silver Lady looked back over her shoulder to make sure Allison was following, and entered the keep.

Momentarily, Allison hesitated. She could not see into the interior. She knew that this portion of the castle was structurally sound, that in fact it had housed servants and even minor relatives as recently as Thorne's father's time. Still, the fate of Thorne's father and younger brother and the folk legends that claimed the Silver Lady lured people to their deaths weighed heavily on her mind as she tried to nerve herself to plunge into the darkness and the unknown.

She reminded herself that this was what she had come to do. Taking a deep breath, she stepped through the doorway and into the dim light beyond. The Silver Lady was standing a few feet from her, still smiling and beckoning. Allison saw that she would have to run something of a maze, for the keep currently served as a storage place for unused farm implements and old furniture. Lifting the skirt of her riding habit high to avoid getting a coating of dust, she started toward the ghost, who turned and began moving toward the interior of the castle. The Silver Lady's progress was not impeded by the stored items; she just went through them. She turned frequently, to see that Allison followed.

As Allison was negotiating around a large seed drill, two things happened simultaneously. She became aware that the geese were sounding the alarm. At the same instant the Silver Lady, a look of terror on her face, disappeared.

Much vexed, Allison turned back. The geese's noise increased in volume and was joined by the sounds of men swearing and a woman screaming. Allison returned to the door blinking as she encountered the sunlight of the bailey. The melange of sounds came from the north, and Sergeant Bean's voice had joined the cacophony.

Allison hurried around the ruins of an ancient kitchen that stood between her and the north wall. There she stopped to take stock of the situation. The geese were ignoring Sergeant Bean's efforts to call them to order. Instead, they were flapping and nipping at two men and a woman. Ian stood nearby, arms folded, laughing as if it was all a show put on for his benefit.

As Allison watched, the hysterical woman leapt into the arms of a slender, elegantly dressed younger man, who staggered under the burden. After struggling manfully to retain his footing, this man, whom Allison quickly recognized as James Betterton, slipped and fell to the ground, the screaming woman on top of him. They immediately disappeared under a gaggle of geese.

The older man, whom Allison recognized with distaste as Captain Newcomb, kicked viciously at the geese, swearing profusely. Allison found herself cheering for the geese. The gander that Sergeant Bean had christened General Blücher firmly clamped Newcomb's posterior with his bill and whipped him violently about the body with his large wings. Feathers were flying everywhere.

Considering the mood of the participants, Allison suppressed an almost irresistible urge to laugh at the sight. Pity for the terrorized woman finally propelled her forward to help Bean shoo the geese away. It seemed forever before the task was accomplished. Finally, all but the fierce gander had retreated amid loud goose-objections.

"Hold, sir," Bean begged Newcomb. "If you won't hit at him, I'll be able to quiet him sooner."

Newcomb mouthed another pair of expletives as he wrapped one large hand around the gander's neck and detached the general from his inexpressibles. Murder in his eye, he struggled to grip the goose with his other hand. "I'm going to wring this beast's neck, see if I don't." But a large wing tip in his eye forced him to drop the bird with another colorful oath.

"No, you shan't, Captain Newcomb, for they are only doing their duty." Allison interposed herself between the angry man and the equally angry gander.

"Duty! Is it their duty to attack invited guests?" Newcomb's complexion had turned a dull red with fury. Blücher skirted Allison and renewed the attack. Another blistering expletive escaped the frustrated man's lips.

Deeply shocked, Sergeant Bean admonished him. "Ladies present, sir. Mind your tongue." He snatched up the determined gander, pinioning his wings. He wavered under the weight and the difficulty of balancing himself with only one good leg. Finally, Ian stepped forward to take a hand in the situation, though he was nearly doubled up with laughter. He grasped Bean by the elbow, steadying him.

For an instant, Newcomb looked as if he might attack Bean for daring to reprove him. Mastering himself, he bowed to Allison and growled, "Beg pardon, madam. In the excitement, I had not fully realized that there was a lady present."

Allison glanced meaningfully at the trim, attractive woman whom a flustered, red-faced James was assisting to her feet. She arched a challenging brow. Newcomb muttered under his breath. "Ain't no lady." Aloud he said, "She's a Frenchie, ma'am. Not likely to have understand the half."

"Nor did I, Mr. Newcomb, for which I thank the good Lord. Jamie, what is going on? Won't you present me to your . . . friend?" She looked curiously at the woman. About thirty, with disheveled deep auburn hair that had largely escaped its prim knot at the back of her head, she was dressed respectably, after the manner of a lady's maid or a housekeeper, and made a respectful curtsy when she became aware of Allison's presence.

James brushed down his much-abused clothing before responding. "This here's Marie Pollard, Allison. Miss Pollard, you are making your curtsy to the lady I spoke of, Mrs. Weatherby, so you can see that you were not deceived."

Marie launched into a voluble, angry tirade in French. As Allison listened, she realized that the woman's screams had not been called forth, at least in the first place, by the watch-geese. She spoke of a ghostly presence, a fierce, heavily armed man who threatened to cleave them all with his sword. Allison looked around her, half expecting to see such an apparition, so convincingly did the woman describe it. She attempted to calm Marie and question her in her native tongue, but Newcomb stepped forward and gave the Frenchwoman's arm a rough shake.

"Here, stop that foreign lingo. No one can understand a word you're saying."

"But a body can see she is terrified." Sergeant Bean thrust himself between Marie and her assailant. "No way to handle a woman, sir, be she lady or no."

"Hold your impertinent tongue," Newcomb raged. "Get back to your post and leave us be."

"Richard is right," James intervened. "No need for rough handling." He pulled Marie gently away from the two men and thrust her at Allison. "Perhaps you and Sergeant Bean could find some water or something to refresh Miss Pollard, Allie?"

Allison scowled at James. "When she has had some time to compose herself, I mean to have an explanation for this. I take it this is the maid that you spoke of, the one who fled from Hammerswold?"

That name inspired Marie to a fresh spate of hysteria-tinged exclamations. "The very one," James crowed triumphantly. "Newcomb tracked her down. Great gun, ain't he? Wanted to tell you he was on her trail, weeks ago, but Thorne said I mustn't."

Now Allison understood James's vague hints of a solution to their problems. As she led Marie toward the gatehouse, she heard James calling Bean back to pen up the geese so he and his friend could look over the castle.

By the time James and Captain Newcomb joined them, Allison

had heard enough from the distressed maid to be furious with both men. "This is a good deal too bad of you," she rounded on them. "Abducting this poor woman and forcing her to search for ghosts when she is terrified of them. Jamie, I had thought better of you."

"Abducting?" James glared at Newcomb. "Thought you said she came willingly?"

"I can't think what she said to give that impression, Mrs. Weatherby," Newcomb responded in an urbane tone, "but it is not true. Miss Pollard desired to come. She understands the situation perfectly, and expects to be well rewarded if she helps to locate that treasure." Newcomb's smooth manner of speaking was belied, Allison thought, by a slight shifting of the eyes under her scrutiny.

"I expect the geese just upset her, isn't that right, Miss Pollard?" James took Marie's hand and patted it comfortingly. She looked from him to Allison to Newcomb, growing progressively more uneasy as the three stared at her.

"Il ne m'a pas dit que le revenant . . ."

"Speak in English," Newcomb growled.

"M-monsieur never told me that the ghost was a murdering *soldat* soaked in blood. He told me of a pale lady who wished her secret to be discovered."

"That's right! Our ghost is a female. Had you ever heard of an armored soldier lurking about, Allie?"

"I have not, but that is beside the point. Captain Newcomb, you have wasted your time and effort in bringing Miss Pollard here. The treasure was hidden somewhere in the north part of the castle, and you can see that little but a massive rock pile remains. The remainder is quite unstable, which is why the marquess had forbidden anyone to search there. Miss Pollard, would you wish to return to the dower house with me? I will assist you in finding another situation."

"May I have a word with you in private, Allie?" James took her elbow and propelled her a few feet away.

She jerked free. "You are unfortunately showing the effects of bad company, manhandling me this way."

James winced, but persevered. "Thing is, Allie, I owe Newcomb a considerable sum of money. And he did rattle about the country for weeks, looking for this woman. I feel that I owe him the opportunity to at least look around."

"Did you know that he caused her to be discharged, and in such a way that she received no recommendation? Otherwise she would never have accompanied you here."

"Is that what she told you?"

"Yes, and I believe it. How much of the treasure did you promise him, Jamie?"

"I . . . not much. Ten percent. Plus I'm to pay him back my debt, plus his expenses for finding Marie."

"Did you not think you should consult Thorne and me before promising away part of our share?"

"Newcomb figured you'd be grateful to have any of it. And so you should be! It's not as if Thorne were ever going to find it. Only way he'll look for it is to slowly dismantle the north wall and tower. 'Eventually, it will turn up, if it's there,' he said. But you see how little he has done. It'll take the rest of my lifetime to clean up that mess at the rate he's going."

"And how did *you* propose to retrieve it from that mess?"

"I have reason to believe the treasure is somewhere else entirely. Thought the ghost would lead us to the exact spot. Wouldn't be as risky, then."

Allison's eyes widened. "What reason? Where?"

"Did some research among family papers in Thorne's library. As to where, don't know exactly. That's what Marie can show us." He took her hands in his and swung them back and forth, his voice taking on a cajoling tone. "Come now, Allie. Talk the creature into having a look around. Then we'll all be rich."

Allison hesitated. It would indeed be worth ten percent to find the treasure, but she suspected she could find it herself, given the chance, and the help of the Silver Lady. If not for the untimely interruption, she might already be looking at it now.

James's eyes pleaded with her. "Be a brick, Allie. Fact is, I'm going to be in a heap of trouble if I don't let Newcomb and that maid look around. Mean to say, he's been patient about my debts, but he has a servant who is an ugly customer if ever I saw one. I shouldn't be surprised if he'd take it out of my hide if I fob Newcomb off."

"Oh, very well. But only if she will do so willingly. I won't let her be forced to do anything she doesn't want to do. And no one takes any risks, do you understand? Thorne is right to restrict access to the unstable areas. We'll have to ask his permission, then get all the help we need if anything is to be dug up, knocked down, or such."

"Of course!" James was already hurrying away from her as he called back this slight reassurance over his shoulder.

Shadowed by Ian, Allison followed Newcomb, James, and Marie uneasily as they walked around the castle grounds. Marie was fingering her necklace and whispering to herself, occasionally crossing herself and kissing the crucifix as she looked around. She gave no sign of seeing anything, nor could Allison. The Silver Lady had disappeared.

They inspected the dim interior of the keep and made the circumference of the castle's intact inner walls without incident, returning to the gatehouse none the wiser. James's steps dragged, and Newcomb looked thunderous.

"Come inside, if you please," Sergeant Bean requested as he saw the quartet approach. "I've fresh, spring-cooled lemonade and some sweet biscuits sent up by the cook from Thorne Hall this morning."

"The very thing," Allison said, tucking her arm under James's elbow. From the look on his face, he took no pleasure from the invitation. "Oh, and Ian, after you have had a glass, will you ride to the dower house for my gig? I plan to take Miss Pollard home with me."

Newcomb mopped his face with a large kerchief and then surprised Allison by offering his arm to Marie Pollard.

Sergeant Bean led them through an archway and across a sitting room. A table was set up at a window, which had obviously been cut into the gatehouse in modern times. It looked out on the approach to the castle. As Allison slipped into the chair James held for her, Bean lifted a large pottery pitcher and began to pour lemonade into glasses. After filling one for each of them, Bean looked back across the sitting room. "Now, where have the others got to?"

Allison and James turned, too. Newcomb and Marie were nowhere in sight. "Oh, Jamie. I'm afraid he may have dragged her off to the north wall again!"

James frowned and stirred uneasily in his chair, but made no move to go and search for the missing pair. "Doubtless they will join us directly, Allie. Enjoy your lemonade." He lifted his own glass and set her an example by drinking thirstily.

"I'll just go along and encourage them to join us," Bean said, setting the pitcher down abruptly.

"Jamie, you'd better go, too. Newcomb won't mind anything Sergeant Bean says."

"Wait, Sergeant. Let me finish my lemonade, and I'll go with you." James reached for the pitcher, obviously intending to pour himself another glass.

Bean stopped and turned, scowling. "But Master James . . ."

"James Betterton! I'm ashamed of you!" Allison was already on her feet when the screams began.

Chapter Nine

Allison ran as fast as her long, bulky skirt would allow, but James passed her before they reached the exit from the gate-house, closely followed by Sergeant Bean.

As they reached the north wall, Allison realized with a sinking heart that Newcomb and the maid were nowhere in sight, and that the screams were emanating from the crumbling remains of the north tower. A stitch in her side robbed her of breath to cry out to James, though she hardly knew if she would urge him on or urge him to stop before he, too, lost his life to the treasure.

Darting past the overturned hurdles, James charged inside. Allison stopped in the tower entryway, calling to him to be careful. He bounded up the stairs to where Newcomb bent over Marie Pollard, shaking her and yelling, "Shut up, shut up."

A loud pounding sound drowned out his angry shout, James's remonstrance, and Marie's screams. At first Allison thought it was her own straining heart pounding in her ears, but she realized it was the hooves of a galloping horse seconds before she heard Sergeant Bean cry out, "My lord!"

She turned in time to see Thorne riding straight toward her, as if he would run his horse right over her. At the last minute he reined in so hard he forced the animal to its haunches. In an instant he had dismounted and strode up to her. He pulled her into his arms roughly.

"Allison, I don't know whether to kiss your or beat you!"

She looked up into his grey eyes and felt that familiar drowning sensation. "Do I get a choice?" she asked. Even as they moved toward each other, they were distracted by the sounds of the struggle above them. Thorne looked up over Allison's head and snarled, "What the devil?" Above them, Newcomb had his hand over the struggling maid's mouth, and James, just below them, tugged at her waist. An ominous crackle sounded from the tower.

"Get down from there this instant!" Thorne's booming voice carried authority and a hint of panic. The three instantly froze. "You are standing on an unsupported stone structure that is jutting out over a steep cliff. At any moment it may collapse, carrying you with it to your deaths. Come down slowly and carefully, one at a time. James, let the woman pass you and come down first."

At these words, Newcomb suddenly released Marie and shoved her against the wall. He shouldered his way past her and James, hastening down the steps, which shuddered beneath his heavy tread.

James gasped. "Here, now," he protested, at the same time steadying Marie, who almost tumbled down on top of him from the violence of Newcomb's thrust. He helped her to slide past him, then followed her down the steps.

When all three were standing on firm ground beside Thorne and Allison, James began an explanation, which Thorne cut short with, "Quite. Newcomb, I take it you are James's guest? You had best come to Thorne Hall with us, for we are going to discuss this incident in detail. James, Allison, you will attend me."

Having issued these orders, he turned on his heel and followed Marie's retreating figure. She stopped momentarily to speak to Sergeant Bean, then continued on her way.

"Who is that woman, Bean?" Thorne asked as he reached the sergeant. "Have they injured her in any way?"

Bean ground his teeth. "She's a respectable lady's maid. From the looks of her cheeks, she's been slapped around pretty smartly. Master James brought her here to help . . ."

James caught up to them. "I'll explain, Bean. You look to her, please."

Bean turned to Thorne for directions. He nodded his head.

"You've been a wastrel and a gambler for years, James, but this is the first time I've known you to abuse a helpless woman. No doubt the influence of the company you are keeping." His contemptuous gaze raked Newcomb. Allison quickly came to James's defense.

"You have mistaken the matter, Thorne. Let me explain," she begged.

"No, Allison, I saw it with my own eyes."

"Saw, and misunderstood."

He met her eyes, his own narrowed with annoyance. She could just hear him thinking, *Disputatious female!*

So much for any hope of a change of mind on his part, Allison thought, reading cold fury in his expression. Quarreling with him over James seemed to have ended whatever tender feelings he had felt for her a few minutes ago, when he thought she was in danger.

"I shall also wish to know why you involved Allison in such a dangerous business." Thorne stopped and swallowed hard. Allison had the mad fantasy that he fought back tears. "Again, we shall discuss these matters at Thorne Hall. My horse must be looked after—he has had a hard run." Setting his mouth in a grim line, he took Allison's arm in his and began quick-marching her toward the gatehouse, where Newcomb's carriage horses were standing, stamping impatiently in their traces, and her mount was grazing under a shady tree. His own animal followed them without urging, blowing loudly as he calmed from his exertions.

Allison did not protest further. *It will be as well to let Thorne calm down a bit before explaining*, she realized. She dreaded what promised to be an acrimonious discussion. Behind them Newcomb and James exchanged angry words.

At the gatehouse Bean waited for them, a worried look on his face. "She took off, my lord. Just disappeared. Fair terrified, she is, of that Cap'n Newcomb. Terrified of our ghosts, too, poor creature."

"Ghosts?" Thorne frowned at the plural. "No, don't tell me. I'll send some men to help you search. I wish to speak with her, as well as see to her well-being."

Bean sketched a salute instead of tugging at his forelock as most estate employees would do. "I'll see to it, my lord." He set his jaw as Newcomb stalked past, followed by James, his face as grim as Thorne's. "Like to give that fellow a little of what he gave that poor woman," Bean muttered.

"I shall deal with him, never fear." Thorne put his hand on Bean's shoulder.

But he was unable to keep his word on that score. Allison and Thorne were sharing an uncomfortable silence while sipping cool lemonade when James finally stalked into the Stuart drawing room unaccompanied. Before Thorne could ask, he growled, "Newcomb don't have the stomach to face you. He ordered his coachman to drive on as soon as I was out of the carriage." He dropped into a large armchair and stared sullenly ahead of him.

"Allison insists that I owe you an apology for accusing you of abusing Miss Pollard. Consider it done." Thorne watched his cousin expectantly.

James turned his head slowly so that he could look into his cousin's eyes. "I am astonished! You've never apologized to me before! Too bad that this is one time when I richly deserve your censure. Not that I forced Marie up those steps, nor was I beating her, as you seemed to think. But I did bring her here, even though I sensed that she was less than enthusiastic about the project."

Thorne snorted. "According to what she told Allison, he deliberately compromised her to cause her to be discharged from her position."

Allison nodded. "Even then she refused, so he and his coachman abducted her and threatened bodily harm if she did not do his bidding."

James dropped his head into his hands. "She said nothing of this to me. Never guessed he was such a rum touch!"

Thorne shook his head impatiently. "All of this does not enlighten me as to why she and Newcomb were anywhere near Silverthorne Castle, today or any other day."

"We were there to look for the treasure, of course."

"Of course. Just like that. Yet I've told you again and again not to go there."

"I am not your child, nor your servant, nor your slave!" Bitterness laced James's voice. "Though you've treated me as all three for years. I am co-heir to the treasure of Silverthorne, and as such I have a right to search for it."

"The castle and all approaches to it are my property. You have no right to be there without my permission. As for you, Allison, I knew you were sketching around the castle, but you gave Ben your word you wouldn't go near the north tower. To think that you conspired behind my back—"

"I did not . . ." Allison began indignantly, then remembered that though she had not been involved in James and Newcomb's plot, she had, in fact, been searching for the treasure.

Fortunately for her, James jumped in. "Now don't you go accusing Allison. She knew nothing of my plan, didn't even know we were there. I take the entire blame for it, though if you were a fair-minded man, you'd say it was credit I deserved. A rum touch though he may be, Newcomb had a brilliant idea. When he heard about Marie seeing all the ghosts at Hammerswold, he saw the possibilities instantly. Bringing someone who sees ghosts is an intelligent way to approach the problem. We might all be wealthy if only you'd agree to it."

"And we might all be dead! There is no amount of money worth risking more lives! Especially when it is unlikely the treasure even exists."

"It is a good deal easier to give up the notion when you are already rich as Croesus! Why don't you go ahead and level the tower and excavate under it, as you have said so many times you would do? Just think, I'd be off your hands for good, and Allison and her mother wouldn't have to be your pensioners, which I know chafes Allie sorely." James thrust his lower jaw out pugnaciously. "Sometimes I think you like the power you have over us!"

"That isn't fair, Jamie. Thorne isn't like that!"

"Huh! Let him prove it. Let him look for the bloody treasure!"

"Your language leaves a great deal to be desired, James. But blood happens to be the right word. I swore no one else would lose their lives over that chimera. For your information, the delay in razing the entire north wall and tower is precisely for your sake. I had an engineer look the thing over carefully, one who has made a study of geology, too. He found evidence that much of the northern part of the castle stands over hollow ground a few feet below the surface."

"No surprise there! You know full well there are tunnels under the castle. This hardly explains your delay. Only makes it more obvious you are determined to thwart me."

Thorne sighed. "You will think the worst, won't you? As a matter of fact, he doubts that escape passages could account for the amount of empty space his test holes indicate. He suspects a large cavern or possibly the work of sappers during the several sieges the castle endured. He says cannon fire alone cannot account for the collapse of the wall. He told me if I blasted the north tower down to speed the search process, as I had been considering, the entire cliff might collapse, taking castle and treasure with it. It would take an army of men and the rest of our natural lives to go through such massive ruins."

James's astonishment matched Allison's. "Why did you not tell us this before, Thorne?" he demanded.

Thorne shook his head. "Would you have believed me? Would it have kept you away? My father knew the dangers as well as anyone, yet he and Percy . . ." He turned to stare out the window. Allison could see him swallow hard. She longed to go to him and offer him the comfort of her arms.

"Am I to lose my cousin to those ruins, as well as my father and brother?" Thorne's voice throbbed with pain. "Do you have any idea how close you came to dying today? Both of you." He began to pace the room.

"When I heard that woman screaming, I thought it was Allison. To see her in the entry to that death trap . . . To see you standing there struggling on those steps . . ."

Allison could see his jaw working and knew he was fighting tears. She turned to James. "Now that you know, you won't go near that tower anymore, will you, Jamie?"

At first she thought he didn't hear her question. He stared at Thorne, bemused by this exhibition of emotion. At last James shook his head. "Pointless. I don't think that is where it is. Told Newcomb that. But when that maid started shaking and chattering about ghosts, there was nothing for it but he must investigate."

Thorne turned on him. "Not there? Of course it is there! Or was. That is where she is always seen. Dozens have said so. That pathetic frightened woman today confirmed it. Told Allison the Silver Lady was standing behind a monstrous soldier. There may be a ghost, or even two, preposterous as it seems, but if so, their mission appears to be to tempt searchers to their deaths."

Allison opened her mouth to argue, to tell him what she had seen today. How James had arrived at the conclusion that the treasure was not anywhere near the north tower, she did not know, but her experience with the ghost suggested that he was right. Nor did she believe for a moment that the sweet-faced Silver Lady could have been trying to lure her to her death.

But Thorne's impassioned speech continued without a chance for her to interrupt. He faced James, determination carved in granite on his face. "I will bring wagon loads of gunpowder and blast that tower down myself, though it destroy the entire castle and me with it, unless you swear to me on your honor as a gentleman that you will not again attempt to discover the treasure yourself, nor cause anyone else to do so."

James was visibly shaken by this threat. Jaw agape, he could only stare for several moments. Allison's mind raced. There was no point in telling Thorne her own theories now. He would lay a similar interdict on her. She could see the deep concern in his face, hear it in his voice. Unlike James, she had no trouble believing Thorne's threat sprang from genuine fear for their safety. She realized she would have to give up her own search for the treasure, find a position as a governess, and let Thorne pursue his slower, less dangerous explorations.

"If I so swear, will you agree to speed up your own plan?"

"Not by an instant. First a means of supporting the tower must be found, for the safety of the workers. Then we shall take it down, stone by stone, just as we have done that middle section of the north wall."

James groaned. "Then there is no hope for me, none at all! I shall be transported for my debts."

"Don't talk rot. Go to Fairmont as I asked—"

"Not asked, Cuz. Ordered!"

Thorne sighed wearily. "If you would show yourself capable of managing it, and stay away from the gaming tables, I'd sign it over to you."

"Charity! I won't take it from you. I pay my own gaming bills. You put Fairmont on the auction block to get my attention, but I say good riddance to it. Didn't want you to buy it back. I'm not cut out to be a farmer. I want to be a soldier. Plan to pay back every penny you've ever loaned me when I come into my inheritance from Father. Thirty seems a lifetime away, but it will come eventually."

"You'll have encumbered all of it long before then, at the rate you are going."

The two men were nose to nose by this time. Allison began to fear they would come to blows. "Stop it, you two! There is no need

to tear at each other this way." She jumped up and interposed herself between them.

"Jamie, can't you see that Thorne has your best interests at
heart? Thorne, can't you see how humiliating James's position
is?"

Neither man responded, but continued to glare at the other. At
least their loud voices had gone silent. And into that silence came
an unexpected sound.

"There you are. Allison, my lamb, you have frightened your
poor mother so. Thorne, I hold you responsible for this. What do
you mean, snatching Allison up and bringing her here? I told Delphinia you had not given up your dishonorable intentions."

Aunt Agatha's strident voice berating Thorne almost drowned
out Delphinia's quieter cry of "Oh, Allie, I have been so frightened. Ian came home covered with blood and dirt, not knowing
where you had gone. I was sure you had been abducted by Gyp-
sies."

Chapter Ten

Never had Thorne expected to be glad to hear Aunt Agatha berating him. But he saw such resentment in James's eyes, and felt such barely leashed fury suffusing his own body, that it seemed there must be a violent confrontation. Without a doubt he would win a contest of strength with James, but they would both lose, for their relationship, severely strained now, would be irreparably damaged.

The two men relaxed their aggressive postures slowly as they turned their attention to the three women, all talking at once.

"Ian, bloody? What happened to him?" Allison tried to recall when she had seen her groom last. *When we went into the gatehouse for lemonade*, she realized. Too much had happened too fast, and she had not noticed what now seemed a most uncharacteristic absence on his part.

"Why are you here? Are you hurt?" Delphinia asked. She hugged Allison fiercely, then held her at arm's length to examine her.

Agatha demanded, "What has that beast done to you? Mind, if he's harmed a hair of your head, I shall thrash him." She brandished her heavy walking stick as if ready to commence this program immediately.

Thorne bowed toward the two older women. "Won't you both please have a seat, and we will sort matters out," he suggested in his most urbane tone of voice. He led Delphinia to a chair, while Allison coaxed Agatha to sit next to her on the sofa. James retreated to the window embrasure, though he knew he would not evade censure for his misdeeds.

Taking charge of the situation came naturally to Thorne, whose deep voice overrode Agatha's shrill complaints. "Now, tell me exactly what happened to Ian," he commanded Delphinia.

"He came to the dower house with a bloody clout on his forehead. Said he'd been struck by someone named Paddy. When he came to, he could find no sign of Allison or anyone else. Her horse was gone, Sergeant Bean was gone, even the geese were gone." Delphinia's voice trembled. "I was terrified."

"Humph. Thorne's doing, I make no doubt. He—"

"No, Aunt Agatha, none of this was Thorne's doing." Allison spoke with unusual firmness, for she had deeply ingrained habits of respect for her elders. "Indeed, it is because of him that both James and I were saved from harm."

While he appreciated her instinct to protect him, Thorne had no wish to hide behind her skirts. Still less did he want to air James's dirty linen before the viper-tongued Agatha Keisley. "We had some intruders at the castle today, who had a notion of finding the treasure." In quick, economical narration he gave Agatha and Delphinia a modified account of the morning's events, leaving out any detail that would have condemned James to an angry tirade.

"Afterward, we came here to discuss ways to prevent this happening in the future," he finished blandly.

Allison could see James from where she sat, his face a study in dread as he awaited exposure. When he realized Thorne meant to cover for him, he looked at Allison, eyes wide with surprise. She smiled at him and nodded as if to say, "I told you he isn't such a bad sort."

"That poor maid. How like a man to put a woman through such an ordeal just for filthy lucre," Agatha exclaimed. "I suppose you let him carry her off, to torment her with his schemes elsewhere, Thorne."

"She escaped while we were confronting our intruder. Several estate workers are looking for her now. Shall I have Doctor Partiger look at Ian?" Thorne directed this question to Delphinia.

"Perhaps, for he may have a concussion. I put a cold compress on his head before we left," Delphinia replied.

"Probably just malingering. Men will make the most of any injury if they can find a sympathetic female to minister to them."

Finding that he was not cast in the role of villain, James joined the conversation. "I am sorry you were fretted," he offered. "As we were unaware of Ian's injury, we had no way of knowing you would be alarmed."

"You might have sent a servant to apprise us of Allison's whereabouts, Thorne!" Agatha turned once again to her favorite victim. "Next you will be telling us you had invited her for dinner, and without so much as asking Delphinia's permission."

"What a happy thought!" Thorne smiled. "Now I think on it, I have had nothing since breakfast. An early dinner will suit all of us, I think." He rose and went to the velvet bellpull that hung next to a massive armoire.

"The nerve. Without so much as waiting to hear if we will accept!"

Delphinia demurred. "It is but a short drive, after all, Thorne."

"We are not dressed for dinner," Agatha added.

Delphinia stood as if the matter were settled, and Allison followed suit.

Thorne invited them to dress and return, but each of the three had some reason why that was impossible, so he and James escorted them to the front portico.

"Why isn't our gig here?" Agatha demanded of the butler, looking one way and another as she surveyed the empty gravel drive that wound its way from Thorne Hall to the dower house.

Thorne Hall's ancient butler, Mr. Mimmings, directed her attention to the sky. "I did not think you would be wishful of driving home with a storm in the offing."

Agatha looked up at a sky half obscured by a line of black thunderclouds moving toward them. At that moment a streak of lightning illuminated the blackest section, and she shrieked in terror. Mimmings knew Agatha Keisley's reactions to even a tame rain cloud was hysteria, for her parents and younger brother had been killed when lightning frightened their carriage horses into running headlong over a cliff. She had been severely injured in the accident.

"Now, Agatha, it will be a good hour before it begins to rain," Delphinia said soothingly.

"Have a closed carriage brought around, will you, Thorne," James offered helpfully. He wanted the ladies gone, for he still had unfinished business with his cousin.

But Thorne knew Agatha better than any of them, so he did not waste his time remonstrating with her. "Come inside," he said, gently taking her arm. "Of course you shan't go home in the teeth of that storm."

Uncharacteristically, Agatha tamely allowed her in-law to guide her back into the drawing room. She was trembling, so he went to the sideboard and poured her a bracing glass of brandy, which she downed instantly.

Delphina explained the situation to Allison and James as they, too, returned to the drawing room. "I expect we had best return to the dower house and send some clothes around for her, for she will be dining here after all, and spending the night, too, if I am not mistaken."

"I do not understand how I can have gone out in such weather! How could I have been so careless? I must have been sorely distracted by Allison's disappearance." Agatha's words tumbled out rapidly, nervously. "Did I hear you say you were going to go back to the dower house? No, no, you mustn't. I couldn't bear the thought of it. Thorne, we will accept your hospitality for the night."

Although Thorne had not as yet offered his hospitality, he bowed graciously.

"But Aunt Agatha!" Allison had a sinking feeling. *I swore I'd never spend another night under his roof, and for good reason!* "We have neither dinner dresses nor night rails. And I am not the least afraid of storms, I assure you."

"Oh, but you should be! You should be! No, I won't hear of it. Thorne, forbid it!"

"Absolutely. Allison Weatherby, you are hereby forbidden to leave this house until the sky is once more clear."

Swelling with indignation, Allison opened her mouth to give him a severe set-down, when she realized that he was quizzing her.

"There, how is that? Now, if you will excuse me, I will find a maid suitable to the task. Allison, will you make a list of required items? James, could I prevail upon you to order a carriage to convey the maid to the dower house?"

An hour later, six people sat down to dine with the Marquess of Silverthorne. In addition to Allison, her mother, Agatha, and James, they were joined by Thorne's one-time tutor, Mr. Markham

Swinton, now employed to keep his library organized and up-to-date, and carry out the occasional secretarial duty; and his overseer for the home farm, William Smith.

Agatha, having recovered some of her aplomb, let it be known that she was not accustomed to dining with servants. "And so you shan't, Aunt," Thorne assured her. "You shall be my hostess and thus sit at the far end of the table. Mr. Swinton and Mr. Smith shall sit at my right and left hand so that I can discuss the estate business that brought me from London in the first place."

With this, in spite of all her complaints, Agatha had to be content. But she insisted on clustering Delphinia, Allison, and James around her, so that they were, in effect, two dinner parties.

Allison told herself that she was glad not to have to interact with Thorne. Attempts to draw James into a conversation failed. He clearly had something on his mind and replied only in monosyllables. She was left to listen with half an ear to Agatha's tirades and Delphinia's attempts to soothe her. In this situation she began to review the day's events in her mind, from the distasteful confrontation with Newcomb to the noisy battle with the geese. In recollection this event seemed more humorous than it had at the time, and she fought the impulse to giggle out loud at the image of Newcomb struggling to detach the gander from his inexpressibles.

A clap of thunder loud enough to penetrate to the dining room startled a shriek out of Agatha and awoke Allison from her reverie just as she had begun analyzing her encounter with the Silver Lady, which she had as yet not had even a second to contemplate.

"Oh, that poor woman," Delphinia exclaimed, loudly enough to attract the attention of Thorne's end of the table. James looked up, blinking like one just awakened from a nap.

"Who? Me? I am quite all right, I assure you." Agatha ran her hands over her hair as if to reassure herself. "Not usually missish, you know. No danger indoors. Unless, of course, lightning should set fire to the building, and—"

"No fear of that, ma'am," Mr. Smith had the temerity to say to her. "Thorne Hall is well protected. Every spire and corner has its own lightning rod to draw off the electrical fluid into the ground."

"Fluid. Nonsense." Agatha lifted her lorgnette to examine him as if he were a beetle. "Fire. Anyone can see that lightning is fire, coming down from heaven."

"The American philosopher Benjamin Franklin, who designed the lightning rod, believes that electrical phenomena, from the Leyden jar to lightning, can be explained as the motion of two opposing types of fluid." Mr. Swinton raised his hand as if waving a pointer in it. "Fascinating theory. I had the honor of hearing him explain it himself. You can read about it in the *Transactions of the Royal Society*, if you like. Thorne Hall boasts a complete set."

"Americans. Bah." Agatha interrupted ruthlessly to launch a tirade against England's former colonies. "Rebels and traitors. They've a good deal to answer for. It is they who gave the French peasants the notion of revolting against the king the Deity appointed to rule over them. I would put no stock in any invention of theirs, Thorne."

"However reprehensible the colonials may be, the fact is, Aunt, that since the rods were installed, neither Thorne Hall nor the castle has ever once been struck by lightning. Previously, estate records indicate as many as a dozen strikes per year, some with disastrous consequences."

James's face suddenly lit up. "Lud, yes. Remember when the cupola of the swinery was hit, Thorne? No fire at all, yet every pig in there was—"

"I don't think the ladies would appreciate that particular reminiscence, James." Thorne was smiling, in spite of the reproof. "Shall we discuss it after they have retired to the drawing room?"

Allison tensed. Reproving James in that fatherly way could only exacerbate their quarrels. *Really, Thorne! Have you no sense at all? That's the wrong way to go about dealing with James.*

As she expected, the younger man's smile slid into a tight grimace. He nodded curtly. "Actually, I need to speak to you privately on a much more important matter, at your convenience." He lifted his wineglass, which he had heretofore sipped from as anyone else would do at dinner, and drained it without pausing for breath. Then he stood and threw down his napkin.

"If you'll excuse me, I am going to inquire of the servants if Miss Pollard has been found yet."

"Well, what a rude young man," Agatha sputtered.

For once, Thorne and Agatha were in agreement. He scowled and started to rise, intending to call James to book. Just then he noticed Allison shaking her head at him. Impatiently, he waited until

Agatha had partaken of every dessert offered and even asked a footman to crack a few nuts for her. When at last she rose to lead the ladies out, he rose too, telling Mr. Smith and Mr. Swinton to stay and avail themselves of his port. Then he went in search of James and found him in the foyer, listening to Sergeant Bean.

"Have you found her?" Thorne asked, interrupting them.

"Not yet, my lord. Seems to have just disappeared. I hoped we would before the storm broke. Don't see how she could have made it to the coaching road, but . . ."

Thorne could see that Bean was deeply concerned about the missing woman. "Have you let the geese out? If she is hidden around the castle, they will likely find her."

Bean shook his head vehemently. " 'Twas what Mr. Betterton suggested, too, but . . ."

"She was terrified of them," James explained. "Climbed all over me trying to get away from them and turned us both over in the process."

Thorne pulled his hand over his mouth to stop a grin at the mental picture suggested by James's words. "Still, better than her spending the night outdoors. Though it looks to be another of those storms that promise much and deliver nothing." He looked up at the sky. The intense part of the storm had already passed overhead. To the north the sky was beginning to clear.

"Just a bit of a sprinkle, my lord. Enough to settle the dust." Bean looked down self-consciously at his dusty clothing and boots.

"But not enough to do the fields any good," Thorne responded ruefully. "Set the geese free, Sergeant. Newcomb may try to return, and I've had quite enough of ghost hunters for one day."

"Aye, sir." Bean turned and, leaning heavily on his cane, limped down the steps toward his gig.

"Perhaps I ought to help them search," James said. "After all, my fault she's in this situation."

"I thought you wanted to talk to me privately."

James frowned. "It'll keep. Mimmings, have my horse brought around."

Thorne watched his cousin turn away, and not for the first time resented his uncle for giving him control of the young man who once had been like a brother to him.

Thorne spent the next two hours listening to Aunt Agatha complaining and Allison playing the piano. She played in a desultory manner quite unlike her usual self, and Thorne winced more than once at obviously wrong notes. He was not unhappy when Delphinia suggested that he accompany her while she sang something for them.

Allison had a lovely voice. He was sorry when she quit after the third song. It was Tom Moore's ballad, "Believe Me, If All Those Endearing Young Charms," and he heard a slight break in her voice as she sang ". . . the heart that has truly lov'd never forgets,/But as truly loves on to the close. . . ." When the last chord died away on the piano, he lifted his eyes reluctantly, afraid that she might be crying. She avoided looking at him by standing to curtsy in acknowledgement of the applause of her small audience.

"I think I shall turn in," Agatha announced, struggling out of an overstuffed leather sofa. "It has been a draining day. Allison, Delphinia, you would be well advised to do the same."

Apparently of one mind on the subject, the three women withdrew, leaving him to make polite conversation with Mr. Swinton and Mr. Smith. They soon decided upon a game of chess, though, which left him to his own uncomfortable thoughts. Was it Charles she thought of as she sang, he wondered, or me? *Have I hurt her so much?* The thought made him miserable.

Why not marry her? His internal dialogue erupted in open warfare. *You love her.*

Do I? All the more reason to run the other way.

Coward!

If I marry, it must be for an heir. To escape his unhappy ruminations, he walked up to the library and searched for a book that would hold his attention.

Night had completely taken hold of the land when he lifted his head from *Nightmare Alley* because he heard a commotion downstairs. He was glad of an interruption, for he found the supposedly humorous novel sadly flat. He descended in time to see James and Sergeant Bean helping a half-conscious woman into the entryway.

Chapter Eleven

"This is the missing maid, I take it?" Thorne took Bean's place and helped James half carry, half drag Marie into the Tudor room, a small drawing room on the ground floor in which Thorne usually received tradesmen and other visitors not of his social class.

"Some brandy," James snapped to the room at large, and Thorne acted as manservant, since Mimmings was too occupied in scolding Sergeant Bean for bringing "such a person" into the front hall.

" 'Tis the servant's entrance for the likes of her. And you, for that matter," Mimmings complained. Bean ignored him, however, to hover around the maid.

The brandy restored Marie to coherent speech, though the men might have been excused for wishing it had not. She began weeping hysterically and begging them not to force her to look for the treasure. Speaking mostly in French, she repeated over and over that "*ils ne me permettent á vous dis! Laissez moi seule.*"

"Who won't allow what?"

James shook his head. "Not sure. Stop your caterwauling, madam. We mean you no harm." But the tone of his voice only drove her to louder weeping. Between sobs she begged to speak to "the kind lady."

"An excellent idea. Let's get Allison down here, see if she can calm the creature down," Thorne muttered between clenched teeth. "Mimmings, send for Mrs. Weatherby if you please. Tell her it's urgent."

Mimmings snapped his fingers at a footman who was gawking at the door. "Quickly, Murdoch, ask Mrs. Weatherby to step down here."

Thus it was that Allison, who was pacing her room wrestling

with whether or not to tell Thorne about seeing the ghost, found herself summoned to attend him immediately. Alarmed and annoyed by such a peremptory summons, she hesitated over her response. She searched her mind for some answer to send by the footman, for she felt the need to collect her thoughts before facing any more confrontations. Moreover, she did not trust herself to see Thorne alone, and yet had no wish to disturb her mother, who was sharing a room with the poison-tongued Agatha.

The footman nervously urged haste upon her. "They found that missing woman, ma'am, and she was wishful of speaking to you."

Relieved to learn the reason for Thorne's summons, Allison followed him, thankful that she had not yet changed out of her dinner dress. Marie's piercing wail reached her ears before she was halfway down the stairs.

Gracious, what are they doing to her, she wondered, hurrying her steps. When she reached the Tudor room, Thorne was waiting for her and almost dragged her to the sofa where Marie sat, keening and rocking back and forth.

"My dear Miss Pollard," Allison said, sitting beside her and putting an arm around her. "What is wrong? Have these men been beastly to you?"

Marie cast herself upon Allison's bosom, which, since she outweighed Allison by several stone, almost tumbled them both off the sofa.

"Oh, madam," she cried. "Thank you for coming. You will not let them force poor Marie to search for this treasure, will you?"

"Is that what they have been doing?" Allison glared at her relatives.

"No such thing," James denied. Thorne only scowled at her and shook his head.

"Miss Pollard, you must calm yourself so that we can discuss this matter rationally." But Marie began weeping again. Finally, in exasperation, Allison snapped out rudely but unambiguously, *"Tais-toi! Écoute-moi, tais-toi."*

Upon being ordered so firmly to shut up, Marie drew in a deep breath and held it until her face turned an alarming puce. Then she gulped and wiped at her eyes. Gradually, she returned to calm, and as she did so, realized the impropriety of her position. She straightened and sprang off the sofa, begging Allison's pardon.

"It is quite all right, Miss Pollard. Do sit down and explain to us what has overset you so."

Allison's firm voice and imperious finger accomplished what Thorne and James could not. Marie sat down, her hands folded in her lap. *"J'ai vu . . ."*

"Please speak in English," Allison insisted, out of consideration for Sergeant Bean.

"I haf seen the ghost of the lady, the sad lady. She tell me not to seek the treasure, that I am not entitled."

"Where did you see her?" Allison demanded.

"In the donjon, madam. The . . ."

"Keep?"

"Oui, madam. There I hid underneath a table. There the lady came to me, she and that fierce *soldat . . ."* Marie's lower lip trembled. She bit it and struggled to keep her composure. "He stood behind her, glowering at me. She made the motion to me *comme ci*." Marie demonstrated with an outward thrust of her hands. "She say I am not of the blood and must leave. I know there is great danger, madam. I run away. Run and run, until I fall. Next thing I know the so-kind gentleman is helping me up." She turned adoring eyes toward Sergeant Bean. "He put me on his horse and take me home with him. He say I must speak to this m'lord." Her eyes turned from Bean to Thorne. "You are he, I think?"

"I am. Oh, don't get up, Go on with your story."

"That is all. Then I see Mr. Betterton and know he will make me go back to the castle and follow the ghost."

"Did he say so?"

"No, madam, but that is why he and that so bad Captain Newcomb brought me here. And Mr. Newcomb say, after here we go to find a ghost in Scotland. Oh, madam, I cannot bear it. These *revenant*, they frighten me so."

James abandoned his position by the fireplace to go sit by Marie and murmur soothingly, "I shan't make you do anything you don't wish, and Captain Newcomb is gone away."

Marie's eyes grew wide and hopeful. "He does not make me go with him?"

"He'd better not try!" This time it was Thorne who spoke. "Bean, will you ask Mr. Smith to spread the word on the estate that

Newcomb is not welcome on the grounds. You will find Smith and Mr. Swinton dueling at chess in the Queen's drawing room."

"And what about Miss Pollard?" Sergeant Bean looked anxiously at Marie.

Thorne caught Allison's eye and winked as he said, "I will have the housekeeper take her in hand. Mimmings, will you escort Miss Pollard to Mrs. Grimes?"

"I expect Miss Pollard and Sergeant Bean would like something to eat," Allison suggested as Marie hesitated to follow the butler. "Mimmings, you will ask Mrs. Grimes to see to that, please."

"Thank you, madam. I indeed have great hunger." Marie rose and curtsied respectfully to the three cousins before following the disapproving Mimmings out of the room, escorted by her self-appointed guardian.

"Well?" Thorne folded his arms and looked from Allison to James.

"Well, what?" James demanded irritably. "Nothing new there—she didn't find the treasure, only said there was danger in looking for it. Newcomb could have saved himself—and me—the trouble."

"And the hapless maid her distress," Thorne snapped.

Allison worried her bottom lip. The maid had seen the Silver Lady, but instead of beckoning for her to follow, the spirit had warned her off. *What did it signify?*

"Allison?"

"I beg pardon, I wasn't attending."

"Do you think she saw a ghost, or is she merely an hysteric?"

"I don't know. But it hardly matters. As James says, we haven't learned anything new."

"No." Thorne looked searchingly at her, as if he was aware that she was leaving something unsaid. She avoided his eyes lest he see too much.

"I believe I will retire—again!" she said.

"Good night, then." Thorne and James both stood. Bidding them good night, she climbed the stairs slowly, her mind agitated by Marie's account. She had the feeling that important knowledge lay hidden just beneath the surface of the day's events.

After she left, an uneasy silence reigned between the two men for a long moment. James shuffled uneasily, and Thorne noticed that he was clenching and opening his hands.

"Are you going to deck me? If so, may I know why?"

"I may, yet. I want to talk to you about—"

"If we are to come to cuffs, let us find a rendezvous that gives a little more room to maneuver."

James glanced around the cramped, unappealing salon disdainfully. "Lud, yes. This place is hardly conducive to lingering."

"That was the intention. I receive nuisances here, mostly."

"Then I expect we had better stay, for I clearly belong to that category." James thrust out his lower jaw.

Thorne shook his head as he started for the door. "Self-pity is a most unbecoming trait. Let us adjourn to the library."

When they were seated amid a cozy grouping of sofa and chairs, a glass of brandy in their hands, James swirled his contemplatively.

"Thorne, I need you to be candid with me."

"I usually am."

"Why am I your heir?"

A frown line deepened between Thorne's eyebrows. "You know the laws of inheritance as well as I."

"But why have you not married long since? You who are always preaching responsibility—why have you not done your duty and got yourself an heir?"

Thorne tented his hands. "That is not so easily answered."

"Try doing it without lying this time."

Thorne jumped from his chair, furious. "You dare accuse me of such a thing? I had hoped for a rational discussion. If you are here to bait me into fisticuffs—"

James leapt to his feet, too, and they stood nose to nose when they heard Allison cry out.

"You two! Can't I turn my back on you for an instant without your quarreling!"

"Allison, this is private, between James and myself. What the devil are you doing, spying on us?"

She advanced on them, her chin up and her mouth set in a stubborn line. "No, but I expect I should do so, if only to keep you from committing mayhem upon one another." As she approached them, they moved apart reluctantly. "I came down for a book to read. It is the library, not Gentleman Jackson's boxing rooms, you know," she said with a defiant toss of her head.

"It is as well that Allison is here," James said. "What I have to say concerns her, after all, and with her here, you cannot by bluster or denial escape the fact that you told one of us an untruth." He led Allison to the chair next to his and sat down beside her.

Thorne slowly returned to his seat, his mind filled with dread. "If you persist in this discussion with her present, you will hurt her, which I know you cannot want."

"Don't want to hurt her, certainly." James hesitated. "Think she's been hurt already, though. Don't change the subject. You led me to believe I stood between the two of you, so I posted down to Bristol to see if she wished me to offer for her. I was vastly relieved to find that she regarded me as I did her—as a cherished member of my family. Like a sister to me!" James's voice roughened as he reached out to pat Allison's hand where it rested on the arm of her chair.

Allison suddenly wished she were anywhere but here. There had been enough uncomfortable moments in this day. Yet she did need to know the truth. Perhaps then she could face her future as a governess with resolution.

"James is right, Thorne. There is a discrepancy between what you told us, I think." She looked directly at him, bracing herself for whatever blow might be coming.

Thorne dragged his hand down his face. *Perhaps it would be easier to tell her with a third party here. She won't cry, or if she does, I won't feel free to take her in my arms, for who knows where that might lead?* But he found that with those concerned blue eyes on him he could not deliberately hurt her. Instead, he made one last push to convince his cousin to marry.

"It has never been my intention to marry, James. My reasons for that resolve are my own. To this point I have not seen any reason to do so, for I have always felt that I had an heir. I want you to learn how to manage the land, learn protocol, take an interest in politics, and most important, learn to accept responsibility. Because along with the title you or your son will inherit comes a great deal of responsibility."

Thorne's eyes took on a faraway look. "Hundreds of people will depend upon you for their livelihoods. Some of the tenants and estate workers on my various properties have lived on this land since before my ancestors acquired it. Our laws do not protect their right to remain there, though. Only the landowner can assure that. Lose the land by extravagance or gambling, and they can be dispossessed as Lord Vernington's people were. Look at his land now— nothing but sheep as far as the eyes can see, and the people who once lived there dead or migrated to America.

"You seem to regard working for me as some sort of punishment, but I truly need your help. I am deeply involved right now in legislation to create better working conditions for those thousands all over England who have left the land to work in mines and factories. Give up your rakehell friends and help me with some of these burdensome responsibilities. In the process you'll learn how to manage when I am gone, or how to teach your son to do so.

"I am convinced you will find it a very rewarding occupation. You are too intelligent a man to really enjoy the aimless, dissipated life you have been living. Marry, James! If you do, I will see to it that you have the very best of the Silverthorne properties to house your family. Every child will be generously provided for, and—"

James's expression had grown progressively more disdainful as Thorne spoke. "You can just give that up! I will never marry while I am another man's ward. How can I be master in my own household when I am your dependent? How could I look a woman in the face and ask her to marry one who is still being treated as a child by his own cousin?"

"I wouldn't have to treat you as a child if you would begin acting like a mature man."

"You've turned the subject. Just because you have no inclination to marry doesn't free you from the obligation, does it? You expect me to prepare myself to be the Marquess of Silverthorne, though we're so close in ages there is little chance of my succeeding you. Why are you allowed to follow your inclinations, while you prevent me from following mine, which as you well know is to join the army. Marry Allison and get an heir of your own. Then it won't matter to you how I conduct my affairs."

A sudden, dawning comprehension came into Allison's eyes. Thorne braced himself for the pain that would follow.

James pressed on. "Or, if you don't love her, marry some young miss from the schoolroom whom you can train to be the wife of your heart."

"If my heart were to be consulted, it would be Allison I would marry." Thorne's eyes darkened.

James, exasperated, fairly shouted. "Then why not marry her, damn it!"

Thorne's nostrils flared with the reluctant breath he drew in. But before he could answer, Allison spoke.

"It is because Charles and I were childless, isn't it? I don't know why I didn't think of it before. If he will only marry to get an heir, that makes me a less than wise choice for a wife."

The sad look in Thorne's grey eyes confirmed her guess. He lifted his shoulder and held out his hands. "I'm not too surprised you didn't realize it before now, for it was a very sore subject with you. I daresay you have buried it deep, where it cannot wound you as it did when you first heard of Charles's death."

Allison dropped back into her chair, her breath going out on a whoosh. She remembered all too well her grief at losing Charles, and how it seemed to her then that she could have borne it better if she had had a child. Contrary to what Thorne assumed would be her reaction, a spurt of hope surged through her. When he knew all of the facts of the case, he wouldn't think her fecundity so doubtful. There might be hope for them yet.

James stood abruptly. "You don't know what love is, Thorne. You're not looking for a wife—you are looking for breeding stock. Allison, you are well out of it. The two of you really wouldn't suit, you know. You are too independent in your thinking, and he is too dictatorial."

He bent and took her hands in his. "I've an idea. Been thinking about it for a while. We'll go to India. That would serve as well as the army to get me out from under Thorne's thumb. There are fortunes to be made there, and young Englishmen who'd be eager to marry a beautiful Englishwoman without the trouble of returning to England."

Allison let him capture her hands, but resisted when he tried to draw her out of her chair. "It is an interesting thought, James, but may I discuss it with you later? I wish to have a word in private with Thorne."

Thorne sprang to his feet, his expression thunderous. "India! You'd prefer that to learning the responsibilities of my heir?"

"Yes, by God. No good pretending you need my help. You wouldn't really let me shoulder your responsibilities. You'd stand looking over my shoulder, criticizing constantly. Don't know exactly what I'm going to do, but I'm not going to kick my heels around England anymore." James snagged the almost full bottle of brandy and headed for the door. "No more waiting for the treasure to be discovered. It isn't meant to be. Going to take myself off somewhere and try being a man for a change."

"A drunken man, from the looks of it."

James started for him. Allison launched herself from her chair and caught his arm. "No, absolutely not. You've cut each other up enough with words. No fisticuffs."

Thorne had taken up a defensive stance, but was grateful when Allison's plea calmed James. He had no wish to thrash the boy. That would only cause further bad blood between them. James's defeated look and posture as he stalked from the room, brandy bottle in hand, bothered him a great deal. He turned a worried look on Allison.

"Think he means it? About going to India?"

"I hope so. You and he will never rub together well as long as he is your ward. I sometimes think his father's conviction that he would be unable to manage his own affairs had the effect of making it true."

Thorne swept his hand down his face wearily. "I haven't handled him right. What did I know of managing an unmanageable boy? Especially when I was little more than a boy myself. We were friends once. His father's will made that impossible."

Allison longed to put her arms around him, to comfort him, for she knew he cared deeply for James. Instead, she directed her steps to the French doors that led onto the front terrace. They were closed, partially obscured by moisture. "It looks as if the storm has blown over." She pushed the doors open and stepped outside to breathe in the fresh air. "I can see stars peeping out."

She was buying time, trying to decide how to explain why she did not despair of having children. To speak of such matters to a man would be very embarrassing. Even with Charles, it had taken her two years to pluck up enough courage to demand some an-

swers from him. When she did, he was mortified by having to discuss such a subject. A rueful half smile lifted her lips. *He simply
did what he thought best, without asking me.* Young and inexperi-
enced, she had accepted her husband's behavior in the marital bed
without question until a chance remark about *Tristram Shandy* by
another wife aroused her suspicions. After borrowing the scandalous book, which her father had kept in a locked cabinet when
she was young, she raised the issue. Charles confirmed her suspicions, justifying his actions by his lack of a personal fortune,
which made the creation of a large family undesirable.

"But Charles, are we not to have any children?" she had asked
him, near tears.

"Someday," he had responded, pinching her chin. "My method
is not foolproof, so it may happen without our planning it. If not,
when I advance in rank, we will try for a small family." As Allison's thoughts flew back in time, she could feel again the resentment that had built up in her. *It was not that he was wrong, but that
he didn't consult me,* she thought. *It made it difficult for me to feel
close to him.* A distance grew between them, which Charles made
into a chasm when he accepted the assignment to America without
consulting her.

She started when Thorne spoke almost in her ear. "I don't think
it ever rained more than a few drops." He was standing dangerously close. Allison felt her blood heat as it always did when he
was near. She moved restlessly away.

"That's too bad. The fields look as if they could use some rain."

"Will you go with him?"

She looked over her shoulder at him, puzzled by the non se-
quitur.

"To India."

"Oh. I don't know. This is the first I've heard of it. I shall have
to give it some thought." What she wanted to think about was
whether to tell him about her husband's views on filling their nursery. After Thorne confessed the true reason he could not marry
her, her first thought had been a joyful one: *We can be married
after all!* But now she began to worry. *What if I really can't have
children? What then?*

"Don't go, Allie." Thorne put his hands on her shoulders. She
could almost feel his deep voice rumbling in his chest, he stood so

close. Her heart sped up. He was going to declare himself, ask her to marry him in spite of his concerns about the succession. Then she wouldn't have to make a decision fraught with problems. She waited expectantly, but he said no more.

At last, she prompted him, turning in his grasp. "Why not, Thorne? Why shouldn't I go to India?"

For an instant his eyes blazed, then he lowered his head, touching her forehead with his. "It is dangerous. The voyage is dangerous, and that climate is dangerous to Englishwomen. Stay here in England. You can . . . you can find a husband here." His voice roughened; he moved away, walking to the end of the terrace, where he could look up at the cliff and Silverthorne castle looming over the manor house. The thought of Allison married to anyone else clawed at his innards in a way that terrified him.

Disappointment slammed through Allison. *He isn't going to marry me. His responsibilities as the Marquess of Silverthorne weigh too heavily on him.* James's comment took on new validity to Allison: "You don't know what love is, Thorne." *Perhaps he doesn't.* Allison studied his profile as he looked up at the dim outline of Silverthorne to the east. *He desires me. He likes me. But love? What he said before may just have been a sop to my vanity. If he doesn't love me enough to marry me believing I cannot bear children, would he love me enough to withstand the sorrow if that prediction should come true?*

Her throat closed with suppressed tears. She turned silently and reentered the library, selected a book, and climbed the stairs to her room.

The Marquess of Silverthorne did not turn around when he heard Allison leave. He was too close to throwing away a lifetime of resolve. One more moment spent near her, drinking in her woman's scent, with its lilac grace notes, one more look into those luminous sapphire eyes, shadowed as they were by the pain he had caused her, and he would have proposed to her. That marked him surely as much a fool in love as his father. Remembering the way Lydia Keisley had bear-led his father, he laughed silently, bitterly. *You are certainly your father's son, Thorne, to think of marrying at last, only to marry a barren woman, when you need an heir to stand between all you are responsible for and the utterly irresponsible James Betterton.*

He slammed his fist on the baluster. Damn that treasure, which had taken the life of his half brother and left him with James as his heir! Blast Uncle Leo for making him James's trustee.

Most of Thorne's anger was directed at himself, though. It wasn't only Allison's inability to have children that made her unsuitable. He would be sure to marry a passive, submissive creature who would never scold and harry him as Lydia had done with his father. So why had he allowed himself to care for a woman of Allison's temperament? *Get your passions under control, man, before they destroy everything.*

Too many emotions were pent up in him for sleep to come for hours, he knew. He turned and made his way down the steps. There was a three-quarter moon rising—a good time for a long, punishing walk.

Chapter Twelve

It was only ten o'clock when Allison reached her room. She allowed the maid she, her aunt, and her mother shared to help her undress and slip a high-necked, long-sleeved night rail over her head.

"Thank you, Peggy. I'll do my hair. You get some rest." She smiled at Margaret Dorne, the greying maid who worked so hard to keep up with three women.

"Yes, ma'am." Peggy curtsied, a look of relief on her face, and left Allison alone with her thoughts. She went to her window and looked out at the valley spread before her. From here one could not see Silverthorne Castle, but she knew well what it would look like soon in the light of the rising three-quarter moon. A decidedly Gothic place in such light, made doubly ominous by the deaths that had occurred there. Thorne had implied that the Silver Lady's intention was not to reveal the treasure but to keep away those who tried to find it. *Did she lead people to their deaths? Have I had a narrow escape today?*

As Allison drew the brush through her hair, she exhaled a long breath. *I expect Thorne is right*, she thought. *Best not to explore further. Let the engineer he has hired conduct the search.* Even as she tried to convince herself of the wisdom of waiting, the future seemed bleak. *For I really cannot tell Thorne about Charles's efforts to prevent us from having children. For all I know, they were unnecessary. What if I were indeed barren? How could I bear to see Thorne unhappy because he lacked an heir? He would worry himself sick. I love him too much to risk hurting him so.* She loved him even more now that she knew his reluctance to marry her grew from his sense of responsibility to others.

As she slipped into bed, she renewed her vow to seek a position as a teacher or governess, for stay much longer with Aunt Agatha she could not. Her mother and Agatha could contentedly gossip over their whist table all day about the members of the *ton*, past and present, and chew up the reputations of acquaintances and relatives alike, but Allison found that a dead bore. *Perhaps someday I shall have a school of my own*, she thought. *I'll organize it along the principles that Gwynneth espouses, and see what educated women can accomplish.* That notion made the future of a teacher seem more palatable.

Allison surprised herself by falling asleep almost the instant she blew out the candle. Her dreams were not of the castle nor of the ghost, but of Thorne. They stood on opposite banks of a stream, each wanting to cross to the other, but unable to do so because of the full banks and swift current. At last she, in desperation, braved the flood and was instantly swept under. Fighting to get a breath of air, she came awake with a gasp.

A soft light suffused the room, which in itself was not surprising, given the bright moonlight outside. What was surprising was that the light came from the direction of the fireplace, not the window, yet the fire had not been lit in months. The hairs stood up on the back of her neck as she turned her head, for she felt a presence there.

At first she saw only a long, glowing white fog spread across that end of the room, like a banner. But as she watched, the fog shifted, changed, coalesced, until it was recognizable as a trio of figures: one man with the plain dress and close-shorn hair of a Roundhead soldier, another wearing rich velvets and lace after the manner of the Cavaliers, and a woman in a voluminous gown with full sleeves and a round white collar. Her hair was covered by a white cap trimmed with lace, and at her throat lay a magnificent ruby pendant.

The men stood nose to nose, exchanging angry words she couldn't quite make out. *I am still dreaming*, she thought. *That must be James and Thorne, arguing. And that woman must be me. How droll that I would dream myself as the Silver Lady.* For such the woman must be, Allison realized.

Then she dreamed she could hear the woman speaking. Her voice sounded like muted bells, yet Allison could understand. She was remonstrating with the men.

"Cease this fighting," she ordered. "Grandfather meant for all of us to share his estate. Jacques, though you are the oldest, you cannot claim it, or the crown would confiscate it. I am a mere woman. Only Gerard can claim it, for he fought beside the king and thus will not be required to hand it over to the crown. We must trust him to give us our share. Only by joining together can we hope to follow Grandfather's wishes and keep it all intact for his descendants. He will curse us all from the grave if his wealth goes to Uncle Gowan."

The two men barely paused in their quarreling to hear her words. All of the bitterness of the English civil wars, which had divided brother from brother and father from son, seemed rolled up in their fury. Suddenly, they drew swords and began to fight. It seemed to Allison as if she were watching a play.

They are on the walkway of the north wall, she realized. In this dream the wall stood intact, though severely damaged by cannon, all the way to the north tower, also intact. The lady wrung her hands and continued to exhort her brothers to cease fighting.

A moment later, they were joined by a large, fierce-looking man in the armor of a pike officer, leading a troop of armed men. He attempted to break up the fight. Abruptly, the one the lady had called Gerard collapsed, a mortal wound in his throat spilling his life's blood. Jacques then turned to face the new arrival.

At that moment Allison realized the troop served the Roundhead, not the third man, who positioned himself between the woman, her brother, and his troop of soldiers. The Silver Lady called out, "Jacques! You will not gain your purpose with this day's foul work. Now that our brother who served the king is dead, I can never reveal the secret of the treasure to you, whom the king has attainted. Get you back to the Netherlands and your regicidal friends."

This time Allison heard the man's words clearly, though like the lady's voice they sounded like bells, bass bells this time, being plucked rather than rung. "I think a few moments on the rack will reveal to you the error of your ways, dear sister." Jacques strode across his brother's body to face the large soldier. "Sir Broderick, join us. Persuade your wife, before I must."

Sir Broderick thrust the woman behind him, dislodging her cap and releasing long silver blond tresses. "Flee, my love" he ordered her, his voice a deeper note, barely audible. "I will follow."

"No. I shall die here with you and leave the future of my children to God." She drew a small sword and, looking at once brave and impossibly delicate, stood beside her husband. As Allison watched, her breath in her throat, the scene began to waver. *No!* she thought. *Don't disappear! I need to know what happened.* A moment more and she realized that it was not the scene that was wavering, but the north wall. It crumbled before her eyes, taking first the Lady, then Sir Broderick, and lastly the woman's greedy brother and his troop, down with it in a roar of stone crashing against stone.

The silence afterward was deafening. The dust clouds raised by the collapsing wall faded into the glowing white fog with which the dream had begun, and Allison was once more alone in the room. It was then that she realized she was not dreaming. She was sitting up in her bed, perfectly awake, staring at the fireplace.

Horror mixed with amazement and a peculiar kind of exhilaration. *I have seen what happened,* she thought. *The treasure was not found. The Silver Lady died rather than reveal it.*

The disappearance of all three heirs was explained. They had not fled to the Continent with the treasure as some, including Thorne, had speculated. Nor had the second Baron D'Aumont, the first baron's brother, murdered them and spent the treasure, as others had speculated. *Their bodies lie beneath the rubble of the north wall,* she thought. *Neither they nor the treasure were ever found.*

Allison tossed back her covers and got up to pace the room restlessly. *I expect the fierce knight who frightened Marie so was the ghost of Sir Broderick.* Knowing what had happened did not seem to make finding the treasure easier, but it did place it back in the realm of the possible.

Allison pondered the scene until sleep once again claimed her. By then the moon bathed her room in a soft but entirely natural light.

A chiming sound awakened her, perhaps moments, perhaps hours later. She blinked at the bright light hovering near her bed. It quickly shaped itself into the Silver Lady, and she urged Allison to rise.

"Come with me, child," the bell-toned voice urged. "We are running out of time."

Allison sat up and tossed the covers aside, but she did not follow. "I am sorry, my lady ghost, but I cannot go with you."

"Why?" the spirit demanded.

"I am afraid. You have led others to their deaths."

"Never have I done such a thing! Always we have tried to warn interlopers away, but they will not heed us!" The Lady held out her hands beseechingly. "Why do you fear me when you came to Silverthorne Castle seeking me?"

"I did not know all of the dangers then. Do you want the north wall, which claimed you, to take my life, too?"

The Lady shook her head. "You will come to no harm. As our kinsman James has guessed, the treasure is nowhere near the north wall. But thanks to his indiscretion there is one seeking it whom I fear may well find it. I have sworn to give it into the hands of my grandfather's blood heirs. You must come now!"

She means Newcomb. Fear and excitement made the blood throb in Allison's temples. Almost without willing it, she rose and started for her clothespress.

"There is no time to dress. We must go while the moon is shining. You cannot go up the footpath in the dark. Put on your robe and follow me." The ghost went through the door. Allison slipped into her robe and pulled on the sturdy boots she wore to ride in. She opened the door from her suite of rooms cautiously, peering this way and that. The hall was empty; only a guttering candle in a wall sconce lighted it. The ghost stood at the head of the servants' stairs, waiting for her.

Surely the maddest thing I have ever done, Allison thought. But she stealthily followed the ghost out of the manor, pausing only long enough to collect a lantern from the kitchen.

Thorne had succeeded in exhausting himself, but sleep seemed no nearer. He returned to the manor house reluctantly. As he approached it from the ornamental garden, he looked up resentfully at Silverthorne Castle. It was a magnificent sight, its edges frosted by the moon, a Gothic study in light and dark.

Something caught his eye—a light that shouldn't be there glimmered and disappeared, only to reappear a few feet higher on the cliff path. Partly build of wood, partly carved out of the cliff face, the path had been constructed to allow quicker access to the castle than could be had by the road that wound around to the top of the cliff. Thorne began striding toward the castle, keeping an eye on the light as he hurried toward it.

Two someones! As Thorne neared the base of the steps, he saw a second light. A little lower than the first, it moved more slowly and hesitantly, as if the person carrying this lantern was less sure-footed than the first. The windings of the path alternately led into the moonlight and back into darkness, doubtless an impediment to the unsure foot.

A turn in the path brought the lower person into view. Thorne gasped, then swore as he realized that it was Allison. *And James!* For it must be he, leading her up the cliff, and not bothering to stay close to her lest she stumble. *Who else would be so mad as to climb those steps at night? Or have the least reason to do so?*

A cold terror gripped him at the thought of Allison losing her footing on the rocks. A steep but safe climb in the daytime, the stairway was treacherous when darkness obscured the difference between carved steps and rocky outcrops or, worse, fallen chunks of the castle.

He started up the steps and realized that it would be slow going, for he had no lantern. *Drat!* He dropped back and looked upward. Hands cupping his mouth, he shouted at the top of his lungs, "Allison Weatherby! James Betterton! Get back down here at once!"

Startled by his voice, Allison very nearly dropped her lantern. Her heart was already in her throat from this midnight climb. At Thorne's shout, it sped up and shifted to a staccato rhythm. She looked up the path. The Silver Lady had paused, too, and looked back down inquiringly.

Now what do I do? Allison wondered, torn between Thorne's demands and the strong desire to follow the ghost. To her surprise, the ghost motioned that she should go to Thorne. Her voice chimed in Allison's ear.

"I had hoped for this. Ask him to join us, for we will require his assistance."

Though Allison doubted Thorne would cooperate, the night and its terrors would seem infinitely less alarming with him by her side. She made her way down the steps.

As she descended, Thorne climbed. When they met, he reached

for Allison and snatched her from her perch above him. "You little idiot," he growled, holding her tightly against him. His lips pressed against her temple; his right hand burrowed into her unbound hair. "You knew that was a damn dangerous thing to do. And James! To let you take such a risk. I'll skin him alive, which I suppose he knows, for he takes care not to come down here!"

"James?" Allison pulled back, frowning. "James isn't with me."

"Now, Allison, unless you want me to think you are in league with Newcomb—"

"The nerve of you!"

"Or some other conspirator—"

"I am with the Silver Lady. Look just above you on the steps. Can't you see her? She is motioning us to follow."

Thorne scowled. "If you hope to allay my anger by that nonsense—"

"It is the truth." Allison stepped out of his arms and drew herself up proudly. "She is leading me to the treasure."

Thorne looked up to where Allison pointed. All he saw was a particularly bright patch of moonlight. "I see nothing! Surely this is some May Game."

Allison shook her head vehemently.

"She really is there, Allie?" But Thorne knew the answer. The truth was in Allison's eyes.

"She is waiting for us to follow her. She wishes to show us the treasure."

"If you think it allays my fears one bit to know that the family ghost wants us to climb those steps, you are much mistaken! It's a murderous spirit, and wants to see all of the D'Aumont line extinguished."

"No such thing. Oh, don't weep, my lady." Allison spoke soothingly to the ghost. "It isn't true. Now see how you have distressed her, Thorne."

Thorne's teeth flashed in a grimace of disgust. "She has distressed me far more, by luring my father and half brother to his death. Now she tries for the woman I love." He reached for Allison.

"No." Allison stepped away before he could take her in his arms. "You do not love me, and she has lured no one to their deaths. She explained it to me. And—oh, Thorne—I saw what happened to her and her brothers tonight. I will tell you all of it later. But we must hurry. I really don't want to attempt those steps once the moon has set."

"The devil take it! I will not follow her, nor permit you to do so!" Again Thorne reached for her. She nimbly jumped up to the next step.

"Go get a lantern and join me at the top." Turning on her heels, she began to scramble higher. But Thorne caught up to her almost instantly. His momentum contributed to their both falling forward, onto the next step. Thorne took most of the shock of the fall in his left forearm, cushioning Allison from the blow. Miraculously, the lantern did not break.

"Are you hurt?" Thorne took the lantern from her hand and held it up.

"No. Yes. You're crushing me." Allison thrust at his chest. The momentum of their fall had carried her onto her back, with Thorne rolling forward until he was almost on top of her. "Get off, you oaf."

"Oaf, am I?" Thorne stayed where he was. His eyes caressed her in the lantern light. "Allison, stop struggling, or I won't be responsible for the results!"

She stilled, suddenly aware of their intimate position.

"That's better." He eased away from her just enough to lighten the pressure, but not enough that she could rise. "Now, listen to me. Seeing you on this cliff at night has cost me ten years of my life. I love you!"

Allison smiled sadly. "I know you do, Thorne."

He sighed. "I've been thinking about what I said this evening. Perhaps . . ." The proximity of his beloved in the moonlight suddenly made nonsense of his determination not to marry.

"Don't, Thorne. Nothing has changed. But if we found the treasure . . ." She lifted a shaky hand to shape his troubled brow. "Please go to the castle with us tonight."

Thorne felt a flood of warmth at this softly, temptingly uttered invitation. *Perhaps I should,* he thought, his eyes caressing Allison's face as her hand stroked his jaw. He very much feared he would do anything for her when he held her like this.

"Us?" He looked around carefully. Then he lifted his eyes hopefully to where Allison had indicated the ghost stood. *Nothing!*

"Answer me this, Allison, I am one of the heirs, yet never have I seen this ghost. Marie is no relation at all, yet she claims to have seen it and another beside. If it exists . . ."

Allison opened her mouth to protest, but he laid a warm finger against her lips. ". . . and if it is benign, why doesn't it show itself to me?"

She looked up, hoping to get an answer from the Silver Lady, then realized that she no longer stood three steps above them. "Oh! She's gone. But you did see her, a few minutes ago."

"No such thing!"

"You saw something, for you thought James was with me."

"I saw another light preceding you up the stairs," he admitted. "Are you quite sure you aren't covering up for my scape-grace cousin?"

"Quite!" Angered by his distrust, Allison shoved on his chest once again. This time he eased away and let her rise. "You saw her! She glows as if made of light. I could almost see the path without using the lantern."

Thorne rubbed his brows with thumb and forefinger. "I find this very hard to swallow, yet I'd like to think you wouldn't lie to me."

"I am not lying to you, Thorne. She was here seconds ago."

He took her shoulders in his hands and commanded her to look at him. "If so, she has gone because I am here with you, to protect you. If there is a spirit haunting these ruins, it is an evil one, with murder upon its mind."

"And I say that isn't so!"

"Then why has she abandoned you?"

Allison had no answer. Moments before, the Silver Lady had been asking her to talk him into coming with them. She once again looked up the stairs and saw a tiny beam of light swaying back and forth far above them, probably at the level of the castle wall.

"There she is!" Allison stood and pointed.

Just then a voice floated down to them. "Who goes there? Identify yourselves before I fill you with buckshot."

"A rather deep voice for a female ghost, wouldn't you say?" Thorne cupped his hands and called up, "It's me, Sergeant Bean. Silverthorne."

"Is it yourself, then, m'lord? I thought I heard voices."

Thorne held his finger to his mouth to keep Allison silent. "I did, too. Are the geese on patrol?"

"That they are, m'lord."

"Good man. Carry on."

"Now we know why she disappeared," Allison said. "She seems to be shy of Sergeant Bean."

"Humpf!" Thorne dropped his hands and motioned Allison to start down the stairs ahead of him. Allison accepted his unspoken order.

They walked back to the manor house in silence, each lost in thought. Thorne's thoughts ran on vindictive ghosts and the naive relatives who seemed determined to fall victim to them. Allison pondered how to convince Thorne to help her search for the treasure.

They climbed the servants' stairs together, making as little noise as possible. When Thorne motioned she should exit the stairs on the second floor, which held the library and public rooms, Allison balked.

"We need to talk," he said.

"I will speak with you tomorrow," she said.

"Tonight."

The anger in his voice and his grim expression made her distinctly uneasy. The dictatorial manner made her bristle. "I am not suitably dressed for conversation." She drew her robe about her more tightly.

"Nor for clambering up a cliff at midnight," he countered.

"Well, as to that, I am not sure what costume would be appropriate . . ."

He fought the smile, but it won. "That robe is infinitely more modest than the dress you wore to the Collingswood's ball."

After a second's hesitation, Allison nodded her agreement, and Thorne escorted her to the library. He held out a glass of sherry to her, then motioned her to sit beside him on a large leather sofa. Disturbing memories of another sofa prompted Allison to take a nearby Queen Anne chair instead.

He watched her gloomily as she sipped her wine. "I feel a certain sense of betrayal. You promised Bean, and through him me, that you would not—"

"Go anywhere near the north wall." She met his eyes unblinkingly. "And I didn't. Wouldn't! I have no wish to die."

"Where have you been searching?"

"I don't recall saying that I—"

"Allison!"

"I expected the Silver Lady to lead me to the treasure."

"She obviously disappointed you."

"She tried twice today. Just now, and earlier. I saw her at the castle just before the fiasco with Newcomb and Miss Pollard began."

He folded his arms and waited.

"She led me into the keep. I'm sure she was going to show me the treasure, but I suppose Marie's screams frightened her away, as did Bean tonight."

"Think, Allison. What need can a ghost have to flee a human being? If she can show someone the treasure, why has she not done so anytime these last one hundred-fifty years? I still say she wants to harm you. I suppose I really will have to blow the damned thing up, to keep you and James from becoming her victims."

It made her heart ache to see the distress in Thorne's tense features. Allison put her hands to her temples. "I need to think. There is something that is eluding me, something that explains—"

Thorne turned his head. "What is that?"

Allison looked behind him. "You can see her!"

"No, I thought I heard something."

"She's there. Barely visible, but unmistakable."

"It sounded like a bell. Probably a stray sheep has fallen into the ha-ha."

"That is how her voice sounds. She is speaking to us."

A flash of realization illuminated Thorne's drawn features. "Her voice sounds like bells? Can you understand her?"

"Yes, if you will be quiet."

Thorne waited, nostrils flaring, while Allison listened to the soft tinkling voice. As she listened, the Silver Lady, little more than a shining fog, floated toward a corner of the room and disappeared into a large locked cabinet.

"She says the answers to your questions are in there and asks us to join her at the keep tomorrow morning early."

Allison waited for Thorne to scoff or warn her away. But the

look of sudden enlightenment, of awe, became even more pro-
nounced. He stood up and moved toward the cabinet. "I have heard
mysterious bells at the castle all of my life. I used to dream up entire fairy kingdoms on the basis of those bells. Do you think—"

"She was trying to communicate with you? Yes! Oh, Thorne,
what is in there?"

He stopped before it. "I shall have to get the key; it is locked up
in my room."

She stood beside him, looking inquisitively into his face.

"Locked in that cabinet is an authentic copy of the original will
written by the first Baron D'Aumont and a careful genealogical
chart that has been kept through the years, tracing the heirs to the
Silverthorne treasure."

Chapter Thirteen

Allison reverently placed the ancient parchment documents on the long table Mr. Swinton used to catalog Thorne Hall's library. Thorne lit three tall branches of candles and dispersed them around the table. Together they bent over the will.

"I have personally compared this copy to the original, which is sealed in two-sided glass and kept in the vaults beneath my London solicitor's office," he told her.

She read through it swiftly. It was short and contained nothing unexpected. The first baron left his land and livestock to his eldest son. He directed that all gold, silver, and precious stones be divided equally among his heirs, male and female alike.

"Well?" Thorne demanded as she sat back in her chair, frowning.

"That doesn't explain . . ." She stood up, the better to see the genealogies Thorne had spread out on the table. Some ancient, some as recent as her own birth, they spanned many generations of English history.

"I wish you would tell me what you are looking for," Thorne demanded. "Then I could help you look, or more likely, answer your questions out of hand. I assure you my father made me familiar with these documents early on, and I had the painful task of reviewing them at his death."

Allison bit her lip. In her eagerness to discover the truth about the enigmatic behavior of the family ghost and thus find the treasure, she had forgotten that his father and brother had perished in the same pursuit.

"I am sorry to awaken painful memories," she said, placing a comforting hand on his sleeve.

He quickly covered it with his own. "Never mind. I must confess my curiosity has been aroused. So I ask again. What are you looking for?"

"It is what you are looking for. Why, if the Silver Lady truly is able to lead the heir or heirs to the treasure, hasn't she done so before now?"

"In fact, why doesn't she just tell us, instead of making us prowl through all of this lot." Thorne gestured impatiently at the fifteen or so documents.

"Hmmm?" Allison wasn't really attending. Her index finger delicately traced the main family tree, following the line from "Silver" Thorne, knighted by Queen Elizabeth in 1602. His son, the first Baron D'Aumont, died during one of the last battles of the English Civil Wars and was succeeded by his brother. Since then the succession had passed in an unbroken line from father to son down to Thorne. James's pedigree took but one additional line, as his father was the fourth marquess's younger brother. *They were not a prolific family*, Allison noted, *but they always managed to produce an heir.*

Nothing there seemed to answer Thorne's question, so she moved to the next sheet, which traced her own descent from the eldest daughter of the first baron's daughter, Elena, by her first husband, Baron Marpold. Her subsequent marriage to Sir Broderick Ramsey apparently was childless.

"Elena must be the Silver Lady."

"That is the generally held belief."

Next came the descent of Elena's youngest daughter by Baron Marpold. Curious, Allison shuffled briefly through the other papers.

"What are you looking for?"

"I thought there were three daughters."

"The middle daughter's line died out in the 1750s. That genealogy is here somewhere, but surely it is irrelevant?"

Nodding, Allison returned to the genealogy leading from the youngest daughter of Elena to Thorne's and James's mothers, who had been sisters. While she perused this one, Thorne grumbled in her ear, "As you can see, both James and I are doubly entitled to this mythical treasure. So why hasn't this troublesome spirit guided us to it long since?"

"I think she tried. For some reason I can see her and you cannot. But the bells you have heard . . ."

Thorne's eyes widened briefly, an echo of his awe a few moments before when he had realized the significance of his childhood experience. "Well, when you find it, my double descent surely means that I get two shares."

Allison looked at him out of the corner of her eye to confirm that he was quizzing her. "Rather, it means that I get half because I am the one she communicates with."

He smiled, but quickly sobered. "Come, Allison, admit she is a fraud or worse. It is getting late, and—"

"I have it!" Allison clapped her hands together and spun around gleefully. "Something in the tableau I saw tonight—"

"Tableau?"

"Oh, I never told you about that, did I?" Allison proceeded to describe the scene in her bedroom, which she had at first thought was a dream. "They all perished, taking the secret of the treasure with them. Before they did, I heard Elena say that the treasure was left to the baron's descendants, that it must not go to their uncle."

"That's not what the will says," Thorne growled. "It says 'heirs.' Gowan D'Aumont was the only male D'Aumont left after the two brothers disappeared. Elena bore the first baron's only grandchildren, but they were all girls."

"I know. Perhaps it was drawn up in haste, or poorly planned. But if that—vision? dream? whatever it was that I saw in my chamber tonight—is true, the first baron would not have wanted his brother to inherit the treasure."

Thorne nodded. "He despised his brother, that we know from the family history. So you are saying that none of the succeeding barons were entitled to the treasure, that my only claim to it is through my mother."

She nodded, eyes glowing. "Don't you see? Through the years the heirs to the title have believed themselves qualified to claim it, had it been discovered, nor would any have disputed them. Until your father and his brother married your mother and her sister, descendants of Elena, that would have meant that a large part of the baron's legacy would have gone to the descendants of a hated brother."

Thorne walked away from her to pace the room, brows furrowed in thought. At last he said, "It is a great deal to assume on the basis of a dream."

"Not a dream, a ghostly apparition. And there are other clues."

"Such as?"

"I often saw the Silver Lady as a child, though after the first few times I did not mention it because you and Jamie teased me so. That time when I was nine was the only time I was completely alone with her, and it was the one time she tried to lead me to the castle keep, instead of merely looking on with a sad expression on her face. Why? Because there were always others there who weren't entitled to the treasure! Your father, to be specific, for we never went there except in his company."

Once more Thorne paced the room. Allison watched him, trying hard to keep her mind on the puzzle the ghost had set for them, instead of upon the attractive man before her. At last he spoke. "There is a family tradition . . ." He darted to a shelf near the cabinet in which the legacy documents had been kept, grabbed a bound leather volume, and began shuffling through it.

"Here it is!" He laid it on the library table in front of Allison. She picked it up, looking inquisitively at him.

"My Uncle Whitaker appointed himself family historian. He collected all of the family and local lore about the treasure and the ghost."

Allison opened the book and scanned the first few pages, which told the story of the disappearance of the first baron's heirs and the first appearance of the Silver Lady. " 'She was seen shortly after the accession of the second baron, while the king was visiting him.' This is fascinating, Thorne. Literally dozens of them saw her fleeing toward the north wall and into the north tower. And the maid who had served her . . ." Allison's voice trailed away. She dropped her head into her hands.

"That makes for unpleasant reading, I know." Thorne placed a comforting hand on her bowed neck.

"They tortured her," Allison whispered.

"She could tell them nothing that wasn't common knowledge, though. Men will do much evil for the sake of wealth." He paused a moment, then added, "Women, too."

Allison looked up anxiously, her eyes asking. "Do you mean me?"

"I was thinking of my stepmother." He took the book from her, turning the pages rapidly. "Here. This is the part I particularly wanted you to read."

She read the passage out loud.

This story is told of brothers Sylvester and Gerrard D'Aumont, offspring of the fourth earl, who during their childhood years often explored the castle. This was a few years after the family ceased to live in the castle. In the summer of 1717, both boys claimed to have seen the ghost fleeing in the direction of the north tower, which they had been forbidden to explore. Their obedience to this parental decree was reinforced by the sight of a menacing male ghost, an armored soldier covered in blood, whose cold presence frightened them very much.

One day Gerrard, the younger of the two, was walking by himself on the castle grounds. He claimed to have seen this same lady ghost, who beckoned him into the keep. He tried to follow her, but she disappeared. This story was given little credence, for an estate worker who followed the boy into the keep saw nothing.

Allison looked up, eyes shining. "So I wasn't the first heir to be led into the keep."

"Uncle Whitaker included every story he could find, no matter how trivial. There are several deaths reported, caused by rock slides. Searching among the ruins for the treasure has always been a dangerous business. If you'll notice, a loose sheet in the back, added after the book was bound, takes note of your sightings."

Curious, she turned to the back of the book.

Allison Rainsville, daughter of Lord Catherton, descendant of Elena D'Aumont's oldest daughter by Baron Marpold, three sightings. At age four, told her father there was a sad-eyed lady following them around the castle. At age five, mentioned seeing a 'shining lady' near the north wall. When she was nine, she wandered off by herself and subsequently said the Silver Lady smiled at her and motioned her to follow. The ghost attempted to lead her into the keep. This distressed Lady Catherton considerably. She believes the spirit is evil, and that it seeks to lure her daughter to her death.

"She believes!" Allison exclaimed. "I am astonished. She has always absolutely refused to allow that there could be such a thing as a ghost."

"Perhaps she hoped to convince you, to prevent just such a quest as you have embarked upon." Thorne solemnly regarded her, the grey eyes reflecting the same concern.

Shaking off the urge to surrender all interest in the ghost to one who so obviously was concerned for her safety, Allison turned back to the page with the story of Sylvester and Gerrard, and studied it. "I suppose you called Gerrard's story to my attention to show that the Silver Lady also tried to lure a descendant of the second baron into the keep. That would disprove my theory about why the ghost has never revealed the treasure's hiding place." She referred to the sheet that traced Thorne's line. "I see Gerrard died young—seventeen. Did he . . ." She lifted dread-filled eyes to Thorne. "Did he die looking for the treasure?"

"No." Thorne sat down beside her. "He died of the smallpox. I pointed it out to you because his mother, my great-grandmother, cuckolded her husband and was divorced by him in 1720."

Allison had not heard of this bit of old scandal. "Are you saying . . ." Allison's face lit up. "If she cuckolded him then, she might have done so earlier. Another man might have fathered Gerrard." Her joy quickly faded. "But that doesn't help my case."

"There's more. The descent of the middle daughter is not really irrelevant at all, as it turns out." He shuffled through the papers scattered over the table. "Yes, here it is. The last of her line was named in the divorce petition. He subsequently married my great-grandmother in 1722, but they were childless. He died without issue in 1750.

Allison put her hands to her mouth, too bowled over by this information to speak.

"So you see, dear distant cousin, if she planted a cuckoo in my great-grandfather's nest, sired by the man she later married, that would explain why Gerrard, walking alone, saw the lady motioning him into the keep. It may prove your theory that she will only reveal the treasure to direct descendants of the first baron, her father."

"You believe in her."

Thorne sighed. "With great reluctance, I admit I am beginning to do so."

"And, I think, in her good intentions."

"As to that, I reserve judgment. I shall initiate a careful search of every square corner of the keep from tunnels to battlements. But don't get your hopes too high, Allison. You must know that this selfsame search has been made at least once in every generation. I doubt that much of the disrepair of the various castle buildings can be laid as much to treasure hunting as to siege engines."

"Thorne, you can be incredibly thickheaded. Or should I say pigheaded! Such a search is doomed, as all of the others have been, without the Lady's help. We must go there tomorrow, the three of us, at first light, with no other persons on the premises, and let her lead us to it."

He shook his head. "I won't allow you to take the risks that might entail. Given time enough, I will discover the keep's secrets, if indeed, it keeps secrets!"

She ignored his pun. "No, you don't understand. She urged haste upon us."

"After all these years, she can jolly well wait a few weeks longer."

"She says there is someone who can find it now. I think she means Newcomb. Jamie must have read this book." She lifted the volume of family tradition and shook it at him. "He doubtless conveyed the information to Newcomb. What if he also stumbled on something in the family papers that reveals one of those subterranean tunnels you spoke of? Newcomb might carry it off before we can find it."

"I find that extremely far-fetched. Still . . ." He muttered an almost inaudible, scandalously insulting epitaph upon his cousin. "Drat that James for telling Newcomb family secrets! I am going to wake him up and find out exactly what he told the man."

He turned and strode out of the room, carrying a branch of candles. At the first landing he recalled his manners and waited for Allison, letting her precede him up the stairs. When they reached the third floor, he turned to escort her down the hall to her room.

Allison hung back. "I'm going with you to see Jamie," she said.

"Shhh. Do you want Aunt Agatha down on us?"

"No," she whispered, "but I do want to help waken Jamie. I

want to be quite sure you don't murder him." She smiled up at him to soften her words.

The heavy-lidded, slumbrous look crept into Thorne's eyes. "But I was looking forward to putting you to bed."

Allison wagged an admonishing finger at him. "Behave yourself, sir. Else I will indeed rouse Aunt Agatha and tell her of your improper advances." Not waiting for a reply, she turned on her heels, tossing him a saucy grin over her shoulder, and walked rapidly toward the other wing, where Thorne's and James's quarters were.

He caught up with her and stopped her by catching her elbow. "You don't know how difficult James can be to wake when he has imbibed too much. He'll singe your delicate ears." He lifted his free hand and delicately caressed one pink earlobe.

Allison tossed her head and stepped away. *He is in a dangerous mood*, she thought. *With the slightest encouragement he would make love to me.* Aloud, she responded, "More so than you did a few moments ago in the library? I have excellent hearing, Thorne." She was gratified to see that his face flushed with embarrassment.

"A thousand pardons. I never meant . . . Ah, well, if you go with me, perhaps you can prevent the encounter from degenerating into a brawl." He offered her his arm and, holding the candle branch high, escorted her down the hall and into his cousin's suite of rooms.

Thorne looked in the bedroom first to be sure James was decent, then motioned Allison to join him as he stood looking with disgust on the fully clothed recumbent figure slanting across the bed. He handed her the candle branch.

"James, wake up. James! James!" Thorne shook the limp form as he spoke loudly. After several moments of this Turkish treatment his cousin began to stir and mutter.

"James, get up. We need to know what you told Newcomb about the treasure." Thorne half lifted the younger man from the bed and shook him by the scruff of the neck.

"Here, try this," Allison suggested, handing Thorne a glass of water. Not the least pleased to see James dead drunk, she did not bother to suppress her grin when he awoke, sputtering, as the liquid was sloshed in his face.

"Damn you, Thorne, leave me be. Shot the cat, don't y'know."
He swung ineffectually at the marquess.

"You did more than that, dear cousin. You told Newcomb some
things about the treasure which only the heirs have any business
knowing, didn't you?"

" 'S in the keep. Tol' him that. Don't matter. Went straight to
the north wall. Stoopid clunch. Told him—got to be in that tunnel
under the well house. Y'know the one, Thorne."

"The one that leads in the direction of the north wall? I know.
And now Newcomb knows." Thorne's grim expression told Allison this information had alarmed him.

"What tunnel?" Allison looked bewildered.

"There is a secret entrance in the well house. It leads to the system of tunnels under the castle. Some of them go to the towers and
were meant to enable the castle's defenders to move swiftly and
secretly to various parts of the castle. Some lead to sally ports, two
that we know of, both very well hidden."

"Sally ports?" Allison looked back and forth between the two
men, seeking enlightenment.

"Escape passages. The exits are some distance from the castle
and difficult to find if one doesn't know they are there."

"Why didn't I know about this?" Allison put her hands on her
hips. "When were you going to tell me?"

"Never!" The tunnel is choked with fallen debris, particularly
near the north wall. Very dangerous. Dark, damp, with lots of false
turns and blind ends. The ceilings drop rocks upon explorers right
and left. My father took James and me in there once, mainly to
show us how dangerous it was. Until tonight I was convinced it
had nothing to offer in the way of clues."

"Mus' be clues. The Sil'r Lady tried to show 'em to Allison
once, didn't she, Allie? Might again, come to think of it. But no!
Can't. Thorne says." James's grievances began to boil up beneath
his alcohol-induced lethargy.

"I suppose you told Newcomb about the sally ports, too?"
Thorne looked ready to throttle his cousin.

"Tol' him they existed. Well, knew that already, di'n't he?
Stands to reason. All the castles have 'em, don' they?"

Thorne grabbed James by the lapel. *"Did you tell him where
they are?"*

"Thorne!" Allison tugged on his sleeves, urging him to let James go, which he did, after a tense moment.

James fell back on the bed and tried to get up once more. "Don' you manhandle me like that, Thorne. Ain't gonna stan' for it. What if I did tell him, in a general way? Can' find 'em without my help, can he?"

"Oh, good Lord!" Thorne scrubbed at his face fiercely with his right hand. "They've been found before, James. And added their share to the treasure's death toll, too. Not that Newcomb's death would grieve me overmuch, but what if he has told others? Sooner or later someone else will be killed down there."

"Oh, James, how could you?" Allison stared aghast at her inebriated relative.

"Meant well," James mumbled. He had finally managed to stumble to his feet.

Allison touched an imploring hand to Thorne's sleeve. "I hate to pressure you, but the only way to end the search for the treasure . . ."

"Is to find it ourselves. Very well, Allison. An early start tomorrow. We'll give our lady ghost a chance to lead us to it."

James seized Thorne's arm and began to shake it eagerly. "D'you mean to say you actually believe there is a treasure? That you are goin' t'search for it?"

Thorne twitched his arm free, but smiled in spite of his annoyance. "Yes, James. Tomorrow morning the three of us have an appointment with a ghost."

At that, James gave a whoop loud enough to wake the dead and seized Allison by the arms, dancing her around the room joyfully. The brandy bottle on his nightstand began to wobble wildly as they danced. Belying his drunken state, James made a neat catch, though some of it sloshed on Allison, wetting the front of her robe.

"Stop, Jamie. Stop. We'll get brandy on the carpet." Laughing, she struggled to detach herself from James's embrace. Thorne moved to separate them.

Abruptly, James let go of her just as she heard Thorne gasp. "Oh, no!"

"Ouch! Ouch!" James bent down, covering his head with his hands as an umbrella landed repeated blows.

"Assault this poor, defenseless lamb, will you! Wicked debauched creature. And Thorne, too. What beastly work have you two been doing this night? Allison, flee while you may. They shan't harm you anymore, not while I am here to defend you!"

"Aunt Agatha, stop. Please don't. Things are not what they seem. Let me explain." Allison pleaded with the enraged woman to no avail. Her battery continued until Thorne wrenched the umbrella from her hands.

"Foul demon! Hell-born monster! Look what you've done to her, Thorne D'Aumont. Reeking of brandy and keeping two men company in her nightclothes in the dead of the night. Oh, Allison. You are ruined. My poor dear." Agatha lunged for Allison, embracing her in a hug hardly less damaging than her blows had been to James.

While Allison was struggling with Agatha's excess of solicitude, she heard her mother's plaintive voice from the doorway. "Wha'st? Whuh go'n on." Peering over Agatha's shoulder, Allison saw Delphinia rubbing her eyes sleepily. Unhappily she realized that they had been joined by Mr. Swinton, their maid, Peggy, and assorted other half-awake but fully curious servants.

Thorne helped her free herself from Agatha's clutches and then drew her within the circle of his arms. "What is going on is that we are celebrating our betrothal."

"We most certainly are not!" Allison glared up at him and tried to escape the iron hold he had on her.

"A likely story," Agatha barked. "Delphinia, you should take Allison and spirit her away. Living with her cousin William would be preferable to letting her remain in the vicinity of this womanizing—"

"Oh, Allie. I'm so happy for you!" Delphinia rushed forward to put her arms around Allison, who was spluttering indignantly.

"Jolly good thing!" James had somehow retained the brandy bottle in spite of Agatha's umbrella. He waved it around gleefully. "Get you two leg-shackled. Find the treasure. Soon all our pro'lems'll be solved!" He raised the bottle and drank from it for an alarmingly long time.

"Here. Stop that!" Thorne demanded. "You're already drunk as a lord."

"But at least now I shan't be a lord's ward! Gonna find the treasure and be my own man!" James did another little jig, which quickly ended in a tumble onto the bed. He upended the bottle once more, draining it.

Allison finally managed to struggle free from Thorne and her mother. After three ladylike attempts to get everyone's attention, she put her fingers to her lips and let loose the long, shrill whistle her father had taught her to use to call back their gun dogs. Abruptly, the tumult in the room ceased.

"Thank you for your attention," Allison said sarcastically. "First, I am grateful to you, Lord Silverthorne, for being so concerned about my reputation that you would conjure up a nonexistent engagement." She held up a hand as a swell of protests began.

"But it is quite unnecessary, as I am sure that no one in this room will speak of this event once we leave it. None would wish to begin a scandal, and no scandal can begin if there is no gossip." She addressed herself particularly to Mr. Swinton and the servants. "Lord Silverthorne and I heard Jamie cry out and separately came to see what was wrong. We had a bit of a struggle to calm his spirits, which you can see are quite high."

As James had resumed his dancing, though with the slow, careful pace of a man much the worse for drink, his observers could not doubt this remark. Wide-eyed but apparently willing to be convinced, they nodded their heads and murmured among themselves.

"Aunt Agatha, do you understand that you leapt to a wrong conclusion?" Allison bent a severe look on the older woman.

"You may be sure my lips are sealed, my child. I wouldn't wish to see you married to this rake for any reason!"

"Oh, Allie!" Lady Catherton, wide awake now, stamped her feet with exasperation. "What a silly chit you are, to be sure. Well, come to bed now, if you please. Thorne is more than able to deal with Jamie, and for you to come to his room was well intentioned but very improper, you know."

She led her daughter down the hall, ringing a peal over her head the whole way. Allison gave the proper contrite responses, but her mind was on Thorne, whose only response to her denial of their engagement had been an enigmatic smile.

Chapter Fourteen

Allison shrank away from the urgent hand shaking her arm. "Leave me alone," she mumbled. "I mean to sleep in."

"But, ma'am, Lord Silverthorne is waiting for you. He sent you some breakfast."

Allison reluctantly opened her eyes to the feeble light of dawn. *Whatever can have possessed Thorne to wake me at this ungodly hour.* Then she remembered the night before and sat up abruptly, excitement coursing through her. *The Silver Lady! Today we find the treasure.*

"Put the tray on my dressing table, Peggy; I will eat as I dress." Allison made quick work of the toast and ham that accompanied her usual morning coffee. As she munched, she brushed her hair briskly, then pinned it in a simply topknot.

"Oh, Mrs. Weatherby, wouldn't you like for me to arrange a few curls?"

Allison shook her head. "This is not a lover's tryst, Peggy. Lord Silverthorne and I have business to conduct." She put on the habit she had worn yesterday and hurried into her sitting room, only to find it empty. *He must have gone down to order the horses.* She descended the stairs with indecent speed.

Mimmings eyed her as if she were a hoydenish miss from the schoolroom. "May I be of service, madam?"

"Where is Lord Silverthorne?"

"He hasn't yet made an appearance, madam, but he sent down a request for horses, so I assume he will be with you shortly."

"Ah! You are still of a mind to go to the castle this morning." Thorne's deep voice accompanied his rapid footsteps down the stairs. "I wouldn't blame you if you said no, after such a short night's sleep."

"Wild horses could not keep me away. I am relieved that you have not changed your mind." *And somewhat surprised*, she thought to herself. She would not have been too surprised to wake at noon and find that Thorne and James had departed long since, leaving orders for her to stay away from the castle.

Thorne accepted his hat and riding gloves from Mimmings, then urged her out the door. "I want no one else hurt searching for this treasure."

"Is Jamie on the way down?"

"I was unable to roust him out of bed." Thorne's expression turned thunderous. "After he finished off the brandy bottle, he found his way to the wine cellar for seconds. He is totally incoherent. I suppose we should wait another day so he can accompany us, but having made up my mind to search, I confess to some impatience to begin."

Shame on James. No wonder Thorne does not want to leave the future of his estate in such hands. "Yes, do let us go on. The Silver Lady stressed the need for haste. She said someone was dangerously close to beating us to the treasure."

Thorne checked the legs of both their mounts carefully as they conversed. When satisfied, he stood up, his expression uneasy. "Your concern may be justified. Marie Pollard is no longer on the premises. I have several estate workers searching for her, but—"

"Oh, Thorne. What if Newcomb got his hands on her somehow? He could already be ahead of us."

"Allison, I wish there were some way to pursue this matter without involving you. This could be dangerous." Deep furrows marred Thorne's brow as he looked down at her, clearly torn.

"Well, there isn't, so let us have no more roundaboutation. I am the only one who can see the Silver Lady—at least the only one of the heirs. We must hurry." Allison motioned the waiting groom to toss her up, not wanting to give Thorne more time to dream up a solution that excluded her.

Thorne placed two large leather wallets across the flank of his horse and tied them down. The first clanked as he handled it, indicating the presence of tools. The second wafted a pleasant scent as he carefully arranged it. "I asked Mimmings to order a luncheon for us," he explained.

*   *   *

Sergeant Bean was nowhere in sight when they arrived at the castle gate. Thorne rode right on through and immediately aroused the ire of the geese. Allison followed, grinning. The birds' indignation always amused her. Her grin turned into a guffaw when the Lord and Master of Thorne Hall, Silverthorne Castle, and all of the lands and houses for miles in any direction dismounted and found himself the target for a flurry of flapping wings and snapping bills.

"Thunderation," he yelled. "Get these beasts off of me. Bean! I say, Bean! Don't just sit there laughing at me, Allison! They know you. Get them off of me."

Allison dismounted, but doubled over in helpless laughter. "Hoist by your own petard!"

"Very funny," Thorne said repressively, but Allison could see that his lips were twitching as he leapt into his saddle again, though his mount was dancing about dangerously among the agitated flock.

At that moment Sergeant Bean rode through the archway and into the midst of the geese at a gallop. Reining in sharply, he began making profuse apologies to Thorne in between admonishments to the geese. Over the tumult Allison called out, "I think you had better wait outside the gate, Thorne, so that the sergeant and I can corral his troops."

With a grin and a wave Thorne did just that. It took Bean and herself several minutes to calm the indignant geese and lure them into their pen by shaking baskets of corn. By the time they had finished, Allison had learned that Bean had ridden out with the search party, hoping to find Marie.

"Old John Garmon, the miller, said he saw her at first light, riding on the back of a wagon that was carrying some provisions to the men making up the hay on the home farm. So she left of her own free will, but I know 'twas because she feared Newcomb."

"You like her very much, don't you, Sergeant Bean?"

"Aye, ma'am, that I do. A fine stout woman with a good heart. I can't imagine where she'll go, with no references nor much in the way of funds."

"Perhaps Lord Thorne would give you leave to go after her."

His face lit up. "I'm sure he would, for he is the kindest of masters." The two of them walked back to the castle gate, where Thorne awaited, holding a lantern.

Allison listened in approbation as he granted Bean's request. "Is there a groom the geese won't rip apart?"

"Yes, sir. That would be Peter Mason. He often brings me supplies and stays for a game of chess."

"Before you leave, see that he takes your place here to watch out for Newcomb. Tell Miss Pollard she'll have a place here if she wishes. One maid is not enough to serve Miss Keisley, Lady Catherton, and Mrs. Weatherby."

Allison knew she would not agree to allow him to provide them with such a luxury, but Marie did need a position, and Delphinia would be so delighted. *Perhaps by the end of this day I shall be a great heiress and can afford her salary myself*, she thought. "I understand she is an experienced dresser. I know my mother will be in alt to have her."

Bean bobbed his head. "I'd best be off, then. If that rum touch Newcomb is still about, he might find her."

They watched Bean saddle his horse and ride away. "I hope that woman has as good a heart as he thinks she does," Allison observed.

"Yes. From the look on her face last night as her eyes followed him around the room, I suspect his missing limb will not weigh with her. I regret his leaving at this time, however. I suppose we should wait until that groom shows up to watch the gate."

"Oh, no, Thorne. The Lady asked us to be here early." Allison glanced eastward. "It is full daylight now."

"I know." Looking none too happy about matters, Thorne lifted the leather pouches that had previously been strapped behind his saddle, handing the one with the food to her and shouldering the other. It was obviously heavy and gave off a metallic clank. "Tools," he explained unnecessarily. "Bring the lantern, will you? Shall we start at the keep?"

"Absolutely." Allison took his offered arm and crossed the courtyard with a light heart. *Somehow, everything is going to work out. I can feel it in my bones.*

It seemed her optimism was fully justified. The Silver Lady waited for them in the doorway of the castle's keep.

Thorne halted. "She's here, isn't she?"

"Can you see her?"

He squinted. "Not really, but it looks as if there is some sort of haze in the doorway. Is that where she is?"

"Yes, and she wants us to follow her."

"Ask her if Newcomb is here. I don't want to be trapped in some dark tunnel with an enemy at my back."

Allison shook her head. "She's already moving out of sight. But I am sure if he were here, she would not put in an appearance. So faithful to her father's wishes! I have been wondering—has she been denied entry into heaven because of this treasure? It seems not to fit with my slender knowledge of theology."

Thorne shook his head. "Until last night I found it difficult to believe she existed, so I certainly can't pronounce on such difficult matters. I have to fall back on Shakespeare.

"'There are more things on heaven and earth' . . . ?"

"Exactly."

"Or St. Paul: 'Now I see through a glass darkly' . . ."

Thorne nodded his head and waited for her to go ahead of him into the keep. Once inside, they found the light dim but sufficient to navigate around the furniture and machinery stored there. Almost enviously Allison watched the ghost pass through these obstacles.

The ground floor of the keep had been partitioned at some time in the past, and the ghost passed through one of these barriers.

"Did she just disappear?" Thorne turned his head this way and that.

"She went in there." Allison pointed toward the wall ahead.

"I was afraid of that!"

"Why? What is wrong?"

"You'll see." Thorne helped her over a rusting haymow and led her to a door in the partition. It was padlocked. He dropped the leather pouch on the floor and bent to fish around in it. He emerged with a ring of large keys, some of them obviously very old. "Here. This looks like the one." The lock was not ancient; in fact, it looked as if it had been oiled recently. It opened easily.

"Enter the Sultan's bath!" He swept a dramatic bow, ushering her within. There was no light inside except that provided by the Silver Lady, who hovered near a very large marble tub in the center of the room.

Allison looked around in amazement. From the outside, the

rough oak enclosure had given no hint of luxury. Inside there was a tiled floor with elaborate inlays. Even the walls were tiled, and the ceiling was stucco. A quick glance at the figures in bas relief there sent a blush to her cheeks. As for the tub, it was sunken into the floor, a wonder work of marble and tile, with gold fixtures. Dust and cobwebs coated the whole.

As she stared about her, openmouthed, the Silver Lady floated through the wall of the tub and then sank into the floor on the opposite side.

This abruptly threw the room into darkness. Thorne took the lantern from Allison's hand and carried it to the door of the room, where he could see to light it. While she waited, Allison stood in the dark, letting her eyes adjust, and soon could make out enough to circle the tub and study the spot where the ghost had disappeared. She dropped onto her knees and found a break in the flooring.

"Yes, there is a door there." Thorne lifted the lantern as he approached, illuminating the area.

"It is the way to the tunnels, I gather. Tell me about this room, Thorne. It is most unexpected."

Thorne chuckled as he set the lantern down and began to feel his way along the edge of the door. "My grandfather had severe rheumatic complaints. His doctor advised him to seek the waters of Bath, but he built this instead, modeling it on a bath he saw in Italy when on the grand tour."

"Modeled on a seraglio, no doubt!" Allison primmed her lips.

Thorne laughed outright. "Now how did you guess that? I confess, looking at the decor, I regret anew that the prolonged hostilities on the Continent kept me from taking the grand tour."

"But a bath here? Why not at Thorne Hall?"

Finding what he was looking for, Thorne pressed on a piece of tile, which popped up with a click to reveal a small chamber. "The well is beneath here. Very convenient, actually."

"But . . ."

He sat back on his heels and smiled at her. "The artesian well over which Silverthorne Castle is built is a hot spring. I expect it is part of the same underground system that keeps the convalescents coming to Buxton. Now if you will just step aside, the door will be somewhat easier to lift without you standing on it."

"Oh! Excuse me." She stepped quickly away from the area. "I never knew any of this was here."

"No, how should you? It wouldn't have been discussed in front of children, partly to keep us out of the tunnels, and partly because the water is extremely hot. Children could well be injured in it just as it comes from the pipes. I did not learn of it until I was sixteen. Grandfather, and my father after him, always kept it under lock and key."

"It is just as well," Allison said repressively, casting a quick look at the carvings in the ceiling. "That is a disgusting way to portray cherubs."

His eyes flashed with heat for a moment as he looked at her. "Why, I do believe you are blushing, Allie."

"Are you going to open that door, or not?" She gave him her sternest look, then giggled, entirely ruining the effect.

"Are you quite sure you wouldn't like to fill the tub and have a nice soak? Its tile portrays some interesting activities, too. Inventive women, those houris."

"No, I thank you, sir! Not even on a cool day!" For the first time Allison noticed how very warm the room was.

Thorne grinned at her. "Too timid by half. Well, then, here goes." Grasping the handle concealed beneath the tile, he strained to lift the door from the floor. *This was why the Silver Lady said we would need his assistance,* Allison realized.

As Allison peered into the dark space beneath the door, for the first time it dawned on her that her dreams had told the truth: She would be exploring dark tunnels deep within the earth. *How narrow are those tunnels, I wonder?* She shuddered.

After lowering the heavy door all the way back on its hinges until it rested on the floor, Thorne dusted his hands. "If I am not out within the hour, you should have Peter Mason ring the alarm bell. That will summon help."

"I'm to stay here?" Allison straightened up.

"I don't want you going down those stairs. Too treacherous. They are as old as this castle—perhaps older, for there are indications of Roman occupation around here, and they never could resist a hot bath."

Hands on hips, Allison confronted him. "What has that to say to anything?"

"They are worn slick with age, and the railings my grandfather installed are wood, doubtless rotting in the humidity down there. As for the tunnels, they are dirty, dark, and dangerous. I want you to be a good girl and wait here for me, contemplating the lessons of the Sultan's tub." Before she could draw breath to argue, he raised his hand. "In the darkness, I saw her. Dimly, it is true, more as a glowing mist than as a person, but enough to follow her, if she will but appear and lead me."

"Very well. I'll stay if she will guide you to the treasure. Otherwise . . ." Her capitulation resulted less from obedience than from fear of the dark tunnels.

Surprised at her acquiescence, Thorne lifted the lantern to study her. "Good. Don't look so worried. With our ghost to help me, I will doubtless return shortly." He pulled her into his arms for a brief, urgent kiss. Before she could protest—or respond—he put her away from him, then took up the lantern and the pouch of tools and stepped gingerly into the black opening. Slowly he disappeared from view. She moved to the edge and looked in. She could see Thorne, and beyond him in the light of the lantern a wide, spiraling staircase that led down so far that its termination was in darkness.

Thorne eschewed the railing, trailing his hands along the wall as he descended. As she watched him disappear into the darkness, with only the small pool of light to mark his place, she felt a shameful sense of relief that he had insisted she remain behind.

No sooner had this thought occurred to her than she heard a muffled curse. The lamp suddenly began to oscillate wildly, then just as suddenly disappeared, plunging the stairs into darkness.

Chapter Fifteen

"Thorne! Thorne! Are you hurt?" Allison crouched at the opening in the floor and shouted at the top of her voice. No answering shout rang out. Instead, all was silent—a terrible silence that pierced Allison to the bone. *What am I to do?*

She knew the answer, but her mind rebelled at the thought of descending those dark stairs. She looked around her for some source of illumination, but there was none. If there had ever been candles in those ornate wall sconces spaced evenly around the bath, mice had long since consumed them.

She thought of running to the gatehouse. Bean would surely have another lantern there. But she immediately discarded this notion. What if Thorne had fallen into water? If he was unconscious, even an inch or two would suffice to drown him. That thought forced her into action. She would have to make her way down those stairs in the dark, relying on her sense of touch alone.

Taking in a deep breath, she put her right foot out and began feeling for the top step. A soft glow of light suffused the stairwell as she did so. A few feet below her stood the Silver Lady, beckoning, her pale face more anxious-looking than ever.

Allison was very glad to have riding boots on. It would have been impossible to go down those worn, slick steps in slippers. As she descended, she noticed that there were handholds carved into the wall at intervals. She used these to steady herself as she followed the Lady down into the bowels of the castle.

It seemed as if she had been descending forever when at last the ghost bent over a recumbent form. *Thorne!* Her heart stopped at the sight of him sprawled on his back on the stone floor, head turned to one side and a tiny trickle of blood flowing from his nose. Allison hurried down the last few steps and knelt at his side. To her intense relief, his chest rose and fell steadily.

He is alive! Allison allowed herself a breath she didn't realize she had been holding. "Thorne. Wake up, dearest! Thorne!" She gently shook him and was rewarded by a soft moan. He gradually emerged from unconsciousness as she cradled his head on her lap, rocking him and whispering words of love in his ear.

From a great depth Thorne heard his name being called. His eyelids seemed weighted, but at last he succeeded in opening them. He beheld Allison, her head bathed in an eerie radiance, bending over him. "I hope you are not the angel you appear to be; that would mean we are both dead." He smiled up at her, lifting his hand to touch her face.

Allison blinked back tears of joy. "As warm as it is down here, I very much fear if we are dead, we have landed in a most undesirable location." She dabbed at his bloody nose with the handkerchief she always carried tucked into the sleeve end of her habit-blouse.

"Ouch! That hurts too much for me to be dead!" Thorne sat up and looked around. "So she's here. It would have been thoughtful of her to appear when I came down the steps; then I mightn't have tripped over my own feet like a clunch."

"She lighted me down. Oh, Thorne, I was so afraid for you!"

Thorne put his hand behind her head and pulled her forward for another kiss, this time a tender, gentle expression of his emotions. "It is a good thing I was unconscious when you came down those stairs, or I would have been the terrified one." They looked into one another's eyes and Allison thought her heart would break for love of him. He must surely feel the same, to look at her so.

Thorne was the first to turn away. "I'd best relight that lantern, in case she decides to do a flit again." As he struggled to his feet, Thorne marveled at the strength of his feelings for Allison. *I truly do love her with all my heart.*

As he fussed with the lantern, which was dented but otherwise undamaged, he pondered where those feelings should take him. *How I wish she had allowed last night's announcement of our engagement to stand. Everything would be so much simpler—there would be no need for choices and decisions.* But his problems were unresolved; indeed, the stronger his feelings for her, the more he distrusted them. *This is not the time or place to work at something that complicated*, he told himself.

As she watched Thorne fumble with the lantern, Allison struggled with a sense of hopelessness. *What future is there for our love? Thorne D'Aumont is too responsible. He will place his duty above his own wishes and yours, my girl, so stop maundering about him.*

Alarmed that the simple task of lighting the lantern was taking him so long, she decided to end their search. "I don't think we should continue our quest now. A blow on the head sufficient to knock you out is not a trivial matter. We should call a physician, I think, and put this off for another day or two."

"No," Thorne shrugged off this idea. "I have a headache, but have taken no serious hurt, I am sure. I want to find this treasure while our family ghost is in a cooperative mood."

This was the first moment Allison had thought of the Silver Lady since she caught sight of Thorne sprawled at the bottom of the stairs. She looked up and saw the spirit a few feet away. Would Thorne try to make her go back upstairs while he followed the ghost? "Can you still see her?"

"Only that luminous haze. What is she doing?"

"Just waiting for us." At that moment the lantern flared into life. The ghost began to sink into the floor, leaving them alone in the subterranean chamber.

"Good job I got this lit. Not very dependable, is she? Well, perhaps she thinks I can find it now without her." Thorne lifted the lantern up and shined it around the cavern. "Though if it is so obvious, why haven't those who have searched for it over the years found it? Ah, well. I'll know soon enough. I'll go with you up the steps," he said, taking her elbow.

"You do not mean to proceed without me?"

"If this incident hasn't convinced you that this is a dangerous quest—"

"Which you would have made mice feet of already, without my help! I do not think she means to show it to you alone, or else she would have preceded you down the steps. Perhaps she can't make herself clear enough to you."

Thorne considered the justice of this suggestion. "If her role is anything more than to lead me to it, I must admit I would be unable to make it out, no more of her than I can see."

"That's settled, then! Has the well dried up?" Allison didn't wish to continue the discussion, having carried her point. She examined the round stone construction in the middle of the well room. The circular trough was empty and looked as if it had been so for a long time. In the center was a solid piece of stone with a giant boulder balanced on top if it.

"No, my grandfather had it capped and pipes introduced to carry the flow to the bath above." He pointed with the lantern to an area on the other side of the trough.

"Yes, I see them now." Allison moved around the trough to look at the lead pipes in the floor. She then turned her attention to the boulder. There was a chain bolted into the huge rock. The other end of the chain was attached to a long, stout oak handle that lay across a large beam. Both chain and oak were of recent manufacture. She touched it and looked inquiringly at Thorne.

"The stone could be lifted on and off the well, depending on whether water was needed or not." Thorne moved to the handle and grasped its smooth curved surface with both hands. As Allison watched in fascination, he used the handle to lift the huge boulder and swing it over the floor.

How strong he is, she thought in wonderment.

As if hearing her thoughts, Thorne praised their ancestors' knowledge of the power of the fulcrum. "No one man could lift such a stone directly. The construction of the entire castle is a testament to the considerable engineering skills of previous generations."

"It is impressive, but why are the handle and the chain so new? They are not needed now that the water is diverted to the pipes."

"Watch. In a moment you will understand." Thorne lowered the stone to the floor on the very spot where they had last seen the Silver Lady.

When nothing happened, he grasped the handle again, raised the stone into the air a foot, and let it drop with a *thunk* that resounded loudly in the closed quarters of the well room. The sound had not died away before it was drowned out by a grating, rumbling sound. As Allison watched, a section of the floor began to move. Where the ball had landed the floor dropped away. The opposite end of the slab began to rise.

"They also understood the use of the pivot," Thorne called to her over the racket.

When the noise ceased, Thorne led her to the opening in the floor, where another set of steps descended into darkness. Fascination mingled with dread as Allison approached them.

"This leads to the tunnel you told me about."

"Yes." He strode back to the place where his pouch of tools lay, shouldered them, then returned, holding out his hand to her. "Shall we?"

Swallowing her qualms, Allison let herself be assisted down what turned out to be a short, straight flight of stone steps. At the bottom Thorne's lantern illuminated the first few feet of a passageway that appeared to have been carved into the living rock of the cliff. Still holding her hand firmly in his, he led her into the tunnel. "So many have explored the tunnels so carefully, I still do not see how anything can have escaped discovery."

Allison was looking past him, hardly heeding. "She's here, motioning us to follow."

"That sounds promising." Thorne dropped back, letting Allison precede him. He partially closed the lantern's opening, to make the Silver Lady easier for him to see.

The ghost moved through the tunnel faster than they could easily follow. Allison slipped several times on the damp rock, but Thorne's arm always shot out to steady her. The tunnel was intersected by others, and at each crossing the Lady slowed to allow them to catch up.

"She's leading us toward that damned north wall," he muttered after they had traveled for a while. "We may as well turn back."

"She has stopped." Allison let Thorne's hand on her arm detain her, her eyes fixed just ahead. "I hadn't noticed those wall sconces before."

"They're all through the tunnels. Once held rush lights."

"She has disappeared!"

"I can jolly well see that. Why does she come and go so much?"

"I don't know." Allison looked anxiously at the lantern, now their only source of light.

"I have more candles, remember," Thorne said, smiling tenderly at her. "Methinks you are just the wee bit uneasy in the dark."

Allison lifted her chin. "I am not afraid," she lied. Admitting her fear would make her more vulnerable to it. "The secret entrance must surely be nearby." She began examining the wall above her minutely. "She pointed up here before she left. I just now realized this part of the tunnel isn't carved from rock. There must be a hidden door here."

"Hard to believe, but I suppose even such closely laid stones can part." Thorne hung the lantern from the nearest wall sconce and then joined her, running his hands along the stone.

Slowly, carefully they went over the area inch by inch. They could see some promising-looking broken stones and too-regular cracks, but Thorne's efforts to convert these into a hidden door were in vain, even using the chisel and crowbar he had brought with him.

They stopped while he replaced the candle in the lantern. "I told you the castle wouldn't give up its secrets easily, else the treasure would have long since been found. Where is that confounded ghost?"

"Perhaps we are looking in the wrong place."

"Oh, do you suppose so?" He raised his brows in mock astonishment.

"I can't understand why she would lead us here, and then . . . Wait! She's here again, practically on top of us." Allison watched as the ghost held up her hand, pointing, and then making a pulling motion. Then she melted into the side of the tunnel.

"Here! Allison moved to the exact spot where the Silver Lady had stood. "She reached up, like this, and pulled at something with her fingers just before she disappeared." Allison mimicked the Lady's actions.

Thorne's eyes caressed her figure. "Is she as shapely as you?"

"Thorne!" Allison dropped her arms and tilted her head back to examine the wall above her head.

"Do that again," he commanded.

"Behave yourself!"

"That would be a dead bore." Mischief gleamed in his eyes. "But I am serious, Allie. Stretch your arms up again."

She did so, sure that he would put his arms around her and steal a kiss, but instead he began examining the wall sconce just beyond her fingertips.

"Did she touch that ring hanging just below it?"

Allison squinted. "I don't see a ring."

"It is all but invisible for the rust, ashes, and tallow covering it." Thorne took her place and began cleaning the sconce with his knife so that they could examine it. A metal ring hung from the bottom of the sconce. The hole in it was small, too small for him to insert a finger. "Would you say that you are about her height?"

"Almost exactly." Allison stretched up once again, trying for the ring. She could just insert her index finger in it. "Ouch! It cut me." She automatically put her finger in her mouth, sucking at the bloody wound.

Thorne pulled it from her mouth and examined the cut minutely. "Not too deep, I think." He imitated her action, placing her finger in his mouth and laving it with his tongue.

At this sensation, primitive feelings stirred through her. "Thorne, stop that," she remonstrated with him in a low, husky voice.

Thorne tilted her head up, a heated look in his eyes. "I think I am pursuing the wrong treasure." He pulled her into his arms. She responded eagerly to his kiss.

Thorne broke it off, chest heaving. "Allison, I want you so."

"I want you, too, Thorne," she breathed. For the first time she actually entertained the idea of taking him as her lover, since marriage seemed out of the question. She reluctantly pulled away. "But this is not the time or the place."

He smiled ruefully. "True. I'd best bind up that finger for you and proceed with our mission before we both do something we may regret." He took a kerchief from his riding jacket pocket and bound her finger. Then he scrutinized the sconce carefully, holding the lantern next to it.

"I think this is made of tempered steel, rather than iron. That must mean something—they aren't all made like that. Hand me that length of rope in the pouch, will you?"

She did so. It was too large to thread through the ring, so he cut part of it off and unraveled the braids until he had a small section of rope the right diameter. This he threaded through the ring and then pulled.

Nothing. Thorne swore, softly but fluently.

Allison ran her fingers along one of the grooves of stone she had examined earlier. "I think this is a little wider. Try again."

Thorne examined the groove. "I doubt it." But he pulled on the ring again.

"Yes. It has moved. Oh, I see why we didn't spot it before."

Thorne bent over the area she stroked excitedly. "I don't."

"It is irregular. I mean, the opening follows the pattern of the stones. Try once more."

This time when Thorne pulled down hard on the ring, there was a definite scraping sound, and a ragged crack appeared in the wall.

"Another pivoting door, like the one in the well house," he said, excitement in his voice. Once more he pulled, widening the gap slightly, but hardly enough to insert even a file. "It hasn't been used in so long, it may be impossible to open."

Allison put the palms of her hands against the wall and pushed with all her might. "It seems to be moving when I push on it."

So Thorne put his shoulder to the left of the crack and shoved. Amid much groaning and scraping, the wall began to give up its secret. A large section of it pivoted, gradually revealing an opening large enough for one person to step through. Thorne turned and swung her in his arms. "We've found it! The secret passage!" He stopped abruptly, putting his palm to his head.

"Your injury is bothering you." Allison steadied him when he swayed on his feet. "Perhaps we'd better not go on right now."

Her disappointment showed in her voice. Thorne grinned. "It's nothing. A twinge. Though we aren't going on. I certainly won't let you go into an entirely unfamiliar part of these tunnels."

"Nor I you, at least not without someone to help you."

"Agreed." Thorne looked longingly at the doorway they had just made.

"Perhaps we could go on just a little way," Allison suggested.

"Oh, very well," he said, as if he himself hadn't the least interest in continuing. "We can at least take a peek. Then I'll come back with some help."

Thorne bent down and took a candle from his leather tool pouch. He anchored it to the passage floor by dripping wax on it. Holding the lantern out before him, he squeezed his way through the opening, then helped Allison through. They found themselves in a tiny antechamber with an open door before them. Thorne stepped through it.

"By thunder, it exists," he exclaimed.

Allison pressed against his back, trying to see around him. He turned and helped her into a room with a high-domed ceiling supported by several stone columns. Around the edge were vaultlike chambers carved into the rock. These were lined with small caskets and larger metal trunks of very ancient manufacture. The wood had rotted away from the caskets enough so that the gleam of gold and jewels, and the dark promise of tarnished silver, could clearly be seen.

Allison drew in her breath. "Oh, Thorne. It does exist. And more than I'd ever dared to hope for." She started forward eagerly, but Thorne threw up a blocking arm.

"Careful. Let us search for traps." He held the lantern high as they surveyed what they could see of the floor, walls, and ceilings.

"I thought as much. Apparently our ancestors did not trust entirely in the location to safeguard their treasure," Thorne observed as he studied the ceiling. Allison followed his lifted hand with her eyes, but did not immediately see the danger. "They expected an intruder to rush into the room without minding his steps," he explained. "Those columns look strong, but notice the base and tops."

Then she saw that the base of the first three columns, instead of being solid, were balanced on a much smaller rock. Above, they supported, not a solid ceiling, but an arched roof composed of stone blocks with no mortar between them.

"They must be fitted together like a bridge archway," Thorne said. "A brush against one, or perhaps a step on the wrong stones, or even the vibration of walking across the room, could easily topple the columns and bring those stone blocks down on the intruder."

Allison studied the situation in silence for a few minutes. "We can go around the edges, though," she said.

"You just can't wait to get your hands on that gold, can you?" Thorne chuckled indulgently. "I am sorry you noticed that, sweeting, because I can't allow you to risk your pretty neck, nor do I particularly want to risk mine. We have found the treasure. Now we will withdraw. I will bring my engineer and some strong workmen to assist me in recovering it. First we'll need to shore up that ceiling."

Allison nodded, stunned by the implications of their find. Wealth was the least of it.

"You know what this means, don't you?" She turned a rapt face up to Thorne. She started to say that James would no longer be under Thorne's control. He could marry and produce an heir, after which she and Thorne could be married! Her natural tendency to consider her words and actions checked her impulse. She waited for Thorne's response.

Thorne's thoughts ran along similar lines. *No more impediments other than my own distrustful mind*, he thought. The brief silence that ensued was broken not by tender words on either side, but by the unmistakable and very unwelcome voice of Captain Newcomb.

"It means that I am going to be a very wealthy man."

Chapter Sixteen

"Deucedly decent of you to have the geese penned up and your brave sergeant away from his post, Lord Silverthorne. Made following you here a great deal easier."

"Newcomb." Thorne's voice vibrated with loathing. He started to exchange places with Allison, who stood directly in the line of fire of a wicked-looking horse pistol.

"Hold, Silverthorne!" Newcomb waggled the pistol threateningly. "I will keep the lady in my sights, to ensure your cooperation."

"Have you run mad, Newcomb? You can't steal something like the Silverthorne treasure and get away with it. I suggest you take the next available ship to Australia and save me the trouble of having you transported."

"Ordinarily any suggestions of the Marquess of Silverthorne would carry great weight with me," Newcomb said, a sneering grin giving the lie to his words. "But today I see before me what is worth risking even more than transportation for. Now, Mrs. Weatherby, if you will step this way?"

"I will not!" Surprising both men, Allison slipped to the side, avoiding Thorne's attempt to grab her, and moved several paces into the room, until she stood directly next to one of the unstable columns.

"Allie! Have a care. You could bring that ceiling down at any instant. Look up, Newcomb, and you will know that you cannot succeed."

Newcomb looked up at the ceiling. "Yes, a tricky bit of business. As Mrs. Weatherby said, you will have to go around the edge and watch your step. Now, Mrs.—I say, may I call you Allison? Somehow the formalities seem a little silly in this situation."

Allison only glared at him.

"I shall take your silence as permission. Allison, both Thorne and myself would be much more at ease if you would step out into the passageway. Then he and my servant Paddy can carry out the treasure without endangering you."

"You intend to earn the gallows today, Newcomb. You've already said so. I see no point in making matters easier for you."

"If you were to take a more conciliatory attitude, my dear, you might yet live to enjoy the Silverthorne treasure, though not, to be sure, with your intended partner."

"I would never allow you to touch me." Allison moved closer to the column. "I'll pull the ceiling down on us all first."

Newcomb turned the air blue with a string of vituperative curses. "You'd best master her, Thorne, or else watch her bleed to death. A shot to the abdomen is a very painful way to die, I'm told."

Thorne felt his blood freeze. He had no doubt that Newcomb would kill her. "Allie, do as he says."

"No, Thorne, you know I cannot, must not do that."

Grey eyes looked deep into sapphire. "Then I shall join you." He started across the floor.

"Wait! A bargain!" Newcomb's voice rose with frustration. "Don't be a fool, Thorne. All I want is the treasure. You bring it to the door. Paddy will carry it to my carriage, which awaits in front of the door to the keep. You and your light o'love will be unhurt. We'll simply beat a retreat that would make Wellington proud."

"After you've shot us both."

"I resent the opinion you have of my honor," Newcomb said grandly. "If I say I will not hurt you, I won't."

"Leaving us to die a slow death, hidden away here. I thank you, but no."

"Don't be melodramatic, Thorne. There's no way we can seal that door up well enough that it can't be spotted instantly. Come to that, you can probably open it yourself, once we're gone.

Which is my absolute guarantee that you have to kill me before you leave, Thorne thought grimly. Playing for time to think, he continued to bargain. "You'll leave the door into the tunnel from the well room open as well?"

"Word of honor as an officer and a gentleman."

"You are neither," Allison called out defiantly. "Don't do it, Thorne."

Thorne had no reliance on Newcomb keeping his word, either. Still, it gave them time. Time for Bean to return, or the groom he had asked for to arrive, or even James. It was a slim chance of survival, but better than none.

"Very well, Newcomb. Allison, you will go the rear of the cavern, please."

"I think not, Thorne. I want her well within range of my pistol as a guarantee of your good behavior. Ah, here you are, Paddy. Did you take good care of that brave young guard?"

A huge bruiser of a man joined Newcomb at the doorway. "As good as ever his mother did, Cap'n. Put him right to sleep." Newcomb's henchman laughed, an evil dark rumble issuing from a mouth foul with blackened teeth. "You ain't gonna let the woman stay in there, is you?"

"Oddly enough, Mrs. Weatherby has declined my offer to bear her company while you and Lord Silverthorne carry out the treasure."

"Too bad. Right purty gentry mort. Wouldn't mind a piece o'her meself."

"Shut that degenerate up or our bargain is off," Thorne yelled, his fists clenched in impotent fury.

"Shut up, Paddy. The treasure will buy us any number of prettier and more compliant damsels. Get moving, Thorne. Delightful as your hospitality is, I wouldn't want to overstay my welcome."

So Thorne dragged the first of four heavy metal chests around the room, shuddering with fear that the vibrations might knock the columns off their balance. Newcomb stood just inside the opening, pistol at the ready while Paddy hoisted the chest on one shoulder as if it weighed no more than a saddle. He balanced it there with one hand and took up a lantern with the other.

During the time it took Thorne to bring the second chest, moving it more slowly to reduce the vibrations, Paddy had already returned from carrying out the first, which meant he certainly hadn't carried it up the stairs and out of the keep. *He has only taken the chest to the well room. He and Newcomb expect to have plenty of leisure to carry the loot upstairs.* This confirmed Thorne's belief that as soon as he had the last of the treasure in his hands, New-comb intended to kill them here.

Thorne's mind raced furiously as he dragged the chests. A plan began to form. He looked at Allison. Her eyes sought his, and he risked a brief nod and flick of his eyes toward the back of the cave.

If ever there was a speaking glance, the one she favored him with at this moment was it. She slowly lowered her eyelids, which he took to indicate that she understood him. *I only hope and pray that at least this once we are not talking at cross-purposes, my love*, he thought. He set the lantern farther back in the alcove where he was working, causing it to flicker and its light to dimin-ish.

"Here, now. What are you up to?" Newcomb demanded.

"The candle is burning low. I'll need some more."

"I haven't any. Just get on with it."

"I have. They are in that leather pouch at your feet."

Newcomb didn't even look down. "Nice try, Thorne. But you won't distract me so easily. If your lantern goes out, you'll have to make do with the light from mine."

"That's crazy. I can hardly see now."

"I am touched by your dedication to your task," Newcomb drawled sarcastically.

"I am clear across the room. What harm can I do you? Just toss the pouch along the wall a few feet."

This time Newcomb glanced down, and seeing that there was indeed a leather pouch at his feet, bent to feel around in it. He tossed out the tools and then slid it several feet down the side of the wall. "Very well, brighten the place up. Might as well have a cheery atmosphere in here." He chuckled at his own joke.

Thorne placed the extra candles and his pocket tinderbox at the back of the alcove, behind the lantern. Then he started dragging the third chest.

After Thorne had brought all of the chests to the opening for Paddy to carry out, he turned his attention to the smaller caskets. When he tried to pick one up, the wood crumbled at his touch. "I'll just put as much as I can in the pouch, shall I?" he asked New-comb, already beginning to stuff it. His plan called for it to be heavy.

"It won't hold enough. Allison, you are wearing petticoats, I ex-pect?" Newcomb waggled his eyebrows suggestively.

She did not answer, but rather lifted her chin and gave him an indignant glare.

"Because I would not wish your modesty to be offended when you take that skirt off and give it to Thorne to bundle the loose bits in. Hate to leave behind so many pretty baubles for want of a container."

Allison remained motionless, merely tilting her chin up defi-antly. She hoped Newcomb would not notice that each time his at-tention had been drawn, however briefly, to Thorne, she had edged backward an inch or two.

"Your lover will suffer from a gut shot just as much as you would. I have a king's ransom already. Do you not accommodate me, I will make life very unpleasant for both of you." Newcomb trained his pistol on Thorne. "Do I make myself clear?"

Lips compressed, Allison untied the skirt, letting it sink to her ankles. Her petticoat was both long and full, but she still felt terri-bly exposed.

"Good. Now throw it to him. Thorne, I am sure you can fashion a commodious carpetbag of that."

Thorne had never been so furious in his life, but though the veins stood out in his head from his desire to attack Newcomb, he controlled himself for Allison's sake. He did as instructed and loaded as much of the booty as he could into the bag he had made of her skirt. *It will actually serve better than my pouch,* he thought. When he had finished filling the makeshift bag, he walked slowly toward Newcomb. He stopped about two feet away, holding the bag chest high.

"Stop dawdling, Thorne. Bring it over here."

"Come and get it, Newcomb."

"Now, none of that. Give it to me, or I fire." Newcomb waved his gun menacingly in Allison's direction.

"Don't you think it would be generous to leave a little for the true heirs?"

Thorne could see from the corner of his eye that Allison had made more progress toward the back of the cave. Either she had grasped his plan, or she had one of her own. *Good girl! Up to every rig and row!*

Newcomb's eyes shifted to Thorne. His gun shifted slightly,

too, as Thorne counted on it to do. "I would have shared. Offered James a percentage. Didn't know you two would try to steal a march on him. Now hand it over!"

"Oh, very well, then." Thorne pushed his arms out with all the force he could muster, hurling the heavy bag fashioned from Allison's skirt directly at Newcomb's head. Instantly, he whirled and started for Allison. Newcomb's pistol rang out. *Oh, God, please let that shot go astray*, he prayed silently, even as he hurtled across the room. The bullet struck the ceiling and ricocheted wildly.

Before Newcomb could fight free of the skirt, Thorne scooped Allison up and deposited her at the back of the cave. She needed no urging to crawl into the nearest alcove. Thorne started back, intending to push over a column, but there was no need. His heavy footfalls, or the bullet, or both, had already started the process. The column nearest the door went down, tumbling rocks between them and Newcomb as he fired his second shot.

"Thorne!" Allison screamed. Heart in her throat, she watched him retreat before the falling rocks. Had Newcomb's shot hit him? At least he was still on his feet. "In here! Quickly!"

The second column went down. A boulder caught Thorne a glancing blow on the shoulder as he dove for the relative safety of the edge of the room. Allison started for him as the third column, the one nearest them, began to topple. He struggled into a half crouch and flung himself toward her as the roar of the falling ceiling reached a crescendo.

She pressed herself back against the wall of the alcove and pulled with all her might, urging as much of Thorne's big body into shelter as possible while the world seemed to turn to dust and stone and destruction around them.

The lantern went out. In the blackness they began to cough and choke on the dust. Without ceremony Thorne reached down and pulled her petticoat up. He pressed the fabric against her face, then caught up a handful of it to hold across his nose.

It seemed like forever before the ceiling ceased disintegrating and the last of the rubble settled. When it did, a faint illumination from Newcomb's lantern showed through cracks in the mass of boulders. They could barely hear his vexed exclamation. "They survived, damn it. I can hear them coughing." They couldn't make out the rest of the hurried conversation between the two men, but heard unmistakable sounds of stone being moved.

"Not, I think, a rescue attempt," Thorne muttered in Allison's ear. Allison shuddered against Thorne. "Wh-what do you think they are doing?"

"If he can clear enough of that mess away, he'll try to shoot us. Let's make it a little harder for him to find us." He took her hand firmly in his and helped her out of the alcove. They felt their way along the wall for several feet, until they came to a large pile of boulders. As soon as they had crouched down in this new position, both of them covered their noses and mouths with the petticoat, for the dust in the room nearly choked them.

"Were you hit?" Allison whispered. "Oh, Thorne, you risked your life to save me."

"Now how could I live in this world with you not in it?" Thorne's voice was low and tender. He pressed a kiss on her cheek through the folds of her petticoat. The honest truth was that he did not know whether his shoulder hurt so much because of a shot or a falling boulder. He touched it tentatively.

"Too many. Too heavy. Can't budge 'em," they heard Paddy growl. "Let's get out of here."

Newcomb's reply was muffled, but the sounds of stone on stone continued. It was a few moments before Allison realized, to her horror, that their purpose had changed.

She moaned. "They're walling us in."

She felt Thorne's head bob assent. "Shutting the door to the tunnel. I expected that."

"Thorne!" Newcomb's shout turned both their heads toward the entrance to the vault. "We're closing the door now. It makes a nice, smooth seal, or will once we've done a little cleaning up. Without your Silver Lady to guide them, no one will ever find you. I hope you take a nice long time to die. And Allison, I expect by now you are regretting your choice of lovers, but it is no use. I can't rescue you now. Not that I think I would. You're more of a Long Meg than is quite to my taste." Newcomb laughed nastily, and his henchman echoed the sound. Then there was a scrape and a thud, announcing the replacement of the door.

Allison's worst nightmare had become reality. They were trapped in a place where all traces of light had disappeared. "Oh,

Thorne. It's so dark. I don't think I can stand it." Her voice rose in panic.

He put a comforting arm around her shoulders. "We have the lantern and the candles, remember? I'll light them when that pair of villains have gone and the dust has settled a little bit. In the meantime, love, close your eyes and pretend we are embracing at midnight."

She turned into his arms, letting the petticoat drop. But before she could press her lips against his, a violent cough overtook her.

Thorne pressed the petticoat back against her mouth. "I am afraid romance will have to take a backseat to survival, sweetheart. Let me tear that flounce off and we'll prepare masks to wear around our noses and mouths."

Pulling the petticoat high again, he began tugging on it, to no effect. "Stronger than steel," he muttered. "Good job I still have my knife." She felt him tugging at the cloth, and then a loud tear.

Allison doubled over with another coughing fit. None too soon, he lapped a double layer of cotton cloth over her mouth and nose, and deftly tied it at the back of her head, just above her much abused topknot. Another ripping sound told her that he was preparing a similar mask for himself.

"I am going to be a walking scandal when we get out of here," she gasped, feeling to see how much of her petticoat was left. "Perhaps you'd best not light those candles after all."

He chuckled. "All the more incentive for me to do so. Stay right here. Don't move."

She clutched at him, suddenly terrified. "What if a hole has opened up in the floor? Please stay with me."

Thorne considered that idea. "A reasonable fear, but it seems to me I recall that the floor looked solid all around the edge. If it is not . . . that damned ghost! Still think she is benign?"

Allison felt tears well up. "I'm not sure now. Oh, it's my fault you are here! I've led you to your death."

"Now, where has my brave girl gone? The one who joked about her scandalous petticoat?" Thorne rubbed her back soothingly for a few moments, then started to move away in search of the lantern. Allison began to shudder all over. She couldn't help herself; chills ran through her frame so that her teeth chattered. Thorne swore a soft oath. "Which do you need worse, Allie? Comfort or light?"

For answer, she clung to him. "Stay a few moments. I shall come about."

He folded her closer against him, and they stretched out along the edge of the room, Allison's back to the wall that held the alcoves. She moaned, "This is all my fault."

"Oh, dear God, Allie. I don't blame you, nor will I let you blame yourself. I chose to break my oath never to permit another search for the treasure." In a lower voice he muttered, "I have been very backward in obeying oaths recently. I truly am my father's son."

Diverted from her troubles, Allison asked what he meant.

"The most solemn oath I ever took was on my father's grave. I've renewed it several times in the last months, but it seems every time I come within five miles of you, I break it."

"What . . . what oath was that?"

"I swore never to love a woman as much as my father loved Lydia Keisley."

Intent as she was on his words, Allison's chills subsided. *Again he says he loves me*, was her first delighted thought. But then she realized that his words hardly bespoke a man happily in love. "What do you mean? I don't understand."

"He loved her so much he let her lead him around by the nose. Don't you remember? Her dislike of your father caused him to break off a lifelong friendship. It was she who convinced him to search for the treasure in a place he knew was unstable."

"A treasure that neither of you needed." Allison felt sick at the thought that she had done the same to Thorne. She began to weep. "How terribly guilty she must have felt."

Thorne pressed her head harder against his chest. Silence reigned, interrupted only by the occasional plop of a rock just then breaking away from the ceiling. At last he said, "Yes, I expect that is why she drank herself into a stupor every day. Though she was prone to like spirits altogether too much long before then. As a child I wished he would take her in hand, for her drinking often led to embarrassing incidents or to vicious attacks on him or me. But he couldn't, of course. He loved her too much to be severe with her."

"You saw his behavior as that of a man weakened by love."

"Do you have another name for it?"

"Weakness, certainly. But I dispute that it is love that prevented him. It isn't loving to let someone do that which is harmful, to himself or others. You love Jamie and me, I think."

"Not in exactly the same way." She heard a half-suppressed chuckle rumble in his chest.

"So you always tried your best to prevent us from doing what was likely to be harmful to us. You insisted I leave Bristol and return here. In Jamie's case—"

"Not as successful there, was I?"

"No, though you tried. I almost think you would have succeeded better if you had tried less. He always fought you because it seemed as if you were treating him like a child. Men don't appreciate that."

"No." Regret laced Thorne's voice. "I wouldn't, in his place. I should have asked you for advice."

"Mercy, I don't know what to do. It is easier to see what not to do."

"True. It is easy to see that I should not marry a woman I adore every bit as much as my father adored Lydia, but I find I cannot help myself. When we are out of here, Allison, I intend to make you my wife."

"Not the most gratifying proposal a woman has ever received," Allison muttered, pushing her hands against his chest. He only held her the closer, chuckling in her ear.

"Sorry, sweeting. I should be horsewhipped for my lack of tact. After I am horsewhipped for bringing you down here! I'll make you a more romantic proposal later."

"What about your need for an heir?" Allison held her breath. That seemed to her to be a much greater impediment to their marriage than his silly fear of marrying for love. Vanity whispered insinuatingly in her ear that he could not possibly love her too much. Self-interest told her that there was little resemblance between her and Lydia, not to speak of how different he was from his father.

Thorne fought down a wave of revulsion at the thought of James succeeding him. He knew he should say it wasn't important, but he could not. The best he could manage was, "It is a matter for concern, but not the main reason."

"My poor unhappy love." She stroked his head comfortingly. "You grieved so much for your father. I know you adored him. It must have been sadly disillusioning to see that he had feet of clay.

I know how you feel. It is still hard for me to believe that my father squandered all of his fortune and left mother destitute, for I always thought he was the best of fathers."

"You don't know how often I have struggled against my anger and resentment of both your father and husband for leaving you so badly situated. Catherton thought of no one but himself after your brother died. And Charles was without the least ability to manage money."

Memory made Allison sigh. "Ah, what did such mundane things matter to me? He was so handsome in his officer's uniform." She smiled against Thorne's chest as she remembered her first season. How her heart would beat when she saw the handsome officer coming toward her!

A rattle of falling rocks recalled her to their terrible situation. A sob escaped her lips. "I know now how Lydia must have felt. Here you are, shut up in this terrible place, just because I wanted so much to have the treasure. I wanted to escape the humiliation of being your pensioner. And then, Jamie needed it so. Besides, I hoped . . . I hoped that Jamie would marry, and then you could wed me. Oh, I am unbelievably selfish."

"No, Allie. No, my little love." Thorne held her even closer, pressing kisses against her temple through his petticoat-mask. "Damn these things!" Abruptly, Thorne pulled down Allison's mask and then his own to kiss her urgently. She melted against him, answering passion with passion.

"I love you so much," she gasped when they had to break apart for air. "We may die here. I cannot die without expressing my love to the fullest. Make me yours, Thorne. Now!"

Chapter Seventeen

Thorne drew in a sharp breath. Here in this dark, dust-filled tomb he was being offered heaven. Every fiber of his body wanted to reach for the love she offered, to take it with both hands. But how could he take what she offered out of terror?

He groaned. "Oh, darling girl! If only I could! But I won't take advantage of your fear that way. Instead, I must see what I can do about getting us out of here."

As if to underscore the urgency, Allison fell into another paroxysm of coughing.

Thorne sat up. "Cover your mouth and nose again, Allison, while I try to find the lantern." He slid past her and began feeling his way back to the alcove where he had put the lantern and tinderbox.

"Thorne, please!" Allison protested. "The floor may have collapsed. At any moment you may fall into a chasm."

"As far as I can stretch my legs, I feel solid rock." He moved away from her. "What the devil . . ."

"What is it?" Terror made Allison's voice shake.

"The alcove where I left the lantern seems to have filled up with rubble, even though the ceiling debris doesn't come back this far."

"What does that mean?"

"I'm not sure. Reach up and find the alcove behind you. Is it still clear?"

Cautiously, Allison first tested the floor in front of her. Solid rock. Gathering her courage, she got to her knees, then crawled carefully along, pressing her body against the wall, while she felt above her for an alcove.

"Here's one. No, it is clear of debris."

"Of all the rotten luck."

"The lantern?" Allison tried to keep her voice from quavering.

"Buried, along with the candles and my flint box. I'm going to try to pull this debris out of here."

"I'll help." Perhaps activity would keep her mind from descending into the dark, mad place it seemed to be hurtling into in the midnight of the dusty vault. She made her way to him and felt around for a rock of a size she could lift. For a few moments they worked in silence. Suddenly, more rocks began falling out of the alcove from somewhere above them.

"Look out!" Thorne jerked Allison to one side and helped her out of the onrushing danger.

"The rest of the ceiling must be collapsing," Allison gasped.

"So it appears. I want you to slip up into one of these alcoves, out of harm's way."

"Only if you will be beside me."

He knew he should say no. He knew where such tight quarters could lead them. But he was not immune to the appeal in her voice. She was being very brave, but she was terrified, as how should she not be? So was he.

"Very well, my temptress." Thorne helped her into the alcove, then slid in beside her. By working his left arm under and around Allison and pressing their bodies as close as could be, he could just barely keep himself from slipping back out of the alcove.

They lay together, hearts beating as one, while they listened for falling rocks. But very quickly the rock slide was over and silence reigned again.

Cautiously, Thorne eased himself out of the alcove and helped Allison out after him. "That seems to be the end of it for now. We had best sit quietly and await rescue, rather than risk making things worse." He put his arm around her.

"Do you really think they can find us?" Allison asked.

"Yes. Newcomb and Paddy won't be able to close that door as smoothly as it had been closed back when the treasure was placed in here." Thorne was not entirely sure this was true, but he wanted to reassure Allison as much as possible. "I doubt if they can remove all traces of recent activity in that part of the tunnel, either. There will be dust tracks, scrapes along the wall, and so forth."

"I hope you are right. Oh, Thorne, I am so frightened. This pitch black darkness oppresses my spirits so!"

He drew her near him. "You have been remarkably brave, my love."

"I don't know how much longer I can keep from hysterics. Now I know why some women have them in crises. Letting go would be such a relief!"

"You shall have them, then. Though I would be very grateful if you could delay them until we are out of here."

She laughed just as he exclaimed, "Poor dirty little coal miner! I suppose I am just as filthy."

Allison's eyes flew to his face. "Oh, thank heavens. We can see again. You are not only black, you shall soon be blue, my poor darling." She slid a loving hand gently along his jaw. "Look at those bruises."

Thorne stood up. "Do you suppose the light means the last rock slide created an opening? Let's look around." He stood and reached down for her hand. When he did so, she could see past him to the source of the unexpected light.

"She is here! That is why we can see. She is here!" Allison scrambled to her feet. "My lady ghost, we need your help. Can you . . ."

The ghost moved swiftly to the alcove where the lantern had been buried under rock. Looking back to be sure Allison was observing her, she disappeared into the rock pile, her feet rising as she moved.

"Gone again! I tell you, Allie, she is either a malevolent spirit or a mere dumb show." Thorne clenched his fists, feeling the strong need to smash something.

"She isn't gone completely, else we could not still see one another." Allison started for the spot where the ghost had disappeared.

"Stay back! That is where—"

"Where a great many rocks fell. Could that mean there is an opening above the alcove?"

She got as close to the spot as she could. Of a sudden the ghost reappeared. She motioned to Allison to follow, then again entered the debris that hid the alcove.

"Did she do what I think she did?"

"She wants us to follow her."

"I'll try to clear those rocks away. I hope that will-o'-the-wisp doesn't disappear completely again. I can work much more quickly and safely with some light."

Suiting action to words, he began tossing rocks off the pile. Allison joined him, tilting her chin defiantly when he opened his mouth to protest. They worked efficiently side by side, Allison dealing with the smaller stones, Thorne with the large ones.

It was hard work, but within a half hour or so they had cleared the alcove. Allison gave a cry of dismay when they uncovered the lantern. It was smashed beyond usefulness.

Thorne continued excavating. "I put the candles at the very back of the alcove," he said, "along with the tinderbox." After a few more moments of effort, he gave a gleeful cry. "Most of the candles have survived intact! And the tinderbox is no longer a decorative object, but I think . . . yes!" He examined the tinder and flint wheel eagerly, then employed them in lighting a candle. "In case she does a flit again," he explained to Allison as he put his head into the alcove and looked up. What he saw made him whistle, long and low.

"What is it?" Allison crowded forward eagerly. "Oh, there *is* an opening up there. The Lady is motioning us to enter it. Could it be a tunnel?"

Thorne eased his way upward. "Yes—a low, narrow one. I'll have to go on hands and feet. The question is, do I trust that ghost enough to try?" He crouched back down, his brow wrinkled.

"If you don't, I do." Allison made to enter the alcove, but Thorne stopped her.

"Don't be ridiculous. I must go; it may be a death trap. She may have come back to finish us off. Here, I'll light a candle for you and leave you the tinderbox."

"Thorne! You certainly will not leave me here by myself! I couldn't bear it." Allison's voice shook. "And you can't make me stay. Once you are in there, I will follow you, no matter what you say."

"I could tie you up," he growled. Their eyes met and held. At last he sighed. "Putty in your hands, just like my father's disastrous weakness with my stepmother."

Allison shook her finger at him. "It is because what I ask is reasonable. You know that. She reveals herself most clearly to me.

What if there is another trick exit? How would you know which way to go?"

"There is something to that." Thorne studied the floor as he thought, jaw flexing nervously. "Very well, but I will go first. If either of us is to go plunging headfirst into oblivion, it must be me. I could never live with myself if you were to die that way."

"Nor could I." She put her arms around him and lay her head on his chest. "You must be very careful."

He returned her embrace. "I will."

She stepped back, blinking her eyes rapidly. "Let's go. I am getting hungry and thirsty. That picnic basket is calling my name."

His teeth flashed white in his begrimed face. "Now that you mention it, I can hear the siren call also." Handing her the candle, he worked his way into the opening with some difficulty and crawled into the tunnel, which led away from the alcove at a downward slant. The misty light, which was all he could see of the ghost, hovered a few feet in front of him.

"Can you get up here on your own? I don't think I can turn around to help you."

"I think so. Move forward some. Give me room." Allison reluctantly blew out the candle and tucked it in the front of her bodice, as she could not crawl and carry it.

"Intrepid female!" He did as she asked and soon felt her nudging against his feet. He pressed against the side of the tunnel. "Can you see past me? Is she just ahead?"

"Yes. As usual, she is beckoning us on." A momentary shudder passed through Allison's body. *Each time she has beckoned us, it has led us into deeper danger! Perhaps Thorne is right.*

But the idea of returning to the dusty darkness of the vault had no appeal to her. *Better to be doing something than just awaiting fate.* So she said nothing, and followed Thorne when he began to crawl forward.

"It falls off steeply here," he said. "Fortunately, there are plenty of rocks to slow our progress."

"My knees had noticed," Allison said, laughing to show she was not complaining.

"Wait a moment. She dropped out of sight. Allison, move up here as much as you can and tell me if you see her?"

Allison squeezed herself in so that she could peer over his shoulder. "No, but I still see the light. Go very carefully."

Thorne did not require her words of caution. "Give me that candle. I want to see what I am up against. There may be drop-off here."

She passed it to him. He stretched out on his side and awkwardly lit it. He then rolled over and inched along on his stomach, holding the candle out ahead of him.

He grunted with satisfaction. "A cave of some sort. Not much of a drop, either. Jolly good thing, since I have no choice but to go headfirst. Here, take the candle."

Allison squeezed her eyes shut and prayed fervently for his safety. She didn't open them or cease praying until she heard his voice calling her.

"Come on, sweetheart," She crawled forward. His head and shoulders filled the opening to the tunnel. Gently, he helped her slide out and set her on her feet. In the candle's shadowy light she saw that they were in another tunnel, much like the one that had led them to the vault.

"Our ghost has disappeared again," Thorne grumbled.

Allison looked around him. The Silver Lady stood a long way down the tunnel, urging them on. "No, she is still here, but she has faded so that she appears as a mere foggy outline."

"Good thing I let you come along," he observed grudgingly. He took her hand and they began following their ghostly guide.

"I've never seen this tunnel. It must surely lead out of the castle," Thorne surmised as they walked. The tunnel angled downward and curved sharply. It was hard to know what direction they were going. *Damn her if she isn't leading us to the north wall. Doubtless hopes we'll finally be crushed out of existence.* But he said nothing of this suspicion to Allison. No point in upsetting her.

"I wonder where it can come out?" Allison's mind was on the same problem. "As you have said, generations of D'Aumonts have searched the area around Silverthorne, looking for a hidden exit."

"It must be very well hidden," Thorne agreed.

"Or buried in the rubble of the north wall." Her voice was matter-of-fact. Thorne halted and looked down at Allison. She smiled, but it was a bleak smile.

"Too clever for your own good, my girl. I have often said it." He gave her shoulders a reassuring squeeze. They walked on in worried silence until a sound ahead of them caught their attention.

"Water dripping," Allison said.

Tension built as they continued walking. The ceiling of the tunnel began to show cracks and irregularities in its surface, and drops of water plunked down on them with increasing frequency. It was like being in a hot shower, for the water evidently came from the same source as the artesian well. It took close attention to keep the candle burning.

Suddenly, the tunnel floor was a puddle of water, and the puddle deepened rapidly. As Thorne paused to study it, Allison moved up beside him and he took her hand.

"How deep is it?" she asked.

"And how hot?" Thorne reached down and tested the water. "Merely warm. Well, my valet would probably have thrown away these boots anyway. Ready?"

Allison nodded, and they waded carefully into the water. By the time it was ankle deep, there was enough water dripping from the ceiling to mimic a heavy mist, obscuring their view of the tunnel ahead.

Thorne paused, peering into the gloom. "That ghost had better not abandon us now, for I doubt we can keep a candle glowing much longer in this."

As if to prove his point, the tiny stub of candle Allison held chose that moment to fizzle out. "Drat! We'd best not try to light another one, lest the tinder get wet." Thorne scrubbed at his face distractedly.

"She's beckoning us as usual. But something is different about the tunnel ahead."

They walked forward slowly until they came upon a cavern. Through the dripping water they could just make out the disturbing sight of a rock slide on the other side of a wide pool of water. The tunnel appeared to have collapsed directly ahead of them.

Thorne groaned despairingly. "What did I tell you. A dumb show! That is all she is capable of. She's passing right through the rocks, isn't she? She's not aware that we cannot."

"She knows." Certainty firmed Allison's voice. "She is making motions as if she were moving the rocks. Once we move them, we will find an exit somewhere, beyond that rock slide."

They looked at one another mutely. In the dim light Thorne could see that Allison's face was now streaked with mud. Her hair hung limply, almost entirely out of the topknot she had begun the day with. Her clothes were plastered against her body, outlining her figure in a way that in any other circumstances would have made his loins tighten with desire. But all he could see now was the fear and near-exhaustion graven on her features. How much more of this could she take? For that matter, how much more could he take? Thorne rubbed his left shoulder and winced with the pain. He had taken a hard blow there when the vault ceiling had collapsed. Would it be better to retrace their steps and wait for rescue in the vault?

Allison frowned at his gesture. "You're hurt. Let me see."

"Just a bruise. My whole body is a bruise." He smiled at her. "Never has a hot mineral bath sounded more enticing. I'm tempted to lie right down in yon small lake!"

Allison laughed. "And I, to join you."

"An almost irresistible inducement." He waggled his eyebrows at her suggestively.

"The Silver Lady does not appreciate your humor, I think." The ghost had emerged from the rock pile to pantomime walking across the pool of water. Allison explained her actions to Thorne. "She is motioning us to hurry."

"Then I had best go on. Wait here while I see how deep this water is."

"Trying to get your hot bath without me, I see." But she made no motion to follow, as Thorne moved forward until the water was up to his knees. Abruptly, he disappeared from sight, the dark water closing over his head and leaving Allison alone with the ominous echoes of the splash.

Chapter Eighteen

Surprise and horror held Allison motionless for a moment. Then she surged forward in the water, though she could not swim. She forced herself to feel carefully for the drop-off that had swallowed Thorne and peered in. She could not see him clearly, but she could see the water roiling, indicating a struggle. Bubbles rose up from the depths. Heart in her throat, Allison started to jump into the deeper water, when Thorne suddenly shot to the surface.

Tossing his head and wiping his hair out of his eyes, he quickly took his bearings. Two strokes of his long arms brought him back to the underwater ledge, where he hoisted himself up.

"Thorne! I was never so terrified in my life." Allison pressed herself into his arms without regard to his soaking clothes.

"Yet you were coming after me." Thorne tipped her chin up. "Foolishly brave once more." He kissed her and wrapped her in his arms. "I must confess to more than a small twinge of fear myself," he murmured against her hair. "I had to take my boots off, else they'd have carried me downward to my death."

"Once more she led us into danger. I am so sorry, Thorne. I should have listened to you. We probably should return to the vault, though how we are to do it without candles, I cannot imagine."

Thorne slapped his hand against the pocket of his riding jacket. "Wet!" He took the tinderbox and opened it. "Ruined, of course. But we won't be going back. This time I must take her part. She knows what I didn't until I barked my shin and hands on it."

"What?"

Thorne held up his right hand, which was scraped and bloody. "There is something very solid beneath the water, just to the right of where I fell. Unless I miss my guess, we will find stepping-stones there."

A joyous light came into Allison's eyes as the import of this sank in. "You mean there's a way across! The rockslide may not be what it seems?"

"I'm guessing it disguises an exit. Where is she, by the way?"

Allison looked past him, across the wide pool of water. "On the rock pile, urging us on as usual."

"Well, she won't have to urge me twice. I want out of this place. Stay here, love, while I try to find the passage without taking another hot bath."

Thorne moved very cautiously this time, finding the drop-off with his toes. Then he stood at that edge, feeling around beneath the water. "Found it!" he shouted. Cautiously, he put first one and then the other foot on the underwater stone. He repeated this process several times, and soon reached the other side.

"I am going to sorely miss my boots when it comes time to step out onto the rocks," he said as he turned around and returned to Allison.

He held out his hands, and Allison inched slowly forward until her toes touched the edge. They both leaned forward until their hands touched, and then Thorne slid his around until he had a firm grasp on her wrists.

"Now try to put your right foot between my feet. Once I've got you, I'll back up to give you room." He led her across the underwater bridge, walking backward himself until they reached the spot where the stepping-stones ended and the mass of fallen rocks fanned out into the pool.

He helped Allison slide past him and steadied her as best he could as she struggled to climb the low, rocky incline. She had to go almost on hands and knees, but eventually was able to clamber to the side of the cavern, beyond the rocks.

Thorne followed her, grumbling softly as he did so. When he had stumbled to her side, he sat down abruptly. "I've got to get my breath before attacking that pile of rocks. What is our lady ghost doing?"

"I can't see her clearly. She seems to have faded. She does that—begins to look almost real when we need to see her clearly, then fades to a sort of glow when we don't."

"Why, I wonder? Dashed inconvenient at times."

Allison jumped up. "I've just realized! That's why she's constantly urging us to hurry."

"Actually, I hadn't realized it yet. What—"

"It is difficult for her to make herself visible. She . . . tires, I suppose. Perhaps she is like a candle—she can't last indefinitely. It could explain why she pantomimes rather than talking to us— perhaps talking wears her out."

"That means if we can't get out of here before she fades . . ." Thorne rose to his feet and started for the water. "I've been studying that pile. If I can pull a few key rocks from the base, a good deal of it may just roll into the water."

"Taking you along with it. I wish you would not try that, Thorne." She placed an entreating hand on his arm. "I can help you remove the rocks the way we did in the vault. Let us take the safer approach."

"No. As you said, our ghost may be running out of time. So are you, my love. You look quite done in."

Allison was country-bred, but her physical strength had never been challenged to this extent before. Fatigue limned her eyes with shadows, but she shook her head vigorously. "I'm fine."

"Nevertheless!" He made his way back to the water and swam to the edge of the rock slide. "The largest game of jackstraws I've ever played," he quipped, flashing her a grin over his shoulder.

"And the most deadly," she whispered, once again praying earnestly for his safety.

Thorne tugged out several large rocks protruding from near the bottom of the pile. When the rocks began to roll on their own, a powerful backward thrust of his arms carried him out of their path. He swam swiftly away, returning to Allison's side to watch the small avalanche he had caused.

"Can you see anything?" He wiped the water from his eyes.

"Yes. Oh, yes! She is there. The tunnel continues on the other side!"

They immediately began clearing a path through what remained of the rock pile. When they gained the other side of the rocks, they found the unexpected. Rather than a tunnel, they now stood in a small room.

"The tunnel ends here," Allison said, dismayed. "We are

trapped once again." She bit her lower lip, which had begun to tremble. *Mustn't turn into a watering pot. Thorne has enough to contend with.*

Thorne looked around him carefully. "She hasn't led us all this way to find a dead end, surely." He examined the three sconces around the room. They looked no different from the hundreds of similar sconces that lined the tunnels, waiting for over a century to hold rush lights that were never lit.

"Just as I suspected." Retrieving his knife from his jacket pocket, Thorne cleaned one hastily. "Allison, can you reach it? It obviously is designed for a woman's hand." He held his breath as she pulled down on the ring hanging from it, just as she had on the one that opened the vault—it seemed like eons ago. And just like that one, the tug produced a small but distinct grating sound, and Allison's sharp eyes quickly saw that a tiny crack had appeared in the wall.

Thorne saw it, too, and let out an exultant shout. He put his left shoulder against the wall and pushed, then groaned and stood away, rubbing it ruefully. "Forgot," he explained.

Allison passed her hands gently over the injury. "Perhaps I can push it."

Thorne shook his head. "My other shoulder is fine." He switched sides and pressed steadily with all his might. Slowly, the wall began to move in the same way as had the other one, emitting loud grating noises as it did so.

When it had opened enough for them to step through it and into whatever lay beyond, the Silver Lady's light vanished. It was pitch black. Allison pressed close to Thorne, once again fighting her fear.

"I hope she's just resting," he growled. "I'm going to feel my way around . . ."

"Be careful." Allison released her hold on him reluctantly. Trembling began again as she once more stared into utter darkness. She fought back long-ago memories of a dark closet. *Not now. Must stay brave.*

Before long Thorne cried out, "Ah! Stairs. Steep stone stairs. A narrow passageway, so no need for rails. Can you come to me, Allie, or shall I . . . ?" Before he could finish, she stumbled into his arms. He led her two paces forward and guided her hand so that she could feel the stairs. She looked upward as if she could see anything in that inky blackness—and found that she could!

"Oh!"

"What is it?" Alarm tightened Thorne's voice.

"I think she is ahead of us. Or at least . . . it seems I can dimly make out something above us."

Silence stretched for moments as Thorne stood beside her. Finally, he expelled a long, relieved sigh. "Yes, I can see light, too. She is there. Or perhaps . . . it doesn't look quite the same. It could be daylight above us." He pointed out handholds carved in the wall and urged her to go ahead of him.

Allison struggled up the steep steps, feeling the way with her hands. Her leg muscles began to tremble with exertion, but the growing light above them urged her on.

Thorne called words of encouragement to her as she toiled up the steps. When she reached the last step, he placed his hand on her rump and gave a push.

"Thorne!" she exclaimed with affronted dignity before crawling out of sight. Hoisting himself after her, he sat on the edge and looked around. Allison, panting but triumphant, stood in a tiny room that did not appear to give him space to stand fully erect. Part of it was of the same stone construction as the exterior curtain wall, but part of it had been carved out of the living rock of the cliff face.

"What do you see?" He crawled toward her as she peered through one of several cracks in the outer wall, the source of the light that had guided them up the stairs.

The first thing that Allison did was draw several deep breaths. "Fresh air. I never thought it could smell so delicious." She put her eye to the largest opening. "I can't see much. Rocks. Some clumps of grass. I could touch them if the crack were larger. Enough to see we aren't on the north side." She moved aside to give Thorne room to look out.

"Thank God for that." Thorne studied the limited view he had, then whistled in surprise. "I have been completely turned around by all the many twists and turns in those tunnels. There is only one place on the castle perimeter where one might see vegetation, and that is where the south face joins the bluff."

He sat down and looked at Allison. "Our troubles are nearly

over, my love. We are, if my calculations are correct, close enough to the cliff path to drop down onto it if we can but find the exit."

"Near the top?" Allison massaged her trembling calf muscles surreptitiously through her damp, ragged petticoat, which she had tugged down over her knees for modesty's sake.

He frowned. "Yes, more's the pity, for I am persuaded you will barely be able to make it down."

"Down? Don't you mean up?"

"By no means. I shan't risk getting you in Newcomb's gunsight again."

"But he must be long gone with the treasure by now."

"You are probably right, but . . ." Thorne pulled a watch out of his jacket pocket, then shook his head. "Not working. It stopped at twenty after eleven, which must have been when I plunged into that pool. Can't tell how long it took us from there, but surely not a full hour, though it seems like an eternity. There is an outside chance that he could still be loading the treasure."

"Let him have the treasure! Don't risk yourself against him. You are unarmed and exhausted, and he has pistols and that brute Paddy. I couldn't bear it if something happened to you!"

"Don't worry so much, love. I won't go after him myself. I'll go down with you and get some men to go with me as soon as I have you safely installed in Thorne Hall.

"Even if he has departed," Thorne added half to himself, "our chances of catching him are good. In our short acquaintance I have come to know him well enough to know he will try to put all of the treasure in his rickety carriage. Greed won't allow him to take only what he can speedily drive away with, especially if he is driving the same spindle-shanked cattle he had yesterday.

Allison frowned. "I hope it may be so. But somehow the treasure doesn't seem so important to me now."

For that sentiment Thorne pulled her to him and kissed her tenderly. Then he broke away on a sigh. "First we have to get out of here." He began studying the small room carefully. There was no wall sconce to tug upon, nor any other obvious means of egress.

"It looks as if these rocks must be removed," he said at last. "Perhaps when I push on them . . ." His face turned red with effort, but the rocks remained firmly in place.

"Let me help." Allison moved to Thorne's side.

Though he doubted she could add much force to the project, Thorne once again admired her spirit. He smiled at her. "Very well, my Amazon. On the count of three." So saying, he put his right shoulder against the rock that looked the loosest. Allison stood next to him, and they both pushed with all their strength. Still nothing happened. Thorne called a halt and dropped back on his heels to reconsider.

"If the rocks were made to drop out, they might have done so during a cannonade," Allison said, moving beside him to study the situation. "And once they had been pushed out, wouldn't the opening have been seen?"

"Probably. Like the collapsing ceiling in the tunnel, this escape route would only have been used as a last resort. But there must be an opening somewhere, or it would have been of no use."

As one, they began to examine the room inch by inch. When they reached the opening to the stairs, they looked at one another across the gap. Frustration had Thorne grinding his teeth. Disappointment had Allison biting her lower lip.

"Don't despair, sweetheart," Thorne said, skirting the opening to go to her side. He pulled her into his arms. "If we can't get out by our own hands, at least we know that we can shout and get someone's attention. I can even push my shirt partway through that crack. That will catch someone's eye, especially since they will be searching for us soon."

"I know, but I want out now!" Allison slipped from Thorne's arms. She could just barely stand erect, being a few inches shorter than Thorne's six feet. "There has to be a way . . ." She reexamined the wall intently, continuing past where the cracks could be seen and into the carved-out area. As she did so, her hair snagged on something on the ceiling.

"Ow. Drat!" She reached up to free it, but couldn't.

"Here, let me." Thorne moved beside her, stooping to avoid hitting his head. He couldn't see what her hair was snagged on, for her head was snubbed up tight against the ceiling, so he probed carefully with his fingers, watching Allison grimace in pain as he did so.

"Have I told you that you are the bravest woman I know?" He kissed her briefly while working with both hands to pull her hair free. Finally, the tension was released, and Allison ducked away with a grateful "Ahhhh."

"Thank you, kind sir. I look bad enough, without being snatched bald-headed too."

"I'm afraid you've left quite a little hank of hair here." He craned his neck so he could examine the little tuft of silvery blond hair hanging from the ceiling, then exclaimed in surprise. "Something here. Take a look, will you?"

A moment's study yielded results. "Yes!" She inserted a fingernail into the crevice where she had caught her hair. Carefully, she teased out an irregular chunk of stone. Under it a steel ring like the ones on the wall sconces lay waiting. Allison gave it a hard tug, but nothing happened. "Why can't I budge it? It was made to fit a woman's fingers."

"Time has doubtless had its way with the mechanism." He cast his eyes around for a tool. "Your petticoat is entirely too long, madam," he said.

She looked down at the bedraggled garment ruefully. "Why do I think you wish to remedy that situation?" Thorne brought out his knife and soon had a strip of the damp fabric. Twisting it to give it strength, he inserted it into the ring, wrapped it around his hand, and pulled. A familiar grating sound drew their attention to the part of the room that had been chiseled out of the cliff face. A gap had appeared—not in the cracked section of the curtain wall, but in what had seemed like solid rock.

"Another pivoting door, no doubt." Thorne moved to the rock and pushed hard with his right shoulder. It gave slowly, reluctantly, a few inches. "Damned clever," he exclaimed, feeling the lower edge of the opening. "There is a metal bar here that probably anchored a rope ladder. I'm guessing there is a trompe l'oeil effect from the outside. Tie the right knot, and the rope could be loosed once the escapees climbed down." He shoved hard on the rock again, and it gave a few more inches.

Allison could insert her body into the opening and peer out. "It is so far down, and there were no stairs then. How could they expect any woman to manage it . . . ?" She withdrew, her face pale at the idea of climbing down that sheer cliff.

"When your life is in danger, you acquire extra strength, I expect. However, I surmise that the plan would have been to use a rope harness to lower anyone incapable of going down hand over hand. Would that I had a rope at my disposal, because if I am wrong about our proximity to the cliff path, we may have to wait for rescue." He shoved once more, and suddenly, with a sharp crack, the rock lurched forward and began toppling out of the opening.

With a short scream of terror, Allison grabbed at Thorne, catching his coat as he teetered on the edge. He quickly regained his balance, and the two peered out.

"I was right!" Thorne sat on the ledge and swung his legs over. "We are just over a landing." He dropped down so that Allison could see only his head. Whatever he saw made him drag his hand down his face and groan loudly.

"What is it, Thorne? Did you hurt yourself? Oh, drat you! Don't keep me in suspense."

"Look for yourself. What incredible luck, though I am not at all sure it is good luck." He hoisted himself back into the room, knocking his head against the ceiling as he stood. Muttering to himself, he held on to her blouse as Allison leaned out to view the situation. The huge stone had fallen onto one of the wooden landings his grandfather had placed at various points along the stairway.

"But it is perfect. Why did you wonder about our luck? Oh, do let us go. I am so hungry and thirsty!"

Thorne's stomach growled its agreement, and they both laughed.

"Look again, love. The rock has dropped down in such a way as to block access to the stairs below. It wasn't intended to fall out, of course." He pointed to broken metal inserts at the top and bottom of the opening. "My guess is that cannon fire and time weakened it. There is no way we can go down the steps, at least no way I would care to risk just now. I don't fancy a dive off the cliff as a grand finale to this adventure."

"But we can go up, can't we?" Allison looked anxiously out the opening.

"Yes, but I told you, I don't want you to go up there. Very likely Newcomb has left, but—"

"Pooh! He is not brave enough to linger."

"Not deliberately. But suppose there was some delay? The man is ruthless, Allison. You spoke truly when you said he planned to earn the gallows today. It would be safest for you to remain here, just until I make sure."

"If . . . if you think it best." The large blue eyes filled with tears, and Allison turned away. The thought of being left in this small room alone did not appeal to her, nor did the thought of Thorne facing those two vicious men. But she did see that her presence could only complicate matters for him. Blinking frantically to suppress her tears, she faced him with a smile.

"I'll just wait for you out on the landing, shall I?" At least she could escape the confines of this small room.

Thorne considered the matter. He was gratified that she was deferring to his judgment, but that made it imperative that his judgment be correct.

Chapter Nineteen

Allison did not argue with Thorne about accompanying him, but her eyes spoke her feelings eloquently. He shut his mind to their appeal as he tried to figure out which way she was least likely to come to harm. He didn't think the steps had been weakened by the fall of that heavy stone, but he couldn't be sure. If so, they might collapse while she waited. On the other hand, was this room hiding any nasty little traps for the intruder? He finally decided the best thing to do was to get her away as soon as possible.

"It isn't far to the top. Will you swear to me that you will remain out of sight on the walkway while I reconnoiter the castle?" At her vigorous nod, he held out his hand to her. "Out you go, then. I'll wait until you have reached the stone steps, just in case the wooden section has been damaged. Wait for me outside the gate."

Allison felt as if a ten-stone weight had been taken off her shoulders. She held his hand while she maneuvered out of the opening. He lowered her slowly, instructing her, once she stood on the rock, to sit and slowly slide off onto the landing rather than jumping down. To her immense relief, the wooden structure held firm. When she reached the carved stone steps, she turned around, waving to Thorne. Her heart in her throat, she watched him gingerly climb the stairs.

When he reached her side, they quietly proceeded to the gateway that had been cut into the battlements along the south wall. They crouched as they slipped through the gate, so that anyone standing in the courtyard could not see them over the top of the balustrade. Thorne motioned her into a sitting position, then carefully raised his head and peeked over—and ducked back down again immediately.

"Are they there?" Allison whispered. She could scarcely believe it.

Thorne whispered a colorful oath. "Yes, and Jamie is with them." He motioned her to be silent and tried to hear what was being said, but they were too far away. "I'm going to sneak down to the tower and creep closer." He started moving to the south, but Allison grasped his jacket and tugged hard.

He sat back on his heels and glared at her.

"The geese," she whispered. "Their pen is beneath the shade trees that grow by the south tower. You must go by the west tower."

"Thank God you thought of that. Can you imagine the noise those birds would raise?" Thorne hugged her. "Stay out of sight, Allie. Promise me?"

Allison nodded. "Be careful, Thorne." As she watched him, bent at the waist, make his way to the tower, she silently prayed for his safety. When he disappeared from sight, she crept to a small gap in the rocks and peered out at the tableau in the courtyard below.

I can hardly believe this of you, Jamie, she thought as she watched. James was helping Newcomb's servant reposition a carriage wheel that had almost fallen off, probably a casualty of the weight of the treasure. Paddy strained with all of his considerable might to lift the axle high enough that James could straighten the wheel. Newcomb stood nearby, his back to her. The team of four horses quietly stood in their traces, heads drooping.

Thorne was right, she thought, studying them. *It will be a wonder if those nags are able to pull that coach with such a heavy load of gold and silver.*

She could not see Thorne, but something made Newcomb uneasy, for he suddenly straightened and put his right arm out. A peculiar mingling of relief and terror washed over her when she saw that he had a long, lethal-looking pistol in his hand, pointed directly at James. *Jamie hasn't betrayed us, but now I have two loved ones in danger.*

Paddy suddenly bellowed loud enough for Allison to hear him. He stood, shaking his hand violently. It had obviously been injured in the process of trying to work the wheel onto the axle of the heavy carriage.

To Allison's surprise, James launched himself directly at Paddy from a crouched position, butting his head into the man's vast midriff. They were so badly matched that it seemed almost suicidal in James to attack the burly servant. Paddy fell backward, and they struggled with one another, briefly rolling under the wheels of the coach where Allison could not see them. Almost immediately, James clambered out. His right hand closed over a large rock just as Paddy grabbed his ankle and jerked him onto his back, then dove over him, his huge right fist raised. James brought the rock up hard against the man's temple. He wilted, collapsing on top of the smaller man. Even unconscious he was a formidable opponent. James struggled without much success to get free of Paddy's bulky form.

Newcomb shifted his position, pointing his gun at the corner of the stables nearest him. He shouted loudly enough for Allison to hear. "Thorne, step forward and surrender, or I'll shoot." When there was no immediate response, he added, "First your cousin, then you." His gun hand swung back to point the pistol at James. At that, Thorne emerged from behind the ancient stable wall, his hands raised over his head.

It is like a nightmare, Allison thought as she watched helplessly. Paddy stirred even as James finally succeeded in throwing him off. They renewed their struggle, and Newcomb's burly henchman quickly gained the victory. Soon both James and Thorne were within Newcomb's gun sights. He pressed them both into service unloading the coach of some of its burden of treasure under Newcomb's watchful eye, while Paddy nursed his injured hand. Then they replaced the wheel.

I must do something—but what? Allison put her fist in her mouth to restrain the scream that wanted to break out. *As soon as they get that wheel on and the treasure reloaded, Newcomb will shoot them.*

She must summon help. If she could reach the paddock by the gatehouse, she could ride Firefly to the hay meadow, the closest place where she was sure to find estate workers. *The only way to get to the paddock from here will expose me to Newcomb's sight for part of the distance.* What she needed was a distraction.

The geese! A sudden picture of white wings and strong beaks came into her mind, and almost without thought she crouched and ran along the balustrade toward the south.

When she emerged cautiously from the south tower, the geese stood up and began murmuring among themselves. They crowded toward the opening, complaining about having been penned up for so much of the day. She knew from experience that they would go first to the center of the courtyard, where Bean usually fed them.

She opened the pen and watched them stream out of it, wings lifted and necks stretched forward. When she heard the first loud, indignant squawk at finding strangers in their kingdom, she ran as fast as she could toward the edge of the buttery, from which she must cross open ground. There she stopped for a minute to see if Newcomb's attention was focused elsewhere. It was! She moved as fast as she could across the open space to the next building. To her chagrin she found that her legs almost wouldn't support her. As she caught her breath, she peeped out to see what was happening.

The geese mobbed all four men, calling raucously as they attacked. James took advantage of the distraction to swing the heavy sack that had been fashioned from her petticoat right at Paddy's head. At the same time Thorne dove straight for Newcomb, who fired his pistol without hesitation. Heart in her mouth, she watched Thorne connect with Newcomb so hard the force knocked him to the ground. Thorne seized his gun hand at the same time he landed a hard blow to the man's jaw, and then another and another.

Having subdued Newcomb, he turned to James, who was valiantly struggling with the huge servant. He shouted as he aimed the gun he had wrestled from his opponent. James jumped aside and Thorne called out a warning, which Paddy answered by charging directly toward him with a bellow of fury. Thorne fired, his bullet hitting the man in the chest. Paddy sat down abruptly, his hand clutching at the wound.

The first shot had sent the geese half running, half flying in all directions. Newcomb's team had begun to rear and plunge at the rush of frightened geese beneath their feet. At the second shot they bolted, racing around the courtyard and out of sight, the coach bouncing along behind them. Gold and silver showered from the carriage as they rounded the stables and disappeared from view.

"Go after them, James!" Thorne shouted. "They're heading for the north wall. If they go over, the treasure will be—"

"Never mind about that." James turned his attention to Paddy, who was struggling to his feet in spite of his wound. James gave one mighty swing of the petticoat full of treasure, and at last the massive man was defeated. He fell forward, unconscious.

James bounded toward Thorne. "You're hit," he shouted, seeing that his cousin grasped his left shoulder, grimacing in pain.

Allison left her sanctuary to go to Thorne on trembling legs. *Please God, don't let it be a serious wound*, she prayed as she hurried across the courtyard.

Thorne shook his head, his eyes crinkling in rueful amusement. "No, just a bad bruise. Fortunately, Newcomb is an abominable shot." The two men embraced, hammering each other on the back so hard Allison feared they would both be injured. She studied Newcomb and Paddy carefully as she passed them. Both men were breathing, but unconscious. She joined the cousins, and Thorne put his uninjured arm around her.

"Let me guess. You are the goose girl?"

She nodded. Wary of his reaction, she buried her head in his chest. *Once again I failed to obey him*, she thought.

"Clever creature, you saved our lives." He kissed the top of her head.

"Allie, is that you?" James plucked her from Thorne's grasp and stared down at her.

"What a sight I must be," Allison cried. "Is my face as dirty as my hands and legs?" James did not answer, but only looked, openmouthed, at her torn, dirty, and still somewhat damp petticoat.

"I must look like Haymarket ware," she moaned, wishing there were a place to hide.

"Never!" James drew her into his arms. "I can't tell you how worried I have been! When Newcomb told me where you were, I feared your sanity might not survive. I know how much you fear dark, enclosed places."

James rocked her back and forth while she hugged him and at last gave way to tears. Blinking back tears himself, he looked over her head at Thorne, who found himself fighting back intense jealousy. *I should be the one to comfort her!* But he could think of no seemly way to reclaim her from his cousin's possessive grip. James's words sunk in, and he asked for an explanation.

"She was once locked in a closet by a governess," James said.

"She was left there for several hours and since then has always had nightmares about close, dark places."

"I didn't know. Allison, you should have told me."

Allison scrubbed impatiently at her tearstained cheeks. She hated above all things to turn into a watering pot. "I didn't want to put my fears into words; they might have overwhelmed me."

"You were even braver than I guessed, to go through all that you did. You'd never know it to see her now, James, but she was a regular Trojan!" He traced the tear tracks on her cheek with his forefinger tenderly.

Allison pulled away from James and smiled tremulously at Thorne. "Thank you. I sadly fear I don't deserve that praise, though."

"Brave and modest, too! Come here!" He pulled Allison into his arms for a hug and a kiss that didn't in the least resemble the embrace James had given her.

At last she pushed free, breathing heavily and knees buckling. Out of the corners of her eyes she saw James staring at them. She smoothed her hair reflexively and stepped away. "I need to find something to cover me before the estate workers begin to converge on us. They surely heard those shots."

Thorne drew in a deep breath. "That would be best. Bean likely has an overcoat of some sort in the gatehouse that you can put on for the nonce. James, I will tie these two varlets up if you will check on those unfortunate horses. I hope the poor creatures haven't gone over the cliff."

Thorne entered Allison's bedroom tentatively. Her mother was there, sitting on the bed stroking Allison's hair, which foamed around her head, damp and curling wildly from its recent shampoo. James and Aunt Agatha stood just behind Delphinia. Allison sat propped against a stack of pillows. Several bruises and small cuts on her face did not in any way diminish her beauty, he thought. He yearned to send her other three visitors out of the room and make love to her.

"And then Thorne fell in and disappeared from sight," she was saying. "I was never so terrified. That is when I got so wet, Mama, trying to help him."

"She waded into the water after me even though she can't swim.

Do you think that means she cares for me?" Thorne sat on Allison's other side and took her hands in his. "I certainly hope so, for I mean to make her my wife as soon as it can be arranged." He felt a sense of peace in making this announcement. Once again his hand was forced by concern for her reputation, freeing him from a decision he otherwise might still have avoided.

"I should think so," Aunt Agatha snarled. "What you can have been thinking of, to put her through such an ordeal in the first place, I cannot fathom, but it is unavoidable now. You must wed her right away." She turned a pitying face to Allison. "I am sorry, dear, but there it is. Soon the world and all will know you were shut up alone with him in the dark for hours. Your good name will be lost forever if you do not marry this . . . this . . . seducer!"

Allison straightened on her pillow. "I am very sorry, Aunt Agatha, but I must ask that you never criticize Thorne in my presence again. If it were not for him, I should have perished several times over—"

"If it was not for Thorne, you never would have been there in the first place."

"It was my insistence that landed us in the situation," Allison snapped.

"Either he hoped you would perish as his brother did, leaving one fewer to share the treasure with, or it was one more example of the bad judgment that is in the D'Aumont blood!" Agatha's eyes gleamed as she attacked Thorne with almost fanatic fury. "You are as weak as your father was. He gave in to Lydia on every little thing! In the end, his lack of resolution led to the death of himself, his son, and my sister." Agatha's chins quivered with indignation.

"Agatha, do be quiet." Delphinia rose from the bed to confront her friend. "Both Allison and Thorne have been through a terrible ordeal, and they behaved heroically, both of them. We should all be grateful they are both alive and unhurt. That is . . . are you badly injured?" She motioned toward Thorne's left arm, which his physician had put into a sling.

Thorne could not reply. Aunt Agatha's words shook him to the core. *She is right*, he lamented, shame washing over him. *If I had not allowed Allison to talk me into searching for the treasure . . .* All of his old fears reasserted themselves. He realized that Delphinia had repeated her question, and answered hastily, "Just a dislocated shoulder. That and a few bruises. Everything will heal soon enough." *Everything but my susceptibility to petticoat governance.*

James had been listening silently all this time. Thorne's eyes met his and saw something there he had not seen since they were boys. Could it be . . . admiration? Thorne recollected James's gallantry and felt an answering emotion stir in his own breast.

"Speaking of heroes, you showed sheer raw courage in fighting with that bruiser Paddy," he said.

"Wish I hadn't been too busy to see you hammer Newcomb into a pulp," James replied. "Must have been quite a mill."

Thorne waved his hand dismissively. "Not really. In addition to being a very bad shot, the man must have a glass jaw." Modesty propelled Thorne to change the topic. "At least that wheel fell off and his team of horses stopped short of the breach, so not only are we all three decidedly the richer today, but we shan't have to undertake a tricky recovery mission to claim our wealth."

Agatha erupted again. "How dare you gloat? There were others who should have shared in that treasure. This ghost Allison praises so much led them to their deaths. There is blood on every gold cup and every silver tray." Bitter tears slid down her cheeks.

"She did not!" Allison quickly came to the Silver Lady's defense. "She tried to stop them. She tried to stop Marie and Newcomb yesterday, and she did the same for any and all who attempted to search for the treasure when they were not entitled to it. It is not her fault that people were too stupid or too greedy to pay attention to her."

"Not entitled . . ." Agatha bristled.

"Not entitled," Thorne echoed. "New information has surfaced that explains why the ghost has been so elusive through the years. The descendants of the second baron had no claim to the treasure until my father married my mother. The same is true for James. It is only through our mothers that we have a right to it."

Agatha's eyes bulged. For a few moments she was uncharacteristically speechless, and Thorne turned his attention back to Allison. Before he could speak three words, Agatha's booming voice interrupted him.

"Do you tell me that my nephew died searching for a treasure to which he had no claim? Why didn't Silverthorne just say so, and put an end to Lydia and Percy's dangerous aspirations?"

"I don't know," Thorne responded, suddenly sorry for the woman's pain. "He may not have known. My grandfather arranged his marriage to my mother, you know. Perhaps my grandfather suspected the truth but did not confide in my father."

"I don't understand any of this," James said.

"Last night Allison and I found a document that traced our mothers' lineage included with important papers relevant to the treasure. I'll explain it in detail later."

"Be sure that he did know!" Agatha interrupted again. "He feared to tell Lydia the truth. I see it now. He was a spineless man, and you are just like him. Oh, Allison, how deeply I regret that you must marry this man. With a fortune at your command, you would be much happier alone."

"Agatha! You mustn't—" Delphinia roughly shook her friend by the shoulders. "Why would you seek to wound Thorne so, when he has been so kind to you?"

Agatha continued remorselessly. "You speak of his wounded feelings. How do you think I felt, knowing that Lydia caused my darling Percy's death by her greedy manipulations. Then she pined away—"

"Drank herself to death," James inserted.

"Pined away, I say, with regret for what she had done, leaving me alone and friendless. And that was your fault, too, Thorne."

"Aunt Agatha, that is totally unreasonable. I must insist that you stop attacking Thorne in this way."

"It isn't unreasonable. Lydia knew what she had done. She couldn't stand for you to be so good to us. She shriveled up a little more inside each time you tried to comfort her." Agatha turned away from Thorne's furious glare. "And I? I had to accept your kindness day after day, knowing how undeserved it was. It is the fate of a poor relation." She laughed, a dry, painful chuckle. "Be glad that you are free of such a fate, Allison. She stalked from the room, leaving four shaken people behind.

Allison dropped her head back on the pillow wearily. "Such a day," she sighed.

Delphinia touched Thorne gently on the arm. "Do not take her words to heart, Thorne. Your father was a brave and honorable

man. If he did not tell Lydia that Percy might not be entitled to a
share of the treasure, it was because he didn't know it himself. And
if you will but recollect, he always regarded the treasure as legend.
He told it to others as an interesting story, not as a truth."

Thorne felt a sudden, intense need to be by himself to think. "I
have much to attend to. We . . . we will discuss our nuptials later,
Allison. Get some rest." He bowed formally and left the room.

"Well, that was hardly a loverlike leave-taking," Delphinia
huffed. "But we must excuse him, my dear. Poor man, I expect he
is worn to a frazzle."

Allison looked thoughtful. "It wasn't in the least loverlike, was
it?" Thorne's manner had changed completely after Agatha's attack. For the first time Allison took seriously Thorne's fear of a
love match.

James stepped to her side in Thorne's place. "If he doesn't
marry you, he is a great fool. I would marry you in an instant if you
would have me."

Allison searched James's face for signs of newly kindled affection. All she saw was the determination of a dear friend to keep her
from suffering society's strictures. She held up her hand and
grasped his, carrying it to her lips for a kiss. "Dear Jamie. I am so
happy for you. Now at last you can be independent of Thorne."

"It would have been a bitter, bitter pill to swallow if you two had
been killed while seeking that wretched treasure."

"I know what you mean. When I thought I had led Thorne to his
death, I was overcome with guilt. I think he is feeling something
of the same thing now. I do wish Agatha had not been so savage
about it. He is severe enough with himself, without her to lash his
guilty conscience into terrible proportions."

Silence reigned for several moments as the three pondered the
day's events. Finally, Allison turned wondering eyes on Delphinia.
"What do you think, Mama? I am an heiress."

Her mother patted her cheek. "I agree with Jamie. The price was
almost too high. But all has turned out well. A fortune and a title.
I shall preen myself no end on having a marchioness for a daughter."

"As to that, Mama, you must surrender that particular point of
pride, at least for the present. I have no intention of allowing

Thorne and myself to be forced into marriage. We will marry for
love, or not at all."

Allison grimaced as she massaged her calf muscles, which still
hurt a full week after her adventure in the tunnel. It had been a
week of self-recrimination; she bitterly regretted insisting that they
search for the treasure. True, she was a rich woman, but at what
cost? Thorne had looked so stricken when Agatha railed at him for
his lack of manly resolution. He had left the room, looking quite
crushed. The dream in which she had been forced to choose between Thorne and the treasure seemed to have come true, and she
had chosen the treasure.

*The true treasure would be Thorne's love, but I sadly fear I have
destroyed what little hope I had of it, and helped deliver a fatal
blow to his pride as well.* Tears welled up in her eyes. The day they
had found the treasure had been the last she had seen of Thorne.
She had expected him to call upon her after supper that night to
check on her well-being, if not to renew his proposal. Instead, he
had sent over some liniment with his compliments and said that he
would call on her after he and James returned from delivering the
treasure to London for safekeeping.

Now he was back and expected momentarily. She did not look
forward to that interview. Before excusing herself to give them
privacy, Allison's mother had lectured her at length about accepting his proposal, but she still did not know what she would say.

"Lord Silverthorne, madam," Peterson intoned grandly. Thorne
entered the room, a look of cool hauteur on his face.

"I have obtained a special license," he informed her as soon as
they were alone. "We will be wed the day after tomorrow."

Allison had spent the entire week vacillating back and forth
about her answer to Thorne's proposal. This cold command had
the effect of crystallizing her thinking.

"I'm not going to marry you, Thorne. At least not right away."

Thorne glared at her from his lofty height. "Yes, you are. You
heard Agatha. Whatever your reservations, or mine, we will face a
terrible scandal if we do not wed."

Not a word about love! "Agatha said a great deal she shouldn't
have that day."

"She spoke some home truths, though. Not least about my

spineless behavior. I should not have allowed you to go into the tunnels. I knew the risks. Believe me, I shall take better care of you in the future."

"If women are not to be allowed to take risks, Thorne, why do men allow them to bear children? Speaking of which, what about that need for an heir? Nothing has changed in that regard, has it?"

Thorne's jaw worked. He clenched and unclenched his fists. "I am hoping that James will turn over a new leaf. Certainly he has the means to marry now and has as good as promised me to do so soon. Stop trying to fob me off. It is my responsibility to protect you. I failed to do so as regards the treasure, but I at least can protect your name. It is as Agatha said. Gossip will have already begun . . ."

Allison shook her head. "You took what she said too much to heart."

"It is no more than I've said to myself many times. Surely you recall what I told you there in the vault. The fear of petticoat governance, much more than your barrenness, has held me back from acting on my love for you. But now my hand is forced, and I am glad of it."

Now he speaks of love, but he looks as if he is about to be executed. "I wish you loved me and wanted to marry me because of what I am, not in spite of it! I love you too much to marry you, when it is all too clear you don't want me for a wife. I don't think I will be the bear-leader your stepmother became, but I can never be a meek little hearth-mouse, either."

"You aren't listening, my love. I know you can't, and am resigned to my fate. Surely you will not turn down the chance to be worshiped and adored by your husband?"

Allison did not return his halfhearted smile, but only stared solemnly up at him. Confused by her reaction, Thorne rubbed his eyebrows between thumb and forefinger as if pressure there could bring comprehension. "Talk to me, Allie. Explain yourself."

"Your worship would scarcely outlast our treacle moon. Whether one month, two, six months later—all too soon you would begin to resent what you saw as my dominance. I won't be married to a man who sees love as a trap. I have pondered your concerns a great deal during this week while you were away. You may think you will be to me what your father was to Lydia, but I do not believe it. I do not remember your father well enough to know what he was like before he married Lydia, but if he did in fact marry your mother simply because his father wished it, that indicates a more biddable man than you! You might begin by yielding to me in everything, but you would soon resent what you see as a weakness.

Her voice grew husky with emotion. "I had enough of autocratic treatment in my marriage to Charles, who took every major decision without asking me. But he never questioned his right or ability to command me. I noticed that the officers who treated their men with the greatest severity were invariably the officers who lacked confidence in their own ability to command. My independent thought and forthright speaking might trigger a dictatorial response, such as you often displayed with Jamie. Would you be like the officers who had men whipped for minor infractions?"

"Whipped? That is nonsense!"

"Is it? Perhaps, but there are other unpleasant ways for a husband to enforce his will upon his wife. Before I began to love you, I was often annoyed at your autocratic assumption that you had but to speak and your will would be done. Frankly, I think it far more likely that you would be a dictatorial husband than an indulgent one."

She rushed on before he could marshal his thoughts. "Even if it were not so, I don't desire to wear the pants any more than I desire to be dominated. A weak husband would not suit me."

Allison opened the door, indicating that he should leave. "You seem to think there is no other alternative in marriage than for one party to rule over the other. What I want is a marriage based on respect and love, not power. Would you respect my need to think for myself, to express myself freely, when you are frightened by it? If you can't dominate, will you think you are dominated? Marriage should be a partnership. I thought we functioned that way in the tunnels, but you look back on it and see your role as one of abject surrender. I think we need to give ourselves some time, to see if we can learn to find a compromise, a middle ground."

Thorne's grey eyes were full of sorrow. He felt something precious slipping out of his grasp and questioned his right to reach for it. "You may be right, Allison. If we can't, we both would be miserable. But what of gossip? Agatha will spread her poison as far and as fast as she can among her numerous correspondents, even if our servants would not. But they will. Gossip about their betters is social coin for servants. Even the best of them cannot resist spending it."

Allison gave her head an impatient shake. "As for scandal, there was already gossip abroad about our relationship before I left London, yet I was received. The tabbies may have a feast, but I suspect my newfound wealth will open up some doors, even if others close to me. I shall be sad if we cannot work out our differences, Thorne, but I won't marry merely from fear of scandal. Mother and I plan to remove to London right away. Perhaps you will call on me there. We can learn to know one another better, then see whether we can learn to compromise."

Thorne looked mournfully down at her. The sapphire eyes were filled with tears. He longed to pull her into his arms and declare that none of the problems they both feared would ever come to pass. But deep inside, he thought it would prove to be a lie. Bidding her good night, he silently closed the door behind him.

Chapter Twenty

Nine people sat around the large, highly polished oak table, listening intently as Thorne's solicitor read aloud while Allison, James, and Thorne followed along on their copies of the settlement papers.

It had taken eight months to reach the point of final evaluation and distribution of the treasure. In that time she had seen Thorne a half dozen times, never privately, and he had always treated her with the utmost formality.

I hoped he would continue to call on us, she reflected ruefully. *I made it abundantly clear that my reservations might be overcome.* But apparently Thorne had not thought it worth his time and effort to do so. Sometimes she bitterly regretted having refused his proposal, but each time she thought their problems through, from the question of an heir, to his fear of marrying for love, to her fear that he might develop into a domestic tyrant, she decided she had made the right decision. As she watched him today, she knew that her refusal had been justified by his subsequent indifference.

"The results of the auction of antique jewelry and plate exceeded our highest expectations," Mr. Holmesly was saying. "It seems that half of the *ton* wished a souvenir piece of the Silverthorne treasure. They bought most of the plate and jewelry at prices far above the value of the gold, silver, and gems as raw material."

Thorne had been one of the most prominent bidders, purchasing many fine pieces for return to the D'Aumont family. She had bought only one item for herself, an emerald pendant the size of a robin's egg, set in a heavy silver frame.

She looked down the table at where James sat, leaning back in his chair with one hand on his hip and his eyebrows raised in astonishment. *Clearly he is pleased at the final amount. I wonder what he will make of himself now?* Allison had seen little of James since the treasure had been found.

"I'm sorry. I've been woolgathering," Allison admitted when she realized every one in the room was staring at her expectantly.

"I asked if there were any last-minute objections to the settlement?"

"Oh, no." Allison shook her head vehemently. "It seems a princely sum to me. I shall be very glad to have this matter behind me."

"Well, then . . ." The lawyer held out a pen to Thorne, directing him and the other two heirs to sign above their names and then exchange copies until all copies were signed. The banker then presented them with a draft and unctuously invited them to leave it in his bank. He began to extol his prowess at investing capital, but Thorne cut him off.

"Thank you, Mr. Lloyd. I am sure we will be in touch with you soon." He stood, a signal that the meeting had ended.

Everyone began shaking every one else's hands, but Allison noticed Thorne carefully avoided shaking hers. As the banker pumped James's hand, he began probing once more about investment opportunities. "I daresay you haven't the least notion what to do with that much capital, my lad. Won't you allow a wise old head to guide you?"

"Know exactly what I'm going to do with it," James asserted, pulling his hand free. "Going to pay off the debt on my estate and purchase additional land. Prices are down now—a good time to add to my holdings. Then I am going to invest in some modern equipment and stock for my tenants. My cousin will advise me on that." He looked at Thorne with admiration. "Knows all there is to know about crop rotation and animal breeding, you see."

"I see." The banker turned expectantly to Allison, who ducked behind her solicitor. She let the banker engage him in a lengthy discussion of possible investments while she made her way to James's side.

"So you are to become a farmer, Jamie!" She quizzed him with laughing eyes, but before he could take it as a criticism, she hastily added, "I think it is famous. Perhaps I shall invest in some land, too. Perhaps you can advise me."

Before a startled James could reply, Thorne joined them. He held out his hand to Allison at last for a perfunctory shake, before turning and clapping James on the shoulder. "He is becoming well qualified to do so, I assure you. And to manage it, though I doubt he will have time, once he adds to his own holdings."

Allison knew her mouth was open, but couldn't help her astonishment. James had become Thorne's willing pupil? Thorne spoke approvingly of him? Finally, she managed to stammer, "I am delighted to see that you are taking such an interest in the land, Jamie." Thorne excused himself to speak to the crown's representative.

"And surprised, I see." James chuckled. "I've said nothing because I wanted to be sure I could give up my wicked ways and become a responsible landowner before I began bragging about it." A pensive look came across his face. "Lord knows, I've caused Thorne enough grief. That day when I thought Newcomb had killed both of you, it shook me to the core. All my sins rose up to accuse me, and I knew I must change my life. Thorne has been a brick! Patient to the fault in training a very inept pupil."

Thorne turned back to them. "Ready to go, James? You promised to help me select a new hunter. Tattersalls is calling. Allison." He bowed quickly, formally, to her and strode out of the room.

James started after him, but Allison stopped him with a hand on his arm. "Would you call on me soon, Jamie?"

"Tomorrow morning? I don't want to fight all of the fortune hunters who flock to your drawing room every afternoon."

Allison's mouth tilted sideways in a half-disgusted smile. "Neither do I. I wish you would tell me how to avoid them. Even mother has fortune-hunting suitors. Eleven o'clock, then?"

Allison was in high fidgets by the time James arrived, forty-five minutes late. Peterson announced him, muttering as he did so, "Always late, is Mr. James."

James followed him in. "Why haven't you pensioned off that old grumble-buss?"

"He refused to go. Said new servants would steal us blind, were he not here to watch over us."

"I daresay he is right. I had to dismiss two overseers before finding an honest one. No wonder Thorne wished I would work for him. I always thought it was just a ploy to get me away from the ivory turners before I gambled away his fortune as well as my own."

"You and Thorne seem to be as thick as inkle weavers now. It is very gratifying to see."

"Yes, ain't it!" James lounged back in his chair, crossing his legs at the ankle and studying his boots thoughtfully. "He's really not such an old stick. Feel sorry for him in a way."

Allison frowned. "Why?"

"Thorne has everything, it would seem. Handsome, intelligent, well-breeched. Everything but love. He's a lonely man." James looked directly at her then, a challenge in his eyes. "Why didn't you accept his proposal, Allie?"

Allison sighed. "Don't you remember the reason he gave from the first for not wanting to marry me? He wants a biddable wife. He feels that I would attempt to rule the roost. He has even managed to convince himself that he would allow it."

"All because of that vicious Agatha. It's rot, you know. True, you are a spirited female, but not an unreasonable, foolish creature like his stepmother. And the notion of Thorne being ruled by you or anyone passes the ridiculous. He'd rule you with an iron hand. Not a pleasant man when crossed, either."

Allison shuddered. "That, I must confess, also seems likely to me."

Blithely unaware of her reaction, James continued. "But what I resented from him, you will find reassuring, for a woman wants a strong man to protect and guide her."

Allison was not reassured. Somewhere between guidance and dominance, between protection and tyranny, lay her ideal relationship between a man and a woman. It was too complex, too subtle a problem to explain to James, so she turned to the other reason for not marrying Thorne. "There is the matter of an heir."

"Been thinking about that. Understandable concern when I was behaving like a hell-born babe. But now he seems well pleased with me. You heard him yesterday. Says he won't need to marry for an heir now."

"And what of the army?"

An odd look came into James's eyes. "Well, as to that . . . perhaps I just wanted to get away from Thorne. Nothing to say that I can't travel later. When I've an heir and a spare tucked away, no one could reproach me for seeing a bit of the world, eh?"

"Oh, Jamie, it is all too ridiculous, isn't it? When I refused him, it should have freed him to find a woman who could give him an heir, and one who would be more the kind of wife who would suit him."

"I doubt he will marry anyone else. He as good as told me he felt it would be unfair, loving you as he does."

"He doesn't appear to be wearing the willow for me. In fact, I haven't seen the least indication that he thinks of me at all."

"Oh, he thinks of you. Speaks of you, too." James sighed. "Tricky business, marriage. I expect I had best begin looking about me, but I dread it. Want to find a good woman, you see. That is, if I can find one to have me after all my excesses of the last few years."

"Silly boy!" Diverted from her train of thought, Allison smiled fondly at him. "Show yourself in London long enough, and we shall have to call out the guards to protect you. You're young, handsome, and now exceedingly wealthy. You've but to snap your fingers to have the pick of the *ton*'s diamonds."

"I hope you are right. A good wife can confirm a man in his virtues, a bad one in his vices. That's what Thorne says, anyway, and I daresay he's right. He usually is."

"Can you really be James, or has some changeling taken your place? To hear you speaking of Thorne so! And I've not heard one breath of scandal about you since we discovered the treasure."

Though this praise obviously pleased him, James waved a deprecating hand. "Easy to behave in the country, looking after business. No time for rioting then. By the by, did you read about the prison ship riots in the paper? Newcomb proved himself as inept at rebellion as he was at robbery."

Allison shuddered. "Hanged. He certainly didn't take advantage of the second chance the crown gave him."

"Gallows bait, that's all he ever was. He and Paddy should have hanged side by side, no matter what his military service to his country. He only got what he deserved. Beg pardon, know you don't approve of hanging."

Allison didn't respond. When it became clear that she was lost in her own thoughts, James stood and crossed to her side. He sat on the sofa beside her and kissed her cheek.

"Have to go. Late for an appointment with Weston. He suddenly finds time to make me all the coats I want, now that I've paid my shot with him. Think over what I said, Allie."

Allison smiled ruefully. "We speak as if I had but to crook my finger and Thorne would come on bended knee. But I have not even heard from him about my finances, much less seen any signs that he wishes to discover how we might deal together. Instead, he has stayed strictly away from me. Whatever he says to the contrary, I suspect he thinks himself well out of it."

"Not true," James declared adamantly. "I'd say he's grieving for you. Seems a pity the two of you can't meet one another halfway." James cocked a questioning eyebrow. When she didn't respond, he gave her hands a pat. "Well, done my part. Up to you now."

They stood, and Allison walked James to the door. "Do you remain in London?" she asked.

"Only for a sennight. Thorne's presence is not required in Parliament just now, so we are going to take a tour of his northern estates."

And that leaves me with a dilemma, Allison thought as she watched James enter his curricle and take up the reins of a fine pair of bays. *How can we discover whether or not we can learn to pull in harness together, if we are never near one another?*

The Marquess of Silverthorne sat at the writing desk in his town house study. Before him a ledger opened to the month's accounts lay unheeded. One of Thorne's internal debates raged in his thoughts.

Shaking Allison's hand at the meeting the day before had awakened all of the longings he had spent several months determinedly suppressing. Since seeing her again, the depth of his craving for her, not just in his bed, but in his study, at his dinner table, with him in his opera box, had overwhelmed him. He even found himself fantasizing about the arguments she would start, the odd opinions she would advocate with such clever logic that he found himself agreeing with her in spite of himself.

That in itself should warn you away before you make the same mistake your father did. The old fear surfaced as always when he felt Allison's strong pull. *We D'Aumonts make the mistake of loving too much.*

But that argument was beginning to lose its force. As he recalled how they had dealt with one another in the tunnel, he more and more agreed with Allison's assessment: They had functioned as partners. Sometimes one, and sometimes the other, had prevailed in deciding a course of action. When her suggestions had been followed, it was because she had reason on her side, not because he couldn't tell her no. When she gave way to him, she never pouted or withdrew from him.

She isn't the least like Lydia. My father was twenty years her senior. He was besotted with her, whereas she married him for advantage, and used his love to rule him. Allison loves me as much as I love her. That makes all the difference.

Does it? Do you really think she could ask you for something, tears in those sapphire eyes, and you would refuse her?

That was the question that haunted him. *Yes!* Thorne sat up and slapped his hand against the ledger. *If I knew what she wanted would harm her, or our children, I could.*

Would you then be the dictatorial husband she dreads?

He hesitated over that question. He knew he had often been short-tempered with his cousin. *But James behaved quite selfishly and irrationally. Allison is an intelligent woman, not a self-absorbed fool. She would bear me no ill will once I explained my reasons.*

Thorne stood up and stalked to the bow window that looked out on the street below. Water on the paving stones rippled as the rain fell. It was May. Thus far the weather had been cooler than usual, but all too soon summer's heat would make London unbearable. *Time to start for the country.* Instead of pleasing him, this usually pleasurable prospect only made him feel more lonely. *Where will Allison be this summer?*

As he stared at the rainy street, he saw James pull up in his curricle, his many-caped driving coat flaring behind him. He turned to greet his cousin, glad now that visits from James were no longer to be dreaded. What a change had come over his cousin in the last few months! Whether because he now had the means to be independent, or because he had earned Thorne's respect and thus respected himself, James had become almost everything Thorne could have wished for in an heir.

James clapped Thorne on both arms as he entered the study. "Good news, Thorne. I took the liberty of speaking to Allison about you. Think I laid her fears to rest."

Thorne frowned, not sure he wanted James acting as his surrogate. "What did you say to her?"

James's guard came up at Thorne's tone. "I say—I hope I haven't raised false hopes and laid that dear girl open to more hurt. You *do* still want to marry her, don't you?"

"Very much!" The answer came quickly. Thorne realized with relief that he no longer doubted his own mind.

"Well, then, I found out why she wouldn't marry you. Gives you a chance to change her mind. Got it out of her very cleverly if I do say so myself."

"I was under the impression I already knew why she refused me." Thorne poured both of them a brandy.

Heedless of Thorne's wry humor, James rushed in. "First, she is worried about the heir thing. I pointed out that was irrelevant, now I've become such a solid citizen, planning to look about me for a wife."

"That sounds hopeful." Thorne swirled his brandy, hoping James would not notice how hard he gripped the glass.

"Second. About this ridiculous notion that you'd live under petticoat rule. Anyone knows that's impossible. Just reminded her how you used to treat my foolishness."

Thorne ground his jaw. "Go on," he growled.

"Not that I didn't deserve your severity!" James sipped the brandy appreciatively. "My opinion is you'd be far more likely to beat her or lock her away than stand the kind of nonsense from her that your father did from Lydia. Told her so."

Thorne's glass came down on the table with a thump. "The devil you did!"

"No need to fly up into the boughs. She wasn't the least surprised. Agreed with me, in fact." James recognized Thorne's pulling his hand down his face as a sign of acute distress. "Don't worry yourself about it, Thorne. Reminded her that a woman wants a strong man in her life."

"And she said?"

"Oh, perfectly satisfied with that. Expressed the hope you might call on her." James knew this statement strained the truth a little, but in his mind the key to a match between Thorne and Allison would be passion, and how could that arise if they weren't together?

Thorne knew James too well. The slight shift of his eyes warned of a prevarication. "Without a doubt! Eager to have her lord and master claim her, wouldn't you say?"

"Just so! Ought to go over there right away." James beamed at him, proud to have played the matchmaker to his relatives.

After James's departure, Allison sat at her writing desk, mulling over a stack of proposals for investing her money. Between them and the requests for charity, she could study every hour of her waking day if she wished. She did not wish!

"If only I could turn all of this over to someone," she complained. Her mother, who sat perusing a letter nearby, made a sympathetic noise. "Nothing in my life has prepared me to handle the huge sum of money now at my disposal, and I feel all at sea."

"I do not believe the female mind was designed to deal with such matters," Delphina observed. "You must find someone to advise you."

"I *can* deal with them," Allison responded with asperity. "I just don't want to. But whom can I trust?" She bent her head again, studying the document before her. She knew that some of the proposals were of value, and others merely schemes to bilk her. Her own solicitor had recommended an investment so much resembling the worst of the fraudulent schemes that she now suspected his honesty.

Her long, loud sigh distracted Delphina's attention from the letter again. "Why don't you just leave it in the bank?"

"Lord Bertland and several others have told me that I must lay it out in a variety of investments, against the possibility that one or another of them may fail."

"As banks sometime do." Delphina tapped her lips with her index finger. "Lord Bertland is a worthy man, but I would not trust him to be entirely disinterested, since he wants you to invest in that tin mine of his."

"Just so. I don't know whom to trust."

"You could trust Thorne, dear."

Allison turned to look at her mother. "Of course I could. I expected him to assert his authority over my newly enriched purse long before this. Nothing could illustrate his wish to have nothing to do with me better than his playing least in sight, now that I have funds at my disposal."

"Nonsense. If you were to turn to him for advice, it would delight him."

"Hmmmm." Allison tapped her pencil against her chin. "I wonder . . ." She leafed through the various proposals in front of her. "I could sort out the ones that sound best to me and present them for his opinion. For instance, here is the prospectus for a rail car that is to be propelled by steam. Don't you think that seems interesting?"

"Umm, hmmm." Delphina's eyes were once again on her letter. Allison could see from the handwriting that it was from Agatha Keisley. Aunt Agatha had taken up residence in Bath with another of Thorne's pensioners, keeping her mother entertained with a flow of gossip from that city.

"And Sir Bertland's tin mine, I think. And the land in Surrey."

"Very good, my dear."

Allison turned so she could look directly at her mother. "You aren't listening to a word I've said."

"Nonsense, dear. I'm fascinated. Please do go on."

Mischief lit up Allison's eyes. She fished through the stack of proposals she had definitely rejected and pulled out the most ridiculous one she could find. "My favorite, I think, is this one. 'A projected voyage to Africa to search out an ape capable of being trained to replace children in factories.' Don't you think that an admirable goal? The children wouldn't have to do such boring, dangerous work, and the apes would require nothing more than food to keep them content."

Delphina surprised Allison by dropping the letter into her lap. "That . . . that is ridiculous."

"Is it?" Allison grinned. "Only think. He proposes to establish a breeding colony in the New Forest. They could fend for themselves there, saving the projectors the trouble of feeding them."

"Allison, you are funning me!"

"He is entirely serious, I assure you. He needs but ten thousand pounds sterling to outfit his ship, build cages, and hire native guides to explore the interior of Africa."

"I beg you will not put this mad scheme in front of Thorne! He would laugh you out of countenance, or forbid you to do it. You would resent that, and the two of you would be at daggers drawn once again."

Allison turned fully around in her chair to stare at her mother. She replied slowly and thoughtfully, "I dare say you are right. Then I most certainly shall present it to him."

Delphina rose. "I am out of all reason cross with you, Allison. You will never make it up with Thorne, and you know you won't marry anyone else. The two of you should be horsewhipped for being so stubborn. I am going to my room, where I can read in peace."

Allison paid little heed to her mother's indignation. She was too busy refining her sudden but brilliant plan. *He won't be able to resist refusing to allow me to invest in this scheme. At one blow I shall show him that he can, indeed, stand up to me, and that I can be persuaded by reasonable arguments to accept his recommendation.*

She picked up her pen and began carefully composing a note to Thorne.

Chapter Twenty-one

"Thank you for calling so promptly, Thorne." Allison greeted her handsome caller nervously. He had lost no time responding to her note of the previous day.

"I intended to call on you in any case, but when you spoke of needing advice, you must have known such an invitation would be irresistible." He winked at her.

Allison laughed. "Particularly as it is financial advice I crave." She picked up the stack of proposals she intended to present to him, her heart beating as if she had run a race. *That wink was almost my undoing.* The sight of him thrilled her as usual; the knowledge of how important this meeting was to her future intimidated her. *I just have to convince him that he will not be putty in my hands. He is sure to object to at least one of these proposals. And if in fact he is utterly autocratic about it, I shall know we can't deal well together.*

As she explained her need for investment advice, Thorne felt like a man who has walked into a dangerous trap. He must advise her wisely and be firm if she sought to do anything too disastrous, else he was of no value to her. But at all costs he must not confirm her opinion that he was an incipient tyrant, unable to bear with disagreement.

"This one comes well recommended," she said, showing him a proposal to link England to France by a tunnel under the English Channel. Allison thought it one of the weaker proposals. She was surprised when Thorne treated it seriously. He discussed all of its positive points first, and then gently pointed out its flaws in such a way that she could but agree with him or obviously play the fool. In the end, he left the decision up to her.

At any other time this would have delighted Allison, for it is just how she would wish them to approach such matters. But as long as he was of the opinion that his love for her put him in her power, it did not accomplish her purpose.

A small worry frown appeared between her brows as Allison picked up the next packet. He could not but approve of the proposal to purchase an estate in Kent; after all, he could hardly deny the value of owning land. Thorne's expression lightened as he read through the survey and description of the estate that Allison was considering. "I know this land. Good, rich land, suitable for corn, and an excellent water meadow. The house is not in good repair, though. Had you planned on residing there?"

Allison's spirits plummeted. *I had hoped to reside with you*, she thought. She shook her head. "No. That is, if I did, I am aware that I would have to build. The land agent said that the house is full of dry rot and sits in an exposed location. He advises pulling it down."

"Your notes are comprehensive—you have studied this proposal carefully, Allison," Thorne said admiringly. "I am not sure that you need my advice, but I certainly would recommend this purchase." *No surprise there*, Allison thought. Yet pleasure suffused her at his praise.

As he picked up the material on Lord Bertland's tin mine, Thorne congratulated himself on having brushed through very well on Allison's first two investment proposals, for the tunnel under the channel, though many hooted in laughter on hearing of it, intrigued him greatly. He thought it would be built someday, though now it would be a very risky venture. As for land, unless it was swampland, it was almost always a good investment.

Thorne frowned as he read the prospectus for the tin mine. "I fear I can make very little sense of this. My advice would be to get the advice of a mining engineer. I can recommend one if you would like to have him go to the site and look matters over." This was far too sensible for Allison to disagree with.

The fourth proposal Allison had chosen because of their recent adventures. She found the idea fascinating, but unlikely to produce profits, for which reason she hoped Thorne would object. "Have you heard of Herr Fromann?"

"The hypnotist?"

"Yes. He has a very intriguing theory regarding ghosts."

"I've heard of him," Thorne snapped. "He thinks hypnotizing people will make them able to perceive spirits. An interesting idea I would very much like to see tested. However, I fear he is not the one I would entrust to test it. Are you aware that I had to stop him from capitalizing on our experience? In both his literature and his lectures he implied that he contributed to your being able to see the Silver Lady."

"Oh! How dare he? But I did not read that." She held up Fromann's pamphlet.

"That is because I told him if he did not change it immediately, I would have him in Newgate."

In her indignation, Allison abandoned all idea of trying to sell Thorne on this plan. "He is just a charlatan then, not a true investigator."

"I am afraid so."

Allison had only one proposal left with which to accomplish her goals. She picked up the folder concerning the expedition to seek useful apes in the interior of Africa. *If he approves this one, I shall join him in fearing his passivity. But he won't.* She confidently laid out the proposal, fighting hard to keep back laughter, for she was sure at any moment Thorne would interrupt her to dismiss the scheme out of hand. She went so far as to pretend a great attachment to the plan, that his refusal to countenance it would give him even greater self-confidence.

Thorne spent a long time reading over it, his mind in turmoil. He was appalled. Never had he read anything so ridiculous. He clamped his jaw shut on a roar of outrage, for he wanted nothing so much as to demand where her usually sharp wits had gone.

This is the side of me she fears most, he thought. For he could but confess to himself that he had a strong urge to ridicule the scheme and refuse her participation in it out of hand. *Not without reason does she believe I have the potential to be dictatorial,* he wryly acknowledged, massaging a suddenly throbbing temple.

Careful, careful. I must counter all of her arguments, but do it gently, convincing her instead of simply overruling her. "Do you really think it is wise to invest so heavily in a scheme that depends upon training an animal that we do not know even exists?"

"But that is why he needs so much money. He must provender a long, dangerous excursion into unexplored territory, capture any simians there encountered, assess their ability to be trained, and then bring back enough of them to establish a breeding colony."

"I . . . uh . . . question whether any creature exists sufficiently intelligent to perform these tasks and yet foolish enough to do it for naught but food and lodging."

"But, Thorne, the children do it."

"Children have parents who insist that they work in the mines and factories. They are given little choice."

"Exactly. They are treated like domestic animals; it would be far better if in fact we could find animals to do such dull and yet dangerous and tiring work."

As she talked, Allison warmed to her subject—not to investing in Mr. Eamon's venture, but to finding a way to relieve children from onerous work.

Thorne drew the conclusion that the scheme appealed to her not as a moneymaking venture, but as a way of helping poor children. As he watched her eyes flash, her hands cut the air, he knew he must swallow a bitter pill and let her throw away ten thousand pounds, or put his foot down and convince her of his cruel inclination to disregard her feelings.

He dragged his hand down his face. At that gesture, Allie felt triumph swell her heart. Though he had not exploded with indignation, he clearly wished to deny her this request.

Thorne's mind raced, searching desperately for a compromise. At last he said, "If you have your heart set on this, Allie, I will permit it, not as an investment, but as a charitable donation. You must expect no return upon your capital, and perhaps must in the end see all of your money go for naught." He hoped if he presented it to her in that light, she would be amenable to other suggestions for ways to spend that money helping poor children.

His eyes caressed her face. He had surprised her, that was clear, but surely once and for all he had convinced her he was no tyrant! Thorne crossed to the sofa where Allison sat, her mouth open in astonishment.

Allison's astonishment had quite a different cause than he supposed. He had given in to her on the most ridiculous scheme in her little bag of tricks. *Poor man. He must be utterly besotted. It would be a heavy responsibility for me to bear, for I would constantly have to watch out never to abuse the gift of his love. Can I be happy with such a passive man?* The tiny curl of disdain Allison felt cast a new light on Thorne's stepmother. Had Lydia demanded so much of Thorne's father out of need to provoke him into standing up to her? Would she one day turn into just such a shrewish harridan, simply out of disgust because her husband had no spine?

"Catching flies, my love." Thorne put his index finger across her open mouth. She closed it abruptly and sprang back.

"I am amazed that you would permit such a scheme!"

Thorne chortled triumphantly. "Listen to me, Allison. I have never been so lonely as in the last few months. Having once admitted I love you, I find it almost impossible to live without you. Will you please marry me?" He attempted to take her in his arms.

Allison pulled away. "Oh, Thorne, don't."

"Don't?" Thorne watched her eyes fill up with tears. "Don't what? Tell you that I love you? Propose to you?"

"Yes. No. I mean . . . It is just that . . ." She lifted her hand to his cheek, cradling it briefly before standing up abruptly. "I do not believe we will suit. You had the right of it, all along. I am far too managing a female to be entrusted with a husband so doting he would allow me to do anything so absurd."

"So doting . . . but I thought . . . you wanted . . ."

"I wanted good financial advice, not passivity and mealy-mouthed acquiescence. If I had been sure of any of these proposals, I would not have brought them to you. I hoped that as we worked through them you would realize that you and I are perfectly capable of reaching rational conclusions together."

"Rational! You speak of rational!" Thorne stood up, his eyebrows nearly meeting as he glared at her. "That trained ape proposal is the most irrational bit of sentimental twaddle that I ever heard of."

"Precisely. Yet you would have let me throw away ten thousand pounds on it."

"If you realized how silly it was, why did you speak so eloquently in defending it?"

"Oh, Thorne, Thorne. I put it before you expecting you to refuse it. Then you would no longer fear that you would be unable to say no to me. Alas, I proved just the opposite. Now I am less sure than ever that we could be happy together. Though I do not wish to be treated as a nonentity, neither do I wish to be married to one."

Thorne was utterly confounded. "I never felt so torn in my life. I wanted to laugh you out of countenance for bringing that thing up, and at the same time I wanted to forbid you even to think of it!"

"Then why . . . ?"

"Because you think I will be a tyrant. It is what you fear most, is it not? Much thanks to James for his meddling! I don't say I blame either of you. I was often dictatorial with him. But I won't be that way with you, Allie. Though that scheme deserves contempt, you are an intelligent woman. I know you would rarely present me with that kind of a dilemma. I thought it was your compassion for the children that clouded your judgment. I hoped to steer you toward a better use for your charity."

Understanding dawned. Allison's tense posture relaxed, her sapphire eyes danced with amusement. "We have been working at cross purposes, Thorne." She closed the distance between them and looked up at him invitingly.

At her approach the Marquess of Silverthorne knew that if he lived to be a hundred he would never feel more relieved than he felt at that moment, seeing Allison go from a woman poised for flight to one poised for kisses. He accepted her unspoken invitation eagerly, pulling her to him for an urgent kiss that left them both breathless.

When he paused for air, she tried to pull away, for there still remained one very important problem. "But Thorne, what about an heir?"

"Shhh, my love. It doesn't matter." He tightened his hold on her and bowed his head, seeking another kiss.

"Of course it matters." Allison pushed on his chest until he released her. "I couldn't bear to see you unhappy, perhaps even bitter, if—"

"I told you true when I said that concern for an heir was less important than my fear of loving a woman too much. But you spoke the truth when you said I am not my father. Nor are you Lydia. I have come to realize that love is not a trap when the love is on both sides. And what do I want with a biddable wife? Compared to you, my challenging, intelligent little love, such a woman would be a dead bore. Perhaps I might become the tyrant with too passive a woman, but you will put me on my mettle."

"Still . . ."

"And James is coming along nicely. You would hardly recognize him as the same person. Besides, you are not such a ninnyhammer as to suppose there is a guarantee that any woman I might marry would present me with an heir. Don't you realize even the most nubile of the season's young misses might be barren, or have only girls? Now kiss me, and let us set a wedding date." He pulled her back into his arms again.

"If you truly mean what you say—"

"What do I have to do to convince you?"

"Then I have some good news for you. Charles did not want a large family."

So caught up was he in convincing Allison to marry him, it took a few long seconds for the implication of this to sink in. "You mean . . ."

She turned her head away to hide the blush she felt rising in her cheeks.

"Why didn't you tell me this before now, minx?" Thorne's hold on her loosened abruptly.

She stepped out of his arms. "What if I might actually be barren? I didn't want to face the regrets if . . ." Thorne's thunderous expression filled her with dismay. Had this confession given him a disgust of her?

"He caused you pain." Thorne touched her face, gently cupping her chin with his hand.

Relief at realizing that Thorne's anger was directed at Charles left Allison weak-kneed. "It is in the past, Thorne."

"I assure you it is! Nothing of that sort is in your future, at least not until you have all the children your heart desires. Come here!"

His face strained with suppressed passion, Thorne drew her into his arms for another kiss, a kiss that ended all doubt that they would be, *must* be, married, and soon.

Epilogue

Allison thought it very romantic of Thorne to bring her to the castle for a private celebration of their second wedding anniversary. Their guests had turned in an hour ago, and after they had gone up to the nursery to look with silent adoration on their six-month-old son, Thorne had led her down the servants' stairs with an air of great mystery. In the gig waiting at the kitchen door, he playfully tried to prevent her from seeing what he had placed behind the seat. In addition to one of cook's famous picnic baskets brimming with delicacies, there was an interesting mound of clothing wrapped in luxurious towels.

He conveyed her up the newly repaired castle road while cuddling her against his side and bestowing frequent kisses. The balmy August evening seemed made for love. Excitement pounded through Allison at his arched brows and possessive smile as he helped her down from the gig. *He can never make love to me too often*, she thought.

Moonlight drenched the keep. "How thoughtful of the moon, to be at the full tonight," he said, tilting his head up appreciatively.

"Either it is shining inside the keep, which casts your repairs in question, or you have caused it to be lighted." Allison stepped over the threshold eagerly. Thorne followed, picnic basket over one arm, mysterious bundle tucked under the other.

The keep's ground floor had been hastily emptied of farm implements and old furniture two years ago, to serve as a reception hall for their wedding breakfast, after their simple but lovely wedding in the old chapel. One of the few to survive the civil wars without damage, the chapel had been the perfect setting for their marriage. Today the ground floor of the keep boasted period furniture, the wall sconces had been fitted out with glass fixtures, and the new gas lighting cast a soft, romantic glow over it all.

Thorne directed Allison toward the back of the great hall, but she demurred. "Wherever you are taking me, and I can't even begin to guess where that is—"

"Little liar," Thorne teased, bestowing another of those kisses that turned her blood to fire.

Allison had often wished they could make love in the Sultan's bath, but it had been badly damaged when Newcomb and Paddy were tromping back and forth over the tile with heavy chests of treasure. She had an idea her wish was about to come true, but not to be seduced before time, she persisted when the kiss ended. "Let us visit the chapel first."

Thorne agreed somewhat reluctantly, to her surprise, for hadn't he caused it to be lighted, as if in anticipation of her request?

"Remember how Marie refused to be married there?" Allison reminisced as they walked toward the chapel. "Claimed there were ghostly presences there. Of course, she sees them everywhere."

"I remember. If it had not been for Bean's calming influence, I doubt she would have remained on the estate. Only the promise of a new cottage convinced her to marry him." Thorne seemed distracted. "I did not ask the chapel to be lighted," he said, frowning.

Allison knew even as she approached the chapel door, from which a radiant light spilled. "Oh, Thorne. She is here."

"I *thought* I heard bells." He looked down at her wonderingly.

They stepped into the chapel. At the alter two figures knelt. After a few moments the couple stood and came toward them. Thorne made to move aside. "It *is* our Silver Lady."

"Yes, with Sir Broderick, if I am not mistaken, though he is not in armor this time." Allison, too, stood aside to let the ghostly pair go by. But they did not pass. Instead, the Silver Lady stopped and regarded them gravely. Sir Broderick stood at her elbow.

Thorne drew in a deep breath. His heart thundered, his mouth had cotton in it. Yet it wasn't fear, but a sort of joyful awe that he felt. "I can see them both, quite clearly," he whispered in Allison's ear. Then he bowed formally to the couple. "My lady ghost, welcome. At last I have the opportunity to thank you—"

The soft chiming voice of the Silver Lady interrupted him. "We rejoice with you on this your anniversary, and wish you joy of your son. We may not linger after this, but it has been my urgent wish to bring you, Lord Silverthorne, some words of comfort."

Thorne bowed respectfully and awaited the Silver Lady's words.

"Your father never believed in the treasure. He married your mother out of love, after your grandfather brought her to his notice. He never told your step-mother that her son had no claim to the treasure because it seemed pointless to him. Nor did he take the boy to the north tower that day. Young Percy had heard his mother demanding that it be found, and took it upon himself to look for it. Upon learning this, your father hastened to save the boy, but instead perished with him. It grieves me to think you believe him both foolish and venal." Thorne could not speak; tears filled his eyes and tightened his throat. He could only nod and bow.

The Lady then turned to Allison. "I leave the family legacy in your capable hands, Lady Silverthorne. I bid thee good-bye and fare thee well, my sister and my friend." The Silver Lady smiled into Allison's teary eyes, then took her husband's hand. With great dignity the pair walked past them and into the castle keep, where they faded from sight.

After the spirit-lovers departed, Allison and Thorne turned into one another's arms and held on as if their survival depended upon it. Long, silent moments passed before Thorne tilted her head up and solemnly began to repeat his wedding vows. Allison joined in, standing in the near darkness of the old chapel.

When they turned back into the hall, arm in arm, Thorne chuckled throatily. "After that, my planned anniversary celebration seems anticlimactic."

"Oh, I hope not, my lord." Allison laughed naughtily. "I believe you have yet to show me the most recent renovation to Silverthorne Castle."

"Someone has given me away." Thorne pretended to be angry. "And after all the precautions I took."

"When that Italian marble accidentally arrived in our shared bath, I began to suspect." She tugged on his arm eagerly. He lifted a key from his vest pocket and handed it to her, picked up the basket and bundle again, and followed her into the Sultan's bath.

PENGUIN PUTNAM

———————————— online

Your Internet gateway to a virtual environment with hundreds of entertaining and enlightening books from Penguin Putnam Inc.

While you're there, get the latest buzz on the best authors and books around—

Tom Clancy, Patricia Cornwell, W.E.B. Griffin, Nora Roberts, William Gibson, Robin Cook, Brian Jacques, Catherine Coulter, Stephen King, Jacquelyn Mitchard, and many more!

Penguin Putnam Online is located at
http://www.penguinputnam.com

• •

PENGUIN PUTNAM NEWS

Every month you'll get an inside look at our upcoming books and new features on our site. This is an ongoing effort to provide you with the most interesting and up-to-date information about our books and authors.

Subscribe to Penguin Putnam News at
http://www.penguinputnam.com/ClubPPI